CAPTURED

G000134522

Niall's glance flicked to h[...] face. "You'll do as I say u[...]

How dare he think he c[...] brothers knew better than to dictate to her; all it did was raise her hackles.

Anger coursed through her, heating her in spite of the moist dampness seeping through her riding habit from the earth. "Don't turn your back on me. I won't sit passively by while you use me to lure my brother to his death. You may depend on it."

A thin smile stretched his mouth. "I like a challenge, vixen." His eyes darkened. " 'Twill keep the next week lively."

Fiona ground her teeth together. She would not be used. Frustration drove her to thrash against him, kicking at the heavy weight of his legs on hers.

In one smooth movement, he rolled her onto her back and raised up above her, his hips pinning hers down. "Don't push me, vixen. I've no love for your family or you, but you're innocent of your brother's acts and I'll try to remember that."

She glared at him, refusing to be intimidated by the brilliant glow of his malachite eyes as they stared down at her. His gaze shifted to her mouth, making her breath catch. The harsh angles of his face spoke of determination and domination as he studied her. His mouth lowered to her . . .

AMBER KAYE

CAPTURED BY LOVE

ZEBRA BOOKS
KENSINGTON PUBLISHING CORP.

Prologue

Boston, 1812

"Lieutenant Currie, yer got ta wake up, sir," the harsh, vaguely familiar voice insisted.

Niall ignored it and swatted at something shaking his shoulder. "Go 'way," he muttered, rolling onto his side away from the irritant.

"Sir," the same voice penetrated the fog blanketing Niall's mind, "the captain wants yer."

Groggy and disoriented, Niall struggled to sit up. The room—no, cabin—spun out of control as he forced himself erect. He grimaced and pushed his thick black hair back from his aching eyes. His head throbbed as if the ship had emptied her guns into it. His mouth tasted as if all the King's fleet had sailed through it, leaving their garbage and refuse behind.

What was wrong with him? Never, in all his twenty-seven years had he felt this bad after a night's carousing. At least, he *thought* he'd spent the night carousing.

Somewhere between the whore on his lap and the

seaman's hand shaking him awake, he must have downed more liquor than his norm because he never felt like this . . . and he never failed to remember.

"Sir," the seaman's voice impinged on Niall's conscience again. "The captain, he said yer was ta come immediate like."

Niall squinted in the dim light of the small cabin and recognized Monty Griff's hoary features, scrunched into worried lines as the seaman shifted from foot to foot.

"Thanks, Monty," Niall forced the words out from his parched mouth. "I'll get dressed and present myself."

"Beggin' yer pardon, sir," Monty said, "but the captain said yer was ta come as yer was and no mistakin' the matter. Sir."

Niall frowned, instantly regretting the action since it caused his head to feel as if hot pincers had tightened on it. He must've had one hell of a night, if only he could remember past the prostitute.

Gritting his teeth, Niall hauled himself out of the small bunk, wondering why he still had his uniform trousers on. He didn't normally sleep in his clothing.

"Sir?"

Monty's persistence brought Niall's attention back to the present. "Just let me put on a clean shirt and clean up a bit."

Without waiting for the seaman's consent, Niall padded on bare feet to the small table where a water pitcher and bowl sat in specially made depressions. He poured out some of the cold water and splashed his face, then ran the liquid through his unruly hair.

The brilliant green of his eyes, rimmed in red, peered at him from the small oval of his shaving mirror. Lines drew his sharply defined lips downward. He looked like hell.

Minutes later, fully dressed, he followed Monty out.

The other man's nervousness was a palpable strain that communicated itself to Niall as they hurried through the ship. Niall's shoulders tensed as he wondered what the captain wanted with him.

They'd docked in Boston two days ago, and the deteriorating relations between the United States and Britain had everyone on edge. That had to be the reason for this summons: Something had occurred between his country and their former colonies.

Feeling more clear-headed by the second, Niall stopped behind the seaman when they reached the captain's cabin, and was mildly surprised when Monty didn't leave him at the door. Instead the seaman knocked and waited for the captain to bid them enter. When he did, Monty stepped back for Niall to enter first, since Niall was the officer, then entered behind.

This wasn't normal behavior, not even if the United States and Britain had declared war on one another. Monty should have left so that Niall and the captain could discuss in private whatever it was that had precipitated this summons. The seaman's actions spoke of keeping Niall under surveillance. Niall found himself becoming more uncomfortable by the moment.

Captain Richford raised his head to pin Niall with hard brown eyes buried in squinting folds of flesh permanently sunburnt and lined from long days spent outdoors peering into distances too great for any man's eyesight. Grizzled gray hair was pulled back from his forehead into an old-fashioned queue, the style when he'd served under Admiral Lord Nelson at the victory of Trafalgar. He was rightly proud of that and never failed to remind his men of Lord Nelson's heroic battle.

"Lieutenant Currie," Captain Richford's deep, rasping voice stated, "you're under arrest."

Niall's eyes widened before narrowing to slits. It must have been one hell of a night. Standing at attention, he asked, "What crime have I committed, sir?"

Captain Richford's face hardened. "Murder."

Niall clenched his hands into fists. He was many things, but a murderer wasn't one of them. Something was wrong here and he'd find out what.

"Whom and when? Sir."

A spark of admiration entered the Captain's brown eyes. "You've never been one to take orders without knowing why, have you, lieutenant?"

Niall lifted his jaw. "No, sir."

"Comes of your Scottish heritage." The captain pushed back his chair and rose. Coming around the corner of his desk, he said, "You're accused of sodomizing—and then cutting the throat of—a woman last night."

Outrage flared in Niall. A helpless woman killed. He lifted his jaw higher. "Who was she and who's accusing me? Sir."

Captain Richford smiled grimly. "The woman's name was Meg. She was a prostitute—well-known and well-liked by the Boston seamen. Two of them found her in her room, a British officer's uniform-button clenched in one hand, your lucky piece in the other. I'm told it wasn't a pretty sight. She'd been beaten first."

Niall gulped hard. He couldn't remember anything, except that the woman who'd been on his lap last night *had* been named Meg. He thought he'd gone to her room. He even thought he'd enjoyed her. But he also thought he'd left her while she dressed to go below and pick up another paying customer.

Through a tight throat, Niall stated, "Someone framed me."

"I'd like to believe that, lieutenant, but you were the last man seen with her and," Captain Richford paused to pick up a shiny round object from his desk, "there's this."

Niall looked at the gold circle resting in the captain's palm. "My lucky piece."

Captain Richford nodded. "Damning evidence, or so the Boston authorities think. Do you have anything to say, lieutenant?'

Niall met the captain's eyes without flinching. "I didn't do it. Sir."

"Can you prove it?"

Niall swallowed. He couldn't even say how he'd gotten back to the ship last night.

"I didn't think so," Captain Richford said. "I'm sorry to have to do this, lieutenant, but murder's murder and the relations between us and the United States right now are too tense for me to do anything else." Turning to Monty, he ordered, "Put him in the brig until we can convene a court-martial. Then notify lieutenants Winter, Sculthorpe, and Macfie that they're to sit in judgment."

Niall felt his blood drain away. He didn't need to know what the verdict would be. The evidence was too damning and his memory of the night too vague. He'd be found guilty and sent to prison for a murder he knew in his soul he didn't commit.

Chapter One

Scottish Highlands, 1815

Lady Fiona Mary Margaret Macfie swayed easily to the irregular gait of her shaggy Highland pony, Mac-Duff. The terrain was rough and isolated, necessitating travel by pony or horse since no carriage could traverse it. Luckily, it was still late summer and the bone-chilling autumn hadn't settled in, though the weather was cool. She had wanted no delays as she set out for Edinburgh from Colonsay, the Highland island her family owned.

The crossing from Colonsay had gone easily, once she'd gotten over the goodbyes with her family. The earl, while resigned to his only daughter going back to Scotland's capital, hadn't liked it. The countess had understood. Love was the strongest force in Mary Macfie's life. Her husband had married her—a poor cottar's daughter—for love, and love had kept them together. Theirs was unlike most marriages of the aristocracy. Mary knew Fiona had to return to Edinburgh and the man she loved.

A breeze, sweet with the scent of heather, freed a strand of Fiona's copper hair. She pushed it behind her ear without thought and prayed she wasn't too late. The man she loved was in pursuit of another woman, and—fool that she was—she'd left Edinburgh and the contest. Now she was returning to fight for Angus.

Somehow she would convince Angus that his being poor didn't necessitate his finding a rich wife. Money was nice, but there was so much more. Although an earl's daughter, she wasn't wealthy; yet she'd been happy all her life. Her parents loved one another, and that love permeated the family. And she loved Angus and knew in her heart that she could make him happy.

But it was four months since she'd last seen her love, and he might be married by now. Her chest tightened, and her hands clenched the reins so that her pony balked. Taking a deep breath, Fiona loosened her grip on the reins and told herself she wasn't too late. She couldn't be.

Her sixth sense would have told her if she'd lost the love of her life.

Ever since she was a child, she'd been fey. One day at the age of two, unable to talk, she'd run crying into her parents' chamber. Her mother, trying to comfort her, had followed a nearly hysterical Fiona to the stables. In a stall, Fiona's favorite bitch was giving birth to a litter, one puppy coming breach. The countess was able to help with the birth; without Fiona's warning, the dog would have bled to death.

The incident and others similar to it had scared Fiona. As a child she hadn't wanted to be different. No child wanted to be different, but to be so in such a strange way had been frightening and very hard. She never knew when her gift would show her something about to happen; and no matter how hard she tried, she was unable to control the gift. Worse yet, was that she usually couldn't prevent the incident from occurring, which was all right if it were good, but more often than not, it wasn't.

She'd matured quickly. Or she'd have gone mad.

More recently, her gift had saved her grandmother's life. That time, the warning had been indefinite and it'd been Fiona's new sister-in-law, Julie Stockton, who'd realized that the storm outside had portended danger. The old woman lived in a valley next to a burn that swelled high with water during heavy rains; but Fiona and Julie had been in time to save Gran and her livestock. That had been one of the few times Fiona had thanked God for her gift.

And there were other disadvantages. People feared her. Oh, not everyone, but enough that she kept her gift to herself—unless something prompted her to reveal it or it revealed itself through a premonition she couldn't ignore.

Angus didn't know about her gift. She didn't think he would take to it. He'd think her either a witch or a bedlamite. He was a Lowland Scot, where the supernatural was scoffed at and the Gaelic legends looked down upon. She wouldn't put his affection to such a test.

Fiona sighed deeply. She focused on the scent of

heather permeating the fresh highland air. Gray clouds flew overhead, their shadows cast to the ground. Trees swayed, and the sun shone. There was a wild beauty to this land that called to her soul.

Several yards ahead of her, her escort of two muttered and exchanged a few words. Taciturn Scots, the men would defend their laird's daughter with their lives, but they did not enjoy leaving Colonsay. Not even the chance to see Edinburgh elicited more than a grunt from them.

Fiona's smile died slowly away as a frisson of fear chased down her spine. Up ahead, the path disappeared into a forest where the trees grew thickly. This was the only part of the journey she dreaded. The two times that she'd passed through this woods, she'd felt as though her entire life were at jeopardy. So far nothing had ever happened, but she always expected something dire.

Fiona shivered in the flitting shadows cast by birch and mountain ash as her pony passed over the invisible line between meadow and forest. The sense of unease was greater than before. Apprehension sat in her stomach like a malaise.

Something was wrong—but what? Eyes wide, she searched the thickly growing trees for the source of her disquiet. Nothing.

Glancing at her two companions, she realized neither man felt anything out of the ordinary. They weren't sensitive to the cool draft coming from the heart of the woods. They didn't feel the urgency and danger infusing the air. It was her gift.

Something was about to happen, something momentous. An involuntary shudder wracked her.

She renewed her efforts to see into the murky depths of the forest, to peer behind mountain ash trunks and around birch branches. Even the birds were quiet. Her gloved fingers tightened on the leather reins, and her pony faltered.

Her shaggy highland pony dragged his hooves, an irritant Fiona didn't need when her sixth sense was already drawing her nerves into sharp daggers. "Come on, MacDuff," she chided the animal.

The pony shook its head and stopped to chew on a tuft of grass growing in a patch of watery sunlight. Fiona dug her heels into the animal's ribs, knowing the futility of her action even as she pressed him forward. MacDuff was stubborn to a fault.

The chill in Fiona's spine became an itch between her shoulder blades. Someone was watching them. Someone she should know, but didn't. Her gift was like a bright flame in her mind.

"Allan. Coll," she said, her eyes darting to all sides, "draw your weapons." As she spoke, she drew her own small pistol, which she kept in a specially made pouch on her saddle.

The men picked up her anxiety. Knowing her abilities and respecting her gift, they did as ordered, keenly alert. Nothing happened.

Fiona wiped the perspiration from her brow with one hand while holding the small weapon level with the other. MacDuff stood motionless, her knees his only guide.

It wasn't long before she tired of waiting, patience

not being one of her virtues. Someone watched them, and she was determined to have that person reveal himself.

Loudly, imperiously, Fiona demanded, "Come out, whoever you are. I know you're there. I can sense you."

She intentionally alluded to her sixth sense, knowing that in the Highlands her gift was both admired and feared. Whoever stalked them, and she was sure someone did, would be nervous about her knowledge, might even leave without confronting them.

Two shots rang out almost simultaneously. The large pistols flew from Allan and Coll's fists. Shaking their hands to ease the pain, the men cursed, but stayed in their saddles. There was no telling what the ambushers would do next.

Fiona nerved herself, expecting the same to happen to her and knowing that if it did, her hand would be taken off in the process. Her pistol was much smaller, a lady's version, thus presenting a very small target. So be it. She wasn't going to throw her weapon down.

Swallowing to keep her voice from wavering, Fiona gripped her firearm tighter. "Come out, cowards, and face us."

It was a brazen attempt at bravado. With their pistols on the ground, her men were prey to the ambushers—and so was she. Her small weapon was only good at close range, if it weren't shot from her fingers.

A man's harsh voice laughed. "I'm at your command, milady."

The mocking words were followed by the appearance of a black-haired, green-eyed devil. He rode onto

the path in front of them, his stallion prancing restlessly. Pistols in both hands, the man controlled his
mount by thighs and knees alone.

Fiona's stomach twisted, and her vision blurred. A
miasma of red shot-through with gray emanated from
the man. Bile rose in her throat as she realized this
stranger brought anger with him . . . and death.

And more.

Without a doubt, this man would change her life.
She saw it in the reckless way he rode his horse, in the
energy that radiated from him in powerful waves. This
man would take control of anything in his way.

Right now, he was bent on having her. She recognized the hard gleam of his eyes and the sardonic curl
of his lip as he watched her.

"What do you want?" She challenged him, determined to fight against the destiny he symbolized. Her
small pistol was no comfort in light of the two primed
guns he brandished so expertly. "What do you want?"
she demanded again.

"You."

It was what she'd expected. Her eyes narrowed,
"What for?"

His mouth became a slash of white teeth. "Revenge."

Fiona gulped. Poverty and heartache were the leg-
acy of revenge. The Highlands was riddled by destruction brought about by men bent on revenge. Thus she
would do her best to see that no one else was harmed
by whatever drove this powerful man.

"What about my men?"

He glanced at the two who still sat their mounts,

their jaws clenched at their helplessness. "I'll let them go . . . if you come willingly and they give me their word they won't follow."

"And why should we trust you?" she asked.

He eyed her, one black brow raised. "You have no choice."

"I can shoot you," she stated calmly, her hand steady, her finger pressed surely to the trigger.

The sardonic smile curving his mouth widened. "If it pleases you. But I have the superior fire power. You'll have to aim to kill and hope I'm not faster, or you'll have two dead men. A high price for your anger."

Every word was true. Frustration gnawed at Fiona's nerves. Her jaw clenched.

Her eyes met his, and their gazes locked. It was a battle of wills she knew she was fated to lose, but one she had to fight.

The pale sunlight filtering through the birch leaves cast a green hue on her opponent, making him seem otherworldly. His black leather jacket and breeches clung to broad shoulders and strong thighs. His gloved hands were steady. His hair was long and tied back into a queue by a leather thong emphasizing the square angle of his jaw, the wide, delineated lines of his lips, and the dominant, hawk-like prominence of his nose. Thick, black waves swept across his high fore-head and highlighted the wide ebony brows which winged upwards at the temples. But it was his eyes that captured her.

Dark green lines radiated outward from the pupils like wheel spokes. Lighter green irises shone in brilliant contrast. He had malachite eyes—bright, polished, and hard.

"Seen enough?" he drawled, the harsh edge of his voice whipping her attention from his features.

Her eyes narrowed, and she glanced away. Allan and Coll sat their mounts tensely, ready if she signaled them to attack their assailant. It was tempting.

"I wouldn't do that," the green-eyed man said as though reading her thoughts. "I can kill both of them before they've moved a foot."

"And I can kill you," Fiona said softly, her attention once more on her adversary.

He met her look coolly. "At the cost of two lives. Not a good trade."

He had all the cards and nerves like granite. Knowing a loosing battle when engaged in it, Fiona tried to draw him out with questions, forcing herself to hold her fire. "What do you intend to do with me?"

His smile faded. "Use you."

Bald words, spoken without inflection. Instinctively, Fiona knew this man's actions would determine her destiny. Her stomach twisted. Apprehension knotted her shoulder muscles.

She raised her chin, but her mouth was stone dry. "How?"

His full, wide mouth pulled into a thin smile. "You'll learn that soon enough."

Without warning, the aura around the man intensified to a bloody hue. Nausea rose in Fiona.

"Death," she whispered, closing her eyes on the sight. "You want to use me to draw someone to his death."

While she grappled with the sensations of losing control, she vaguely heard the man sharply draw in his breath before speaking harshly to her men. "Give me your word not to follow, and I'll let you live. Swear on the Laird of Colonsay's honor. Otherwise, I'll kill you."

He knew who they were, Fiona realized, her disorientation fading slightly. "Do as he says," she managed to say, the nausea held in abeyance. "I'll be all right."

They would return to Colonsay and her father with the news faster than it had taken the three of them to get this far. She could expect help within days. That wouldn't be too long. She could survive anything for that time.

The man looked back at her. "You're a sensible woman."

Fiona thought she saw admiration spark his eyes, but it was gone so quickly she knew she had to have be mistaken. "I've no choice," she said, the bitter helplessness of her situation seeping into her tone.

"Your oath," the man prompted, turning back to the two men.

In sullen tones, Coll and Allan muttered their vow. Grudgingly given, it would hold them only until they reached Colonsay.

The bandit leveled his pistols. "And you, milady—" sarcasm laced the words "—retrieve your men's pistols from the ground and put them on the fallen log to your right with your own weapon."

Fiona dismounted and did as instructed, her back stiff with resentment.

"That's right," his hated voice said, "you must do as

I say. Don't try anything, or I'll be forced to shoot; and there's nothing that would anger me more than having to kill two men because you're a stubborn, selfish woman."

From the log where she laid the weapons down, she cast him a fulminating look. "I'm neither of those things or you'd be dead by now, from a bullet through your heart."

The bark of his laugh rang out in the silent forest. "And your men would die with me, only the bullets would be through their eyes."

Cold. He was as cold as ice.

She glared at him, hating him and fearing him in equal parts. "What do you want me to do now?"

"Stay put. You," he looked at the two men who were still within shooting range, "take yourselves off the way you came. Don't look back and don't double back. The girl's life depends on you as much as yours depend on her." The two servants turned their mounts around, but instead of leaving looked at Fiona. She knew that if she said so, they'd forfeit their lives by rushing her captor. She shook her head.

"Do as he bids," she ordered. "There's nothing he can do to me worth losing your lives." She firmed her voice and added, "Remember that."

Scowling, shoulders held stiffly back, Coll and Allan urged their ponies in the direction they'd already traveled. Fiona watched them with a sinking feeling that made her want to crumble onto the leaf-carpeted ground. They were her only security in a world suddenly gone topsy-turvy.

Instead of succumbing to the weakness, she scooped

up the long skirt of her moss-green riding habit and strode to MacDuff. Taking his reins, she led him toward the log where the pistols lay.

"Not that way," the man said, leveling one gun at her. "Over there." He jerked his head in the opposite direction. There was a boulder reaching high enough for her to use it to mount the pony. "And don't underestimate me again. I've no intention of playing cat and mouse with you. Next time I'll tie you up and cart you around like an unwieldy sack of oatmeal."

Fiona stiffened, but did as he ordered. The man meant what he said. There would be a time and a place later to escape.

Once more on MacDuff's familiar back, Fiona forced herself to wait patiently for her captor's next instructions—no, orders.

Not until her men were out of sight did the man move. His big stallion was perfectly trained, Fiona noticed when it came to within a foot of her pony and stopped. He put one pistol into a holster attached to his saddle.

"Hold out your hands," he said as he fished in a bag by his saddle with his free hand.

He was close enough for her to see the tiny lines bracketing his mouth, as though he used to laugh, but did no more. The lines were white in a face tanned by wind and sun.

Pulling out a length of rope, he grabbed her wrists in one hand. Her gaze went to where he held her. His grip was firm, his hands strong with long, well-shaped fingers. Where the sleeves of his jacket met his wrists, she noted scars.

Curiosity overcame her anger. "Where did you get those?" she asked, nodding at his wrists.

His eyes met hers coldly. "Newgate."

The breath caught in her throat as she stared at him. He'd been in prison and now he was kidnapping her. She should be afraid. She should be fainting from fear. Instead, all she felt was anger. He was keeping her from getting to Edinburgh and Angus. This man was altering the course of her life—or at least trying to.

Still holding her hands in one of his, he put up the second pistol. Then, without hesitation, he tied her hands so tightly together that the ropes burned her skin.

"You're hurting me," she stated flatly, her eyes on his face to see if he enjoyed what he was doing.

Some men liked inflicting pain on others. While she didn't think this man did, it was a possibility she couldn't afford to overlook. It wasn't a pleasant thought.

The lines etching the corners of his wide mouth deepened. "It's a reminder of who's in charge here. Do as you're told, and nothing will happen to you. Fight me, and you'll regret it."

The threat hung in the cool air.

Fiona was the first to look away. She didn't want him to see her intentions in her eyes. She would not only fight him, she'd best him. No man was going to hold her captive for any longer than it took her to figure out a way to escape.

Without another word, he strapped her bound wrists to the pommel of her saddle. He paid out the remaining length of rope, close to four yards, so that her pony was several steps behind his stallion. Turning right, toward the north, he guided them into the deepest thickets of the forest. No sun penetrated here to alleviate the damp chill that hung in the air.

Her taciturn captor kept the pace steady and slow enough for her Highland pony to keep up with his spirited stallion. Fiona had plenty of time to consider her fate.

The man's broad shoulders swayed easily in the saddle, telling her he felt comfortable riding. The leather clothing he wore was well made and expensive, not something a gentleman would wear but too good for a poor cottar. His speech was refined, with only the slightest hint of a burr to speak of his Scottish origins. She frowned.

He spoke and carried himself like a gentleman, and if she didn't miss her guess, he'd been educated at Eton and possibly Cambridge. She knew from her brothers that arriving at the English schools with a Scottish accent was the kiss of death. Any boy thus afflicted was quick to change or daily wear the bruises of his refusal. Her brothers could speak like purebred Englishmen when it suited them.

This man spoke the same, except when he allowed his voice to slip. He also rode an expensive horse.

No, she shook her head, this was no poor man kidnaping her. But whom did he want revenge on? Her father? She didn't think he had any enemies. More like, it was Ian. Thought to be a traitor, he had no dearth of enemies.

It was a discouraging thought. She didn't want to be the bait that drew her beloved older brother into danger. She had no doubt that her captor would prove deadly to anyone he decided to harm. And Ian had a new wife.

Fiona's determination to escape increased.

They'd been traveling for hours and not once had her captor looked back to check on her. Although the forest's thick canopy of branches kept the sun from sight, she knew the sun had set as the cold penetrated her wool riding habit. She wished she could get out her cloak, but she couldn't free herself. Her bonds were so tight her wrists were raw meat. Very likely she would have scars to match his when this was finished.

To make matters worse, although she could ignore the cold, as well as hunger and thirst, she couldn't overlook nature's call. She wouldn't disgrace herself.

"When do we stop?" she asked in her most imperious voice.

It was the closest she could make herself come to asking him to stop. Pride was too much a part of her for her to admit to him, even in so small a way, that he'd won their first battle.

"Soon," he said, still not looking back.

It was the answer she'd anticipated, but anger still knotted her stomach. Under her breath, she cursed, "Bloody tyrant."

"Did you say something?" he asked, his voice rising in a lilt at the end.

He was baiting her, and her temper snapped. "I'm bloody hungry and thirsty. And I've got to relieve myself. Unlike you, I'm human."

At that, he stopped. He slid from his saddle and came back to her. His mouth curved in a lopsided slant that was almost a smile, but not quite. Reaching out, he clasped her waist and swung her down.

He lifted her high and set her down fast, making her stomach lurch. Her toes barely touched ground as his hands remained around her waist, holding her to his hard body. It was a threat of strength that she didn't fail to grasp.

Yet, the heat emanating from him was comforting in the gathering gloom and cold. Fiona found her flesh craving the warmth coming from this man. She cursed herself.

Hands tightly bound, Fiona struggled against his hold. She kicked out at him, connecting with a shin. His grunt of pain was very satisfying.

"Vixen," he growled, releasing her abruptly so that she stumbled back.

"Tyrant," she returned, standing her ground. "Untie my hands so that I may do what we've stopped for."

His eyes narrowed. "If you wish, milady."

The silken tones of his voice made Fiona instantly wary. She held her arms out anyway.

His eyes never wavered from hers. "But if I undo you, you must suffer my presence."

Her mouth thinned. "I expected as much. How do you expect me to lift my skirts if my wrists are bound?"

His smile was cruel. "As best you can. Just as I managed to do difficult things so many times these last three years."

Watching him intently, she saw the darkening of his eyes and the tightening of the skin around them. He'd

been made to suffer and now he was seeking revenge
for it, even if it meant taking it out on her in the
meantime.

"You won't break me," she told him, "just as you
didn't break." She lifted her chin. "At least let out the
rope so that I may go to the other side of a bush
without you. Or do you think that out of your sight I'll
be able to untie your knots?"

Her sarcasm bit at him. "You're too small to fight
me, milady. And I am not afraid of your escaping. The
bonds are tight. I learned them at sea."

A sailor. Probably an officer.

Red emblazoned her cheeks as she stalked the entire
four yards of distance the rope allowed her. When a
large bush effectively separated them, she struggled
with her unwieldy skirts.

She had just finished when she heard the sounds of
another horse approaching. Fiona knew this was her
captor's accomplice; she'd sensed another man's presence from the beginning.

"Damnation, Micheil," her captor cursed. "I told
you to stay out of sight. I've no wish for you to be
drawn into this anymore than you already are."

Chapter Two

Her captor's anger at his accomplice surprised Fiona. Smoothing down her riding skirts with bound hands, she listened unashamedly. Honor was a commodity she couldn't afford if she were to escape.

"I'd never leave you to do it all yourself, Niall," the new man's light tenor said almost in a whine. "You know I wouldn't. I stood by you these past three years; I'll stay by you now even though I don't agree with what you intend."

Her captor groaned. "I know. I know. But I don't want her seeing you. 'Tis bad enough that she'll remember me, but I won't have you endangered, too."

"Niall," Micheil said, "I stayed away until she went behind the bush. You can't keep me out of this. I'm your friend. I care about what happens to you."

Fiona listened intently. She was the prisoner of a man named Niall. Niall. She sounded the name in her mind, letting the gaelic lilt of the word echo in her thoughts. Such a melodic name for such a beastly man.

"Micheil," Niall said, interrupting her consideration of his name, "I never doubt you. You're the only one who supported me through these years. That's why I want you gone before she returns. I don't want you seen."

Fiona's mouth formed a moue. Her abductor was actually pleading.

"I'll go this time," Micheil said, "but I'll not stay away from the camp. She's got to see me sometime."

"Such as now," Fiona said sweetly, stepping around the bush.

Niall watched the flame-haired vixen without trying to hide his irritation. He knew his brows were a V in his forehead and his eyes were as hard as the stone they resembled. He didn't care.

She stood there bold as brass with her hands on her hips and her hair hanging down her back in a tumble of curls. Even her nose was impertinent with its re-troussé tip.

Her moss-green riding habit was dirty and had a rip up one side that showed her petticoats. It was obvious she didn't care. She stood defiantly, her blue eyes like cold aquamarines and her full, pouting mouth just like a ripe peach.

Niall forced himself to unclench his fingers. "Your timing is impeccable."

She mocked him with her curtsy, keeping her balance even though her wrists were tied in front of her. "The same could be said of yours."

Exasperation coursed through Niall. He should have known that any sister of Duncan Macfie's would be a spitfire and a beauty. It was an unholy combination that promised to make the next weeks of his life hell.

"So you're Duncan's sister," Micheil said, coming into the conversation.

The girl looked at Micheil, and her face blanched. She swayed.

Cursing her, himself, and the situation, Niall lunged for her, catching her just before she hit the rock-strewn ground.

Micheil was at Niall's side instantly. "M'God. What came over her? You don't suppose she has the fainting sickness, do you?" His face held all the horror he felt at that possibility.

"Duncan was a strong man; his sister wouldn't be so frail," Niall said, refusing to believe such a thing. "Get me some water. We haven't the time to linger here. Those men of hers will be on our trail before we can say Methuselah."

Niall felt her forehead, which seemed cool enough. Her pulse beat strongly and slowly.

"Here." Micheil handed him the water skin.

Niall took the stopper out and poured the cold water over the girl's face.

"Wha—!" She spluttered, her tied hands swatting at the water streaming down her cheeks and neck. "What are you doing?"

She sat bolt upright, chest heaving, eyes flashing. "You fiend!"

Niall sat back on his haunches. He had to admire her wit and courage, even though he didn't want to. She was a means to an end for him. Nothing more.

He frowned. Rising, he pulled on the length of rope

that bound her, forcing her to stumble to her feet. "We aren't stopping yet."

When she tripped over her long skirts, he grabbed her up by the waist and swung her into the saddle. She landed with a jolt that made his teeth ache in sympathy, but she didn't say a word. She just glared down at him, her blue, blue eyes like chips of ice.

Niall turned away and said to Micheil, "If you insist, I'll meet you back at the camp. But you know I don't like your being seen. 'Tis *my* revenge, not yours."

Micheil, his hair a sandy brown in the fading light, smiled wanly. "You know I'd follow you to hell, Niall."

Niall's shoulders slumped. "I know."

From her perch on MacDuff's back, Fiona watched the tableau. No matter how hard she tried to keep her gaze averted, her eyes kept returning to Micheil.

The man was cursed. There was an aura of black death about him. That was what had made her faint.

Shudders that she could do nothing to stop shook her body and raised gooseflesh on her skin. Cold seeped into her very bones. This man had murder writ on him.

She squeezed her eyes shut to block out the sight of him. Relief washed over her when she heard the sounds of his horse leaving. Her gift abated and she could breath again, belatedly realizing that she'd been holding her breath for some time as though to keep from taking in the taint of his curse.

MacDuff lurched into movement, and she knew that

Niall had mounted his own horse and had set off again. For camp. Wherever that was.

Fiona opened her eyes to keep from getting vertigo and falling from MacDuff's back. It was plain to her that if she fell, Niall would likely haul her back into the saddle by the rope binding her hands. After having water thrown in her face to waken her, she hardly expected any kinder treatment.

The remainder of the ride was hard. The water had dripped onto the bosom and shoulders of her habit, and the air made the material clammy and cold. The sun was barely a glow on the horizon, its warmth long gone. Fiona's teeth started to chatter and, try as she would, she couldn't stop them. She fully expected to get an ague.

But she was no longer hungry. Neither did nature call. She'd gone beyond all of that in her discomfort.

And still they kept on.

It was as though the fiend were fleeing from pursuit. She knew it was too soon for her men to have reached Colonsay. They had to cross the choppy waters of the ocean; and no matter how pushed they were, they'd hesitate to do that in the pitch black. Neither would they follow her themselves. They'd given their word.

Fitful dozing claimed her, the plodding rock of MacDuff's gait lulling her like a cradle. If only it were warm . . .

Niall approached the edge of the sea cliffs and paused, his nerves drawn tighter than a harp's strings. Several feet ahead was the path down to the rocky cove where his camp was and where Micheil waited. He didn't expect ambush, but three years in Newgate made a man value his freedom. It was too soon for the girl's men to have returned, but one never knew.

When nothing moved and the birds continued their calling, he started forward. The seagulls would tell him if an intruder was in their midst.

Glancing over his shoulder, he saw the girl start awake. For some time now, he'd been aware that she dozed fitfully. Dark lines underscored her eyes, making them appear enormous in the pointed angles of her face. Right now she looked transparent from fatigue. But not once had she complained.

He turned abruptly away from her.

Fiona clenched her jaw to keep from moaning at the pain lancing through her hip and back as they made their way down the steep decline to the rocky cove. Dark shadows rose on either side of them as they descended to a place where the last rays of day didn't penetrate.

MacDuff's hooves slipped numerous times before gaining a hold on the path. Countless times, Fiona held her breath, knowing she was inches away from tumbling into darkness.

The cold breeze off the water bit through her habit. She shivered in the night air. It might be late summer, but she'd welcome a blanket tonight.

Her captor angled around a rocky promontory at the base of the path, and she realized they were at the entrance to a cave. Inside a fire blazed, casting jumping shadows on the narrow walls. One was of a tall, hunched-over man.

Micheil was here before them.

Fiona gulped down the bile rising in her throat. She

would have to master her reaction since it looked as though she'd be seeing quite a bit of the man. Her determination to escape intensified.

Niall stopped his stallion just outside the cave entrance. Leaping down, he grabbed his mount's reins and looped them over a piece of driftwood.

Fiona longed to slide down and feel solid ground under her feet, but knew movement was futile. She was tied again to the pommel. And even if she weren't, she knew she couldn't stand on her own. Exhaustion sapped her strength.

She straightened her shoulders, not willing to show weakness to her opponent. However, she couldn't suppress the quiver in her arms or the shivers from the cold.

Her captor strode over to her and unwrapped the rope binding her to the saddle. Before she could say a word, he lifted her down. Her feet hit the ground and her legs buckled.

Niall, with a snort of disgust, hoisted her into his arms. The protest died on her lips as the warmth of his body penetrated his leather jacket and her wool habit. His heat was welcome no matter what type of man he was, so cold was she.

His arms were as strong as iron around her back and thighs. His heart beat slow and steady against her ear through the butter-soft leather of his jacket. Oddly, she felt safe.

It was a dichotomy. The man was a threat to her safety and the life of her beloved brother, Ian. Yet, in his arms, with the deep throb of his pulse in her ear, she felt secure.

Fiona closed her eyes. Only for a moment, she told herself, drifting into sleep in spite of herself. She woke with a start when her captor laid her down.

The fire warmed the small cave. Perched over the flames was a blackened pot from which came the aroma of meat. Her stomach growled.

Niall smiled, an expression almost of gentleness on his harsh features. "Your stomach is more vocal about your needs than your mouth."

Exhaustion was like a drug to Fiona. Her gift was temporarily lulled, even with Micheil nearby. The edge was gone from her voice. "I'm famished and thirsty."

Micheil shot a glance at her captor before moving to her. Squatting down, he undid the rope binding her wrists.

The pain of returning circulation shot through Fiona's hands and fingers, overshadowing the queasiness Micheil's proximity caused. As gently as possible, she massaged her flesh.

"Thank you," she said to Micheil, his kindness at odds with her sensation of him as a murderer. It seemed her vision blurred when she looked at him: Two people inhabited his body, and she couldn't tell which was which.

"You free the vixen at your own risk," Niall said darkly from his position across the fire.

Micheil, his eyes on her raw flesh, said, "She's only a woman, Niall. And she needs to eat."

He handed her a bowl of brown stew and a cup filled with brown liquid. The food was venison. The drink was strong tea.

"Thank you," Fiona murmured, feeling uncomfortable at his nearness but no longer nauseous. The aura around him had abated, and her stomach was more hungry than upset.

She ate the food and drank the tea eagerly. Warmth flowed into her, and with it a lethargy that dragged at her limbs. Setting down the empty bowl and mug, she looked at her captor.

"Do I get to sleep now or are you going to torture me by making me stay awake indefinitely?"

Niall glared at her, his malachite eyes glowing in the firelight. His black hair swept back from his forehead in waves of darkness. His brows winged upward. He had a diabolically handsome face—harsh, yet strongly beautiful. Fiona's pulse sped.

Before Niall responded, Micheil rose and spread a blanket on the ground in a corner, close enough to the fire for warmth, but far enough away to provide some privacy. She was still under view.

Niall rose and strode to her. Squatting, he picked up the rope from where Micheil had dropped it to the ground and said, "Hold out your hands."

A sigh of regret escaped Fiona before she could clamp her teeth shut. Resignation slumped her shoulders, but only momentarily. She held out her arms and defiantly met his gaze.

"You're a cold man," she said as he wound the rope securely about her wrists. She bit down on her lip to keep from gasping as the rough hemp cut into her raw skin.

He glanced up at her, his eyes fathomless pools in the shadow cast by the fire at his back. "I learned the hard way not to trust anyone."

She thought about his words as he checked the tightness of the rope. What had he done to be put in prison? She'd wager he was of noble or landed birth, with no reason to steal. She thought he'd been a ship's officer. Had he killed someone? But she felt her insight linking him with death was involved with his present quest for revenge, not his past.

The scars of his imprisonment were barely visible in the flickering light as he finished binding her. When he was confident that the rope would hold, he reached down and hooked his hands under her arms. He lifted her as if she weighed nothing.

"You're a tiny thing," he murmured.

Fiona didn't consider herself a tiny woman, yet she didn't quite reach his shoulder. He was a tall, lean man with the grace of a mountain cat and the piercing gaze of an eagle. Her skin tingled where he touched her.

When she spoke, her voice was harsh. "If you're done with me, I want to sleep. There's no telling what tomorrow will bring."

His wide mouth curved; his eyelids drooped. "Look into your crystal ball, milady."

She ignored his sarcasm, but couldn't ignore his touch as he guided her to the spread blanket. Breathing was suddenly difficult. He was strangely upsetting to her.

Glancing at Micheil, she saw his eyes on them, a frown pulling his sandy brows together. Even in a crouch, his shoulders hunched, he was tall and lanky, without the sinewy grace of his friend. His hands fidgeted nervously with the silver button on his coat. His eyes were pale and opaque as he watched Niall walk back to his place on the other side of the fire. His nose was a sharp triangle. His need for Niall showed in every line.

As soon as he noticed her studying him, he wiped his face clean of expression. A chill chased down Fiona's spine.

She sank gratefully onto the blanket, pushing Niall and his strange friend from her mind. Fatigue was a drug in her muscles. She needed rest. Later, she'd think about the two very different men and how to escape from them.

The cave floor was hard under her back with little rocks jutting into her spine. The fire's warmth barely reached her, and her wrists ached from the continuing rope binds. Somehow, she dozed off.

On the verge of sleep, in that strange place where thoughts wander where they will, she found herself longing for the nearness of her captor. Even in that borderland, she chided herself for the unusual desire. She was going to Edinburgh to win her love; she shouldn't feel anything but loathing for this man who'd captured her to use in getting revenge on her brother. She should hate him.

"The vixen is mine, Micheil." Niall's voice rose forcefully, waking Fiona from a sleep she hadn't expected to get. "And with her my plan begins."

Keeping still, her eyes closed, she eavesdropped without remorse to the conversation between the two men. This wasn't some Edinburgh drawing room where manners meant everything. This was a life-and-death situation where anything was fair in order to survive.

"Forget this," the other man's light tenor pleaded. " 'Tis the past. Don't endanger yourself for revenge."

She heard the crunch of rock and dirt under booted feet and surmised that Niall had risen to pace the narrow confines of the cave. Through her closed eyelids, the light from the fire darkened and lightened as he passed between her and it.

"I spent three years in Newgate." The pacing stopped. "Three years, Micheil. Do you know what that does to a man—to his honor?"

There was such a wealth of pain and bitterness mixed with his anger that Fiona found herself sympathizing with him. But what had he done to merit such a fate?

Micheil said, "You weren't in discomfort. I made sure you had everything a gentleman would need. I even gave up my own career in the Navy to stay in London near you."

Fiona wondered how Niall could stand the guilt Micheil heaped on him. She wouldn't have been able to.

Niall groaned. "I know you did, Micheil, and I can never repay you for that. But I must have revenge."

"If you kill them, you'll go back to prison." Micheil's voice lowered. "Or you'll have to flee to the Continent. Better to forget it all. You're free now."

"You don't understand," Niall said, sounding harassed. "I lost my honor. My name is smirched beyond redemption." The pacing resumed. "And for what? Why?" He spat the words, the force of his emotions carrying like waves to Fiona. "Because someone killed a woman and framed me."

"I know, Niall. I'm sorry," Micheil said. "But that's no reason to kidnap this woman and use her. What if you get caught?"

"I can go to Newgate," Niall said in bitingly ironic tones.

Micheil tried a new tack. "This is a foolhardy plot. What are you going to do if it works and Macfie comes for her?"

Fiona heard the brutal determination in her captor's voice. "I'll challenge him to a duel . . . and I'll win."

Micheil's laugh was high and caustic. "A duel? A duel?"

Fiona squinted through her lids, trying desperately to see the faces of her captors without letting them know she was awake. Niall's back was to her, but the tension in his shoulders told her how strong the emotions were that he held in check.

"I'll not become a murderer, though many already think me one." His tone was flat, anger and disillusionment spiking through the words anyway. "Macfie will fight an honorable duel with me, as will Winter and Sculthorpe. Those three sat on the court-martial board that condemned me for a murder I didn't commit without giving me the benefit of doubt." His voice lowered. "They didn't believe my word."

The tale was stark and bitter. Fiona felt her flesh raise in goose bumps. There was a wrong here that needed to be avenged; she didn't need her gift to realize that. But if it meant killing three men who'd only done what they were bid to, she couldn't condone it.

Niall continued. "I'll fight all three and I'll win. And

when I win, I'll force each one to recant his decision that day—or I'll kill him."

Micheil went to his friend and laid a hand on Niall's shoulder. "I wish you'd forget this. Nothing you do will erase Newgate and the conviction. Don't endanger yourself by this obsession for revenge. Let it go."

Fury blazed from Niall. He shook off Micheil's hand. "I'll not do it. I'll fight them all—and I'll kill them." His hands clenched into fists. "Or I'll die trying. My honor demands it."

The air in the cave was chill, the fire almost out. Fiona shivered involuntarily in her blanket, her captor's vow ringing in her mind.

Micheil had spoken of the Navy. Her younger brother Duncan was in the navy. Could he be the MacFie Niall was bent on fighting? Duncan was a captain now. He could have sat on the court-martial board that condemned Niall to prison.

She shivered anew. There was no doubt in her mind that Duncan would come to rescue her and that Niall would kill her brother. Niall was too dangerous and too powerful to be bested by any man.

"That's where I need your help, Micheil." Niall spoke again, diverting Fiona from the thought of her brother lying dead from Niall's weapon. "I want you to take a message to Macfie. Tell him I have his sister and if he wants to see her alive again, he must come to me."

"I don't like this," Micheil said, his voice quiet, yet resigned. "What if he won't come?"

Niall's harsh laughter rang out, echoing from the

stone walls. "He'll come. He thinks I'm capable of murder."

"What if he doesn't believe me when I tell him you have her?"

Fiona's breath caught at that. What if Duncan didn't believe it? What would happen to her then?

Niall moved so quickly, she barely had time to shut her eyes completely before he was upon her. She choked back a gasp as he loomed over her, reached down, and took a strand of her loose hair. There was a tug; then he was gone. Softly, she released a sigh of relief.

"Here. Even Macfie should recognize his sister's hair. Especially hair of this copper hue."

Fiona inched her eyes open again in time to see Micheil reluctantly take the strand and put it into his pocket.

"I still don't like it, but I know you're set on this. Where do you want me to tell MacFie to meet you?"

"I'm taking the girl to Skye."

"Your clan's island?" Micheil asked incredulously. "But I thought your father disowned you after the disgrace."

Bitterness etched deep lines around Niall's mouth. "That he did. But there's a ruined castle near the coast. No one ever goes there. It's said to be haunted. I'll take the girl there."

At the mention of the castle, Fiona's gift flared. Perspiration broke out on her palms. Something would happen there, and it would change the rest of her life.

Chapter Three

Fiona lay motionless, listening to the two men discuss the logistics. Micheil was to leave at first dawn and travel to Glasgow, where Duncan's ship was in dock. She and Niall would leave shortly after, headed for the Sound of Sleat which they would cross in a small boat.

She would have to escape before they left. Once they were on the Isle of Skye, she'd never be able to get off. Nor would her father and his men be able to find her. Time was running out for her.

She'd wait until the men bedded down for the couple hours of sleep left before dawn. Then she'd use her teeth on the knots of rope binding her wrists. Even if she had to break her teeth, she'd free herself. While she could run with her hands bound, it would be hard to climb the steep path to the top of the cliffs and even harder to make her way quickly.

Time moved at a sluggish pace before everything quieted down. Surreptitiously, her eyes open for any movement, Fiona began to chew at her bonds.

Each bite rubbed her flesh, sending shooting pains

up her arms. She didn't need to see her skin to know it was like raw meat. The rope cut her lips and gums, but she kept at it. She had to escape.

The fire was dead, and cold filled the cave. The full moon shone like molten silver into the mouth of their hideaway, lining everything in a white haze. Dawn would be upon them soon and her last chance at escape gone.

So far, she'd bitten through several layers, but not enough to break her bonds. Tears of frustration rolled down her cheeks, freezing her cheeks.

She paused to catch her breath. Only then did she realize that someone was up and about. Quickly she pushed her hands deep under the blanket, swallowing the gasps of pain the rapid movement caused her abraded skin.

She strained her ears. Perhaps he was going to relieve himself.

A shadow blotted out the moon's meager light. Belatedly, Fiona squeezed her eyes shut, but she was too late.

The figure squatted down beside her. A finger settled on her lips, indicating silence. Her gift activated, creating a churning sensation in the pit of her stomach. It was Micheil who touched her.

Defeat tightened her muscles, overriding the unease in her gut. He was going to check her bonds; she knew it. Then they'd be tied even tighter. She fought against the tears of defeat forming in her eyes.

Revulsion ripped through her as his other hand moved down her arm to her wrist. For a fleeting second, she wondered if he'd violate her, here in the dark with only Niall to hear. Then his fingers were at her wrists and he was pulling her hands from under the blanket.

This was it. Fiona tensed, ready to fight him. She wasn't going to submit meekly.

Before she could do anything, the fingers of his free hand closed around her neck, thumb and finger pressing her jugular. Her vision blurred. The scream she was about to release, died.

It was only minutes, but it was enough for him to release her wrists. Without a word, he rose and returned to his sleeping pallet.

Fiona lay quiescent, her thoughts sharpening as her blood circulated back to the brain. For some reason of his own, Micheil had freed her. She would have to think about this before acting. There were times when she was precipitate, usually as a result of her gift. This wasn't one of those times.

Something was out of order. Micheil was Niall's friend and was supposed to be loyal to him. True loyalty should mean he wouldn't release her and thus foil Niall's plans for revenge.

Or, this could be a different form of loyalty. Micheil could be loyal in his desire to protect his friend from harm; he obviously thought Niall shouldn't go through with his plan for revenge. Perhaps Micheil was trying to save Niall from the consequences of his bitterness and anger by letting her go free. Without her, Niall couldn't lure Duncan.

It was all so confusing and so much a matter of her guessing as to the reasons behind another person's actions. She didn't like doing that.

But no matter what Micheil's motivations, this was her only chance for freedom. Fiona knew she'd have to act now or give up all hope of escape.

Stealthily, she pushed back the blanket. The rough wool rubbed her bloody wrists. She bit her tongue to keep from moaning until the coppery taste of blood exploded on her tongue.

Rising to her feet, she fought vertigo caused by her abrupt change in position as she inched around the fire, making sure she kept it between herself and Niall. It meant passing right by Micheil.

She glanced down at the man. His opaque blue eyes watched her.

Fiona froze, her own eyes unable to leave his. For long minutes she stood thus. Slowly, he lowered his lids. She took it as a signal that she was free to go, that he'd been waiting for her to escape.

Her chest tightened, and her breath caught. She'd been right. He wanted her gone.

Well, she wouldn't disappoint him.

Sometime later, Niall woke with a start. It was the same nightmare: His trial, Newgate prison, his father's disowning of him. Dishonor and imprisonment, what more could he suffer?

His mouth twisted. For someone raised in the Highlands, where name and honor were frequently all a man had, there was nothing worse than dishonor. He had tortured himself with that knowledge while he rotted in the ship's hold as it made its way to England. He'd thought nothing worse could happen.

He'd been mistaken.

Upon hearing of Niall's court-martial and conviction of murder, his father had disowned him. His chest rose and fell in quick breaths as he strived to contain the bitter pain that memory elicited.

The youngest of four boys, he'd never been his father's favorite, but he hadn't dreamed the man thought so little of him as to believe him capable of beating a woman, slitting her throat, and sodomizing her. He'd been wrong.

Even now, three years later, he could picture the woman clearly. They'd taken him to look at her to try and force a confession from him. She hadn't been a pretty sight. Death never was, but her murder had been particularly gruesome. Her throat had been slit, blood forming an obscene smile across her neck. Bruises had covered her body and she'd been used as a man would use another man.

No, she hadn't been pretty. Nor had the sight of her elicited a confession from him. He knew in his soul he hadn't done those things to her.

But he'd been made to pay for another's crime. They hadn't believed him when he'd denied the act. Instead, they'd found him guilty because his lucky piece had been found in her clenched fist. Clapped in iron until they docked once more in England, he'd been transferred to Newgate Prison, where he'd spent the past three years of his life.

It was there he'd vowed revenge on the three men responsible for having him dishonorably discharged from the Navy and sent to prison. Duncan Macfie was the first on his list. And Fiona Macfie was his key to Duncan.

He should be exultant, his plan was finally being put into action. Instead he felt heavy of heart and disgusted. Revenge was a difficult burden to carry, no matter how righteous it was.

Prince Charlie, Niall's stallion, snorted, rousing Niall from his disturbing thoughts. The animal's paws dug at the rocky ground. A wry smile twisted Niall's lips. The stallion had little patience. He however, had learned about patience in jail, patience and coldness.

He'd need both to deal with Fiona Macfie. The girl, actually woman, was spirited and strong. Damn her. All five feet of her was going to fight him.

Her hair was like a fire's flames, its brightness and warmth beckoning even as it threatened to burn the unsuspecting. Her petite, yet perfect, little figure beguiled with every twist of her body or stiffening of her shoulders.

The ache that had been with him since he first encountered her returned with a vengeance. It was an urge he had to deny.

She was a means to an end. She wasn't a woman he could seduce. She was the daughter of an earl and the sister of the man he'd vowed to kill. She was an object.

With a groan of frustration, Niall hoisted himself out of the blanket and stretched his six-foot frame. The fire was down to embers, and Micheil was still asleep. The corner where his captive lay was empty.

Striding to the mound of blankets, he tossed them aside. Underneath lay the rope, partially gnawed through. Squatting, he examined it. She'd bitten through several strands, but that hadn't been what had freed her. The knots had been cut. By her?

"Wha's the matter?" Micheil's sleepy voice asked.

Eyes narrowed, Niall looked over his shoulder. His friend was bleary eyed, his sandy hair tousled, his clothes rumpled. "Did you let her go?"

He spoke softly, without accusing, yet Micheil's eyes slid away from his. It was answer enough.

Rising, Niall asked calmly, feeling almost as though he were in a drawing room and politeness was of the utmost importance. "Why?"

Micheil got up and busied himself by putting several small logs on the fire and blowing on the embers. He still didn't look at Niall. "Because it's a mistake. You're free now. Don't risk imprisonment or having to flee the country by killing a man in a duel."

"Neither of those thoughts scare me, Micheil. I don't think you understand." He chose his words carefully, wanting his friend to comprehend. "I wouldn't be imprisoned. I'd leave the country first, and I've already lost so much that leaving Scotland would matter little."

Micheil glanced at him, then looked quickly away. His shoulders hunched as he poured water from a leather bag into a pan and set it over the fire. "I understand that you're angry and your pride is wounded. Don't let it ruin the rest of your life."

Niall turned away so his friend wouldn't see the disillusionment in his eyes. He'd thought Micheil could grasp the intensity of the demons driving him. He'd been wrong. Micheil's sense of honor and justness wasn't the same as his. And he had no time to ponder or argue further; he couldn't afford to lose the girl.

"I'm going after her," Niall said, exiting the cave and going to Prince Charlie. "Even on her pony, she can't get away from me. She's only got several hours lead at best."

Micheil followed him from the cave. "I'll head on to Glasgow with your message since you won't listen to sense."

"Thank you, Micheil," Niall said from the saddle. No matter what their differences, Micheil had always stood by him. "You're a true friend to help even though you think I'm wrong. And you're a truer friend for telling me when you think I'm wrong. I won't forget that."

What Niall left unsaid, but hung between them, coloring every interaction they had, was Micheil's loyalty during his trial and incarceration. When men he'd thought his friends had turned from him, Micheil had been there, naysaying the ones who called him a murderer. When his father had disowned him, Micheil had stood beside him. Micheil was the one who had visited him every day of his imprisonment. Micheil was the one who'd seen to it that he had money to purchase the necessities available even in a hellhole like Newgate. He owed Micheil more than he could ever repay.

Micheil gave him a lopsided grin and waved. Niall smiled back before turning away.

Leaning low in the saddle, Niall followed the traces of the woman's escape. Where her mount had passed, the seagrasses were trodden down. Once in the forest, there'd be broken branches and crushed leaves to tell the story of her route.

The morning chill settled over Niall. It was the end of August and winter would soon be on the Highlands. Luckily, he'd already provisioned the castle and laid in a good supply of blankets. There would be snow on the ground soon.

First, though, he had to find the woman. He pressed Prince Charlie to travel quickly while his sharp eyes searched for signs. They were ridiculously easy to find. She was traveling hastily.

His lips twitched. Soon.

Fiona heard him before she saw him. He made no effort to disguise his approach. Her heart sped up, and her fingers instinctively tightened on MacDuff's reins. As usual, the pony balked.

"Blast. Don't stop now," she muttered, kicking his flanks. He plodded on.

The sound of her pursuer crashing through trees and undergrowth was loud. Her breath came raggedly.

MacDuff stumbled, his hoof catching in a rabbit hole. So intent was she on the man following, that she wasn't paying attention. She tumbled over MacDuff's neck and head, hitting the ground with a bone-jarring thud.

Scrambling to her feet, Fiona glanced wildly behind her. He was there. Just clearing a fallen log, he rode his stallion as one. She broke out in a sweat.

She started running, knowing there was no time to mount MacDuff and no way the pony could outdistance the horse. She had to lose her would-be captor by dodging and zigzagging through the trees.

The long skirts of her riding habit tangled in her legs. She tripped, going to her knees. Behind her the sounds of pursuit neared.

Struggling to her feet, she plunged on. With one hand, she held her skirts up to her thighs. With the other, she pushed aside branches and cleared paths through brush. Her breath came in uneven sobs.

He was so close . . . so close.

She didn't dare glance behind; it would only slow her, and she couldn't afford to be slowed. Her feet pumped and her chest pounded. Blood rushed in her ears like the raging wind of a storm. It drowned out the sound of pursuit.

She pressed on.

An arm swooped around her waist, lifting her high into the sky. Her stomach did a somersault. She screamed and flailed with her fists.

She caught him in the mouth.

"Bloody vixen," he cursed, his grip faltering.

She kicked out, her booted foot hitting the side of his calf. He dropped her. She landed hard, her knees buckling and pain shooting up from her arches to her calves. She fell to all fours, hair hanging in her eyes, obscuring her vision.

She scrambled away from the stallion's prancing legs. The crash of hooves sounded from the ground where she'd lain seconds before.

As she pushed herself up from the ground, Fiona's breath came in puffs. She grabbed her skirts in both hands and ran for her freedom. For her life.

With another curse, Niall launched himself from Prince Charlie's back. Landing on the balls of his feet, he sprinted after her. It'd be a good day in Newgate before she escaped him.

She darted between two gnarled oaks. He followed her unerringly. She clambered over a fallen tree trunk. He vaulted over it, using one arm to push off and up. She was within grasp.

His muscles bunched powerfully beneath him. He dove for her in one supreme effort. His arms wrapped around her calves, his face burrowing into the voluminous folds of her skirt.

Fiona flung her arms in front of her face to protect it from the ground that rushed up to meet her. She slammed into it. The air rushed out of her in a whoosh. Lights flashed in her head.

His weight was an anchor keeping her pinned to the bed of leaves beneath them. She squirmed, trying to push away from the smothering forest floor with her gloved hands. He shimmied up her body until she lay under him, his chest pressed to her shoulders and his legs tangled with hers. He placed a hand on either side of her head. She turned to one side, teeth bared, intending to bite him.

"Don't even try," he warned in a soft, deadly voice.

Fiona gulped in air, almost willing to bite him and suffer the consequences. "Then . . ." She dragged in a deep breath. ". . . get off me before I suffocate."

He rolled off her, but he grabbed her wrists and his legs continued to pinion hers. Both on their sides, they confronted each other. His eyes blazed into hers.

"Don't try to escape again."

She stared at him defiantly, her mouth a thin line of rebellion. "I'll do as I damn well please."

His grip on her tightened. She winced, the pain from her still-raw wrists lancing through her.

His glance flicked to her wrists and back to her face. "You'll do as I say until I'm done with you."

How dare he think he could control her? Her own brothers knew better than to dictate to her; all it did was raise her hackles.

Anger coursed through her, heating her in spite of the moist dampness seeping through her riding habit from the earth. "Don't turn your back on me," she warned. "I won't sit passively by while you use me to lure my brother to his death. You may depend on it."

A thin smile stretched his mouth. "I like a challenge, vixen." His eyes darkened. " 'Twill keep the next week lively."

Fiona ground her teeth together. She would not be used. She thrashed against him, kicking at the heavy weight of his legs on hers.

In one smooth movement, he rolled her onto her back and raised up above her, his hips pining hers down. "Don't push me, vixen. I've no love for your family or you, but you're innocent of your brother's acts and I'll try to remember that."

She glared at him, refusing to be intimidated by the brilliant glow of his malachite eyes as they stared down at her. His gaze shifted to her mouth, making her breath catch. He was crushing her; and yet, it didn't hurt.

His muscles were hard against the flattened swell of her bosom, and his thighs were like hewn tree trunks

in their strength against her legs. The harsh angles of
his face spoke of determination and domination as he
studied her. His mouth lowered to hers.

Fiona's stomach knotted as she turned away from
him. Every fiber of her being screamed *no*. He mustn't
kiss her.

Taking one hand from her wrists, he took her chin
between thumb and forefinger and turned her toward
him. He smiled just before his lips covered hers.

It was a hard kiss, his lips never softening as he
pressed against her. His tongue forced entry and plundered her mouth. It was his way of showing her that
he was in charge.

The anger of minutes before became fury. Fiona
was damned if he'd punish her this way.

Her tongue flicked against his, enticing him deeper.
She teased with him, her mouth moving against his.
She sensed the change in him, his punishment was now
his pleasure.

She bit him—hard.

He reared back. "Bloody vixen," he cursed, his hips
still pressing into hers, holding her captive. But instead
of holding her jaw in place for his kiss, he was using
that hand to feel how much blood she'd drawn from
his tongue with her teeth.

"You won't bleed to death," she said coldly.

"No thanks to you," he muttered, releasing her
wrists and rolling off her into a squat beside her.
"Don't try it again."

"Don't kiss me again."

She pushed herself up so that she stood above him.
Looking quickly around, she judged the distance to his

stallion. It was too far. He'd be on her before she gained three feet.

"If you run again," he said quietly, still squatting as though disdaining her ability to escape, "I'll strap you over your pony's saddle like a sack of wheat. You wouldn't like that."

She turned back to look at him. The cold gleam in his eyes and the hard line of his mouth told her he'd do that and more. But somehow she had to get away. Perhaps not now, but soon. She couldn't let him use her to lure Duncan to his death.

With ill grace, she said, "Nor will you enjoy the next days. I won't make it easy for you."

For the first time since she'd encountered him, he smiled. The flash of teeth lit up his face and softened the full line of his mouth. It made him into a rogue with the potential to break a woman's heart.

Fiona's chest tightened, and her hands turned clammy and cold. She jerked away.

When he gripped her arm above the elbow, she jumped. It felt as if a bolt of lightning had struck her, run up her arm to her shoulder, and shot down into her abdomen. She twisted away.

"I can walk on my own."

"But can you be trusted not to bolt?"

His challenging question gave her no alternative but to look at him. It was a mistake. The breath caught in her throat. No matter what she thought of him, he was devilishly handsome. Virility emanated from him in waves that threatened to drown her. She shook her head, to clear it of the ridiculous thoughts. She loved Angus and would go to Edinburgh to win him, as soon as she escaped this fiend's hold and warned Duncan of the danger to his life.

"I can be trusted to honor my word only. Nothing else." She forbade herself to look away from him no matter how disturbing he was.

"Give it to me," he said harshly, "and I won't bind you again."

She laughed, the sound choked. "That would be the same as condemning my brother to death."

He shrugged. "Have it your way."

With those words he strode to his stallion, yanking her in his wake. Fishing in one of the leather bags tied to his saddle, he pulled out a white lawn shirt.

"Stay put," he ordered her. She stared stonily at him. "Stay put or I *will* strap you over your pony."

Knowing she couldn't get away this time, Fiona nodded curtly.

He pulled a knife from his boot and used it to rip the shirt into strips. "Hold out your hands," he said.

Fiona, surprised, did as he bid. With a touch that was almost gentle, he wrapped the fine cloth around her raw flesh. Only then did he once more tie the rope around her wrists. It still hurt because her skin was inflamed, but it helped ease the pain.

"Why?" she asked, quietly, unable to let this act of kindness go without some explanation.

He gave her a sharp glance. "There's no reason for you to wear scars the rest of your life."

"Like yours," she whispered, disturbingly aware of him.

Instead of replying, he hoisted her onto MacDuff's saddle and mounted his horse, the rope once again tying them together. He headed back into the forest where he'd ambushed her. She knew they would be safe from her father's men today since the two servants would be further south near the coastline where they'd man a boat to the Isle of Colonsay. Her captor, not being a fool, knew that also.

But what unnerved Fiona more than anything that had happened so far was that upon entering the dreaded shade of the forest that had haunted her from the first time she had ever passed through it, she felt nothing. Her gift no longer made anxiety crawl along her back in foreboding.

It was as though whatever was meant to happen to her, to change her life, *had* happened. Her fate was sealed.

Chapter Four

Fiona looked sourly at her captor. "This is no weather to be crossing the sound in."

Niall glanced up, but otherwise ignored her. "Pat," he continued speaking to the cottar who would stable their mounts until their return, "you know what to do."

The other man grinned, showing a missing front tooth. His brown hair stuck out from beneath his watch cap. "Aye, laddie. Ol' Prince Charlie'll be noon the worse fer me."

Niall smiled back. "I know. Now we must be on our way before the winds get worse."

Fear stabbed her. Once she was over the water and on Skye, her father would never find her. Even escape would be hard, if not impossible. She had no money for passage back to the mainland, and she knew no one on the island.

Fiona scowled. Nor would this man, Pat, be any help. It was obvious Pat knew her captor from way back and supported him. At least she wouldn't have to worry about MacDuff. She sensed that whatever Pat's human allegiances were, he'd take good care of the Highland pony. It was a bright spot in this nightmare, and she would cling to it.

Never one to worry over something she couldn't change—having learned her lesson the hard way with her gift—Fiona turned her attention to the small boat they were to take. It was barely big enough for the two of them. Looking inside, she saw two oars and an empty bucket.

A wave pounding the rocky shore beside it caused her to flinch. She wasn't as cock-sure of their ability to withstand the anger of the Sound of Sleat as her companion seemed to be.

Still, she wasn't going to show fear. It wouldn't help her cause with her captor and would only lead him to try bullying her the more. At least her hands were unbound for the first time since he'd recaptured her. Another bright spot she'd cling to.

"Milady," the devil's voice said, "those skirts of yours are meant for riding, not sailing in a small boat. Pat's wife has some clothing more fit for what lies ahead."

Fiona glanced down at the ruined velvet skirt of her habit. Much as she hated to admit the man was right, he was.

"That's if you can bring yourself to wear plain homespun."

His voice, deep as the lowest string of a harp, brought her head up. "Don't lay your prejudices on me, sirruh."

He raised one black brow. "Then you'll go change."

It wasn't a question, and she didn't answer. Entering the low-roofed cottar's house, she quickly switched clothes.

To Pat's wife, she said, "Do what you will with my dress. I'll not be needing it."

The woman's smile was radiant. "Thank ye verra much."

While the material might be ruined, it was still thick and warm. It would make good clothing for the woman's children, something Fiona had been well aware of when she'd made the offer.

Back outside, she frowned at the waves that had gotten higher in the short time she'd taken. They promised a very rough crossing, but her gift wasn't warning her of danger. So it must be all right or at least wouldn't permanently harm her or Niall. She hoped.

Niall ordered her into the boat with a jerk of the head. With one dubious look at the vessel, she gathered up her rough-spun wool skirt and clambered in. Inside, a bucket lay on its side, ready to be grabbed by desperate hands. Fiona smiled wryly.

They set off, the wind biting through Fiona's cloak, blouse, and chemise like a knife through butter. The waves lapped against the frail wooden sides, threatening to topple them. She had to admire her captor's skill in guiding the small boat.

Halfway across, the rain started. It was a summer storm—and those could be as deadly as any other kind. Waves lapped over the side, and water poured from the skies.

"Bail," Niall shouted over the whistle of the wind.

Fiona, realizing they were taking on too much water, grabbed the bucket. Kneeling in the shallow craft, she scooped and tossed. She tossed until her back ached and her shoulders were so tight she had a headache. Her arms felt like jelly. And still, she kept going.

In spite of the chill penetrating her clothing, her back was soaked with sweat. Her hair clung to her head in wet ropes.

Glancing at Niall, she stopped bailing. He sat on the one bench that straddled the width of the boat, his face toward her. His muscles strained beneath the rain-soaked leather of his coat so that she could see each ripple as his shoulders and arms heaved on the oars. He was all that stood between them and a watery grave.

His mouth was a rigid line. His jaw was clenched. Squinting into the rain-shrouded distance, he commanded the small boat to go where he willed, not where the storm pushed it.

She couldn't help admiring his power and determination. He was much like her in that aspect.

The wind buffeted him, plastering his leather jacket to his body, revealing the breadth of his torso. His leather breeches were even tighter on his thighs, showing the bulging muscles he used to retain his balance on the narrow bench.

He was an imposing, domineering man with more strength than she'd ever witnessed. He was also wickedly handsome, the harsh lines of his countenance both forbidding and enticing. He was the devil in human form, come to lure a girl's heart from her chest.

He glanced at her, his eyes flashing malachite.

The derision he made no effort to hide brought Fiona up short. She'd been letting her imagination run away with her. This was no time for that. They had to get to Skye before their little craft sank.

Concentrating on her bailing, she shut her mind to all else. If he could persevere, then so could she.

The craft scraped bottom, and Fiona jumped. Relief flooded her as she let the wooden bucket drop from her numbed fingers.

Niall leaped out and pulled the boat onto shore. Fiona, thinking she should get out so it would be lighter, couldn't make her exhausted muscles obey her. It was all she could do not to keel over in a dead faint.

Once ashore, instead of helping her out, Niall said, "What are you waiting for? There's no besotted swain or paid servant to see to you here."

She took that to be his way of telling her to get out on her own. Gathering her limited strength, Fiona forced her legs to work. She managed to stumble out of the boat, but her skirt caught on the wooden edge. Tumbling forward, she was pulled up short of the rocky beach by a strong arm around her waist.

"Oh!" He jolted the last of the air from her lungs.

He lifted her effortlessly, his arms supporting her close to his body. It was the last thing she wanted. Putting her palms flat to his chest, she pushed. Nothing happened. She tried again.

Wearily, she said, "I can walk." The rain and the wind had lessened enough that she thought she could make it.

He didn't bother to look at her. "You can't get out of a boat, but you can walk."

His sarcasm bit with sharp accuracy. She didn't have any energy left. Fiona closed her eyes, accepting that she couldn't stop him from carrying her and that she no longer wanted to. She leaned into him, her cheek against his chest where his heart beat strong and slow. The leather he wore was already warming from his exertions. Although it was still wet, it felt wonderfully good against her cold skin.

The next thing she knew, he was setting her down. She felt bereft. The chill of the wind on her damp clothing penetrated to her bones.

Forcing open her eyes, she watched him go back to the boat and unload their meager belongings. Then he pulled the boat into a sandy crevice that would hide it from view, ensuring that no one learned of their arrival. A shiver chased down her spine and her shoulders sagged in defeat.

In her heart, she knew that if she didn't escape this instant from this beach, she never would.

Commanding her legs to action, she pulled on every reserve of energy in her body. Pulling on the rocky outcropping nearby, she managed to get to her feet. Her sodden skirts weighed heavily and clung to her legs like leeches.

Somehow she managed to move. Shuffling and stumbling on the uneven jumble of rocks underfoot, she attempted to move in the direction opposite the water.

She hadn't gotten ten yards before he was upon her. "Damnation, woman." The words were cold and precise; his hands were iron bands on her arms. "I warned you."

Fiona, too tired to do more than slump in his hold, resigned herself to the situation. He was going to tie her up like a sack of oatmeal and sling her over his shoulder. So be it. Right now, she couldn't do anything more. Later, when she had her strength back she would escape and warn Duncan—regardless of the cost to herself.

His face a mask of irritation, he hoisted her once more into his arms. Again, Fiona found herself comforted by his warmth and the strength of his heartbeat. It was a closeness she should have loathed.

"You'll tire quickly if you try to carry me," she said, all fight wrung from her.

He cut her a glance from under lowered black brows. "I don't intend to carry you. You'll walk, but without your hands to balance you. This being rough terrain, you won't enjoy it."

She met his look without flinching, even though the idea of walking now, when she could barely stand, made her want to lie down and cry. "I have to get away," she said softly.

He ignored her.

Taking both her hands, he once more wrapped part of his torn shirt around her wrists to protect them and then bound them with the rope. He shouldered the small parcel of items that had come with them before taking the end of the rope and pulling her along. They headed toward the interior of the island.

It was a steep climb, made more difficult by her

bound hands. Her muscles protested every footstep, but her mind held sway. She wouldn't collapse.

She faltered and he glanced back at her, even going so far as to take her hands in one of his and haul her over a large boulder. After that, he slowed the pace; not much, but enough.

Fiona was hanging on through sheer willpower, wondering when her body would fall to the ground against her command. Her knees buckled just as they rounded a granite outcropping and a ruined castle appeared. A sigh of relief escaped her parted lips. This had to be where they were headed. It had to be.

Niall made straight for the tumbled mass of rocks and hewn tree logs which were all that remained of the once formidable castle. Past the outer jumble of debris, the tower stood two-stories high. It was still in relatively stable condition.

Patches of grass interspersed with the purple of heather dotted the interior grounds. The sweet scent of heather joined the salty tang of the air to create a perfume more intoxicating than any expensive French fragrance. Fiona found herself being renewed.

Inside the tower it was dark. Small windows cut from the stone allowed in little of the remaining sunlight, but what entered sparkled with dust motes floating like diamond flakes. Propped in one corner were several packs and a mound of blankets. It seemed her captor had provisioned this place in advance.

Fiona cast him a wry glance. "You plan ahead."

Not looking at her, he pulled her to the pile. "Three years in Newgate gave me plenty of time to plot my course."

"I suppose it would," she conceded.

He rummaged in one of the bags to pull out a small jar. "Sit down," he ordered. When she remained standing, he jerked on the rope. She gasped in pain. "I said *sit down,*" he repeated.

Fiona, realizing she was only hurting herself by her defiance, did as he commanded. "You didn't have to be so brutal."

One black brow rose. "You would have listened otherwise?"

It was a snide comment she didn't deign to answer. Instead, she bit her lower lip to stifle any more sounds of pain as he undid the rope binding her and unwound the shirt-strips protecting her wrists from further abrasions. The bandage was rust colored from her dried blood.

"You've a nasty burn," he said, laying aside the cloth and picking up the jar from which he removed the cork top.

"Nice of you to notice," she said, unable to stop the sarcasm.

He slathered the white cream onto her raw skin. "Sometimes stubbornness is no more a virtue in a human than it is in an animal. Next time you should remember how irritating your pony can be and curb your rebellion accordingly. I won't coddle you any more than I'll put up with your continual efforts to escape."

Scathing words hovered on the tip of her tongue. She held them back. He didn't have to treat her wounds, yet he did. Already the burn was easing.

"Thank you," she said softly, showing appreciation when it was warranted.

He recapped the cream. "Don't mention it."

The derisive reply destroyed the small warmth she'd begun to feel toward him. No matter what kind act he might perform, he was still the same black-haired, green-eyed devil

"I won't again," Fiona stated, resting her wrists gingerly on her lap.

His wide mouth curled. Picking up several blankets, he spread them on the ground near her. "It'll be dark soon, and you look like you can use some sleep."

As much as she hated to admit it, he was right. Lying down, she closed her eyes. Her last conscious thought was that she'd be damned if she'd continue to thank him when he was so surly about it.

Niall looked down at the woman, admiring her spunk in spite of himself. She'd stuck with him on the climb here even though she was beyond her endurance. She'd shoveled out buckets of water by hand for hours on end, and he knew how hard that was on back and shoulders. And she hadn't complained once. Not even the pain of her chewed-up wrists had elicited more than a gasp when he'd taken the bandages off. She had more backbone than most men he knew.

He turned abruptly away from her sleeping form. She was bait to get Duncan Macfie. Nothing else.

Fiona woke to the pure, haunting notes of a harp. The sad lament, a Gaelic melody, thrummed in her blood. She recognized it as "The Islay Maiden," one of the songs she'd only recently translated from the Gaelic.

It was a goal she'd set herself, to record the history of her people's folksongs before they were all anglicized. It wasn't easy. She had to go out amongst the crofters and cottars and get them to sing the songs slowly enough for her to write them down. Then she had to translate them with the help of her gran. Many songs she knew from singing them herself or listening to her mother and Gran, but the two older women didn't know all of the songs by a long measure.

Her one regret was that she wasn't musically inclined and couldn't carry a tune. She sometimes thought that was why she strove to record the Gaelic music. It was her contribution to a heritage she couldn't perpetuate by performing it.

The last note of the song struck, reverberating off the stone walls of the castle's keep. Its beauty drove deeply into her chest, and a tear formed at the corner of her eye.

Who could create such magic?

Fiona opened her eyes slowly, her imagination picturing an elven king with flowing white hair and long, narrow face. His mouth would be wide, sad at the corners as befitted his music. There'd be a nimbus of gold around him to symbolize his otherworldliness.

She was being foolishly romantic.

Niall sat cross-legged, his head bowed, the dark waves of his shoulder-length hair free and framing his long, narrow face. His wide mouth turned down at the corners, his eyes shadowed. Behind him, a small fire cast its golden glow on his back, outlining the broadness of his shoulders and glinting from the bronze strings of a Celtic harp cradled in his hands. His long, well-shaped fingers caressed the harp.

Fiona shut her eyes.

Opening them again, she surreptitiously scanned the area of the room that she could see without moving and alerting him to her activity. No one else was here.

She looked back at him. He was fiddling with one of the strings, tuning it by ear, she realized when he plucked it before twisting the peg the wire wrapped around. When he had it tuned to his satisfaction, he strummed the entire set of strings.

The magic began again.

Niall, the hard, vengeful man who had kidnaped her to lure her brother to his death, played like an angel. It was a difficult, confusing insight she didn't want to be faced with.

Blocking the softness, the affinity suddenly forming in her for him, Fiona forced herself to concentrate on the music and nothing else. She wouldn't ponder the contradiction of character that made him at once so harsh and yet so emotional as to be able to play the harp this beautifully.

He wasn't the kind of man who interested her. He was too hard and too vengeful. He didn't know how to let go of the pain, to forgive. And she was still determined to go to Angus and win his love.

Yet, as she listened to the magic Niall evoked from the simple instrument with nothing more than his fingers, she found herself wanting to know him better. She wanted to find out what it was in him that gave him this gift; for it was as much a gift as her ability to sometimes foretell the future.

The melancholy notes soared in the still, smoky air of the enclosed castle keep. Each musical cord seemed to ride on a wave of warm air, wafting from the fire to the ceiling. He played old Celtic songs with the heart-rending, bittersweet acceptance of fate and death that only the best players could achieve. He made magic.

Fiona found her body relaxing, her mind calming. She drifted into a realm of heroic feats and undying love.

She awoke to someone banging pots together. Rising on one elbow, she surveyed the room. Niall squatted by a small fire, stirring a pot of porridge. The smell of hot oatmeal and warm honey made Fiona's stomach growl.

He looked up, his eyes pinning her mercilessly. "You're awake at last. For awhile, I thought you'd be an easy prisoner, sleeping through your imprisonment."

"You aren't that lucky."

She rose and stretched, then grimaced, feeling every ache deep in her bones. She wasn't accustomed to sleeping on the hard ground, just as she didn't bail out leaking boats on a daily basis.

A tiny, reluctant smile tugged at one corner of his long, well-formed mouth. "There's ointment in the smallest bag."

It was said without emotion, but it was a kindness. He could let her suffer.

"Thank you," Fiona muttered, digging in the bag.

She found a small jar. When she removed the cork top, the pungent scent of herbs hit her like a brick.

"Rub it in until the cream disappears. It'll do the trick."

Her mouth thinned. His brief directions were unnecessary. Destined to marry and run a household, Fiona already knew this ointment and what to do with it. Nonetheless, she made haste to turn her back on him and apply it. The only spots she couldn't reach well were the middle and small of her back, and they were the sorest.

Stifling a sigh of regret, she stoppered the ointment and returned it to its bag. When she turned back around, he was holding out a bowl of porridge to her along with a jar of honey. She took both willingly.

"It's a good thing you like it," he said, swallowing a spoonful of his own. "We've plenty of oats and little of anything else, except dried meat. They're the easiest to store."

Fiona scraped her bowl clean, wishing there were more, but not willing to ask. Instead, she stood and tried again to stretch out some of the kinks in her spine.

When he finished his food, she said, "Since you cooked, I'll clean."

He rose to tower over her, his massive shoulders and narrow hips making her feel suddenly soft and feminine. She knew from experience that every inch of him was muscled and hard. Her pulse leaped.

"There's a stream nearby," he said, his deep baritone as smooth as finest Scotch and just as burning to her nerves. "I'll take you. You can wash the bowls and yourself, if you'd like."

Her eyes lit up. It'd been days since she'd been clean. "Do you have soap?" It was impossible to keep the note of hopefulness out of her voice.

His mouth quirked up on the right side. Fiona could swear she saw a dimple in the swarthy skin before the smile faded.

"I've soap. But you'll not get it unless you promise not to try to escape."

Chewing her lower lip, Fiona considered his condition. "I'll promise not to try while we're at the stream. This time."

He frowned, his black brows forming a bar above the malachite sheen of his eyes. "It's better than nothing. You must want a bath greatly."

"I do." She moved with alacrity to gather the dirty dishes.

"How do I know I can trust you?" His soft words were barely audible.

Carefully, she laid everything down at her feet. She rose to her full height of five feet, a good foot shorter than he, and stared him in the eye, hands on hips, feet spread.

"I'm a Macfie. Our word's as good as our life." When he didn't immediately answer, her eyes narrowed. "Do you doubt me?"

"And what if I do?"

It was a bold challenge. He meant to put her on the spot, to make her realize she was totally at his mercy. Fiona's cheeks flamed like ripe apricots. She ground her teeth.

"You're a devil," she said, enunciating the words heavily. "You know there's nothing I can do. You've got me here, trapped. I might as well be Rapunzel in the castle tower; I'm that cut off from civilization and help."

He turned away from her, his words coming loud and clear anyway. "See that you remember that, vixen. Even if you should manage to elude me, it wouldn't be for long." He glanced back at her as he took a sliver of soap from a bag. "You should have already learned that lesson."

Her hackles rose. There was no reason for him to continue rubbing her face in her helplessness. "Underestimate me at your own risk."

Turning back to her, he said, "Hold out your arms."

Her mouth dropped. "You aren't going to bind my wrists again. Not after I've given you my promise."

He unrolled the same rope that had held her captive so many times before. "For the trip. You didn't promise not to try escaping before we reach the water." He paused to let that sink in. "And since I can trust your word when given, I'm equally sure I can't trust you when it's not given. Now hold out your hands."

The salve from last night had eased some of the raw burn on her skin or numbed it enough that today's confinement was painful but not excruciatingly so. Fiona bit her lips to keep from moaning or inadvertently saying anything to let him know it still hurt. She wouldn't give him the satisfaction of holding that over her, too.

Once she was tied, he put the bowls and cooking utensils into an empty bag along with the soap and led her outside. The sun shone on the surrounding grass and heather, glinting on puddles of water beside rocks where yesterday's rain still lingered.

Gazing into the eastern horizon, Fiona could see the Sound of Sleat, and she realized that the castle was built on a promontory. Yesterday she'd been too exhausted to realize that most of their journey had been up, climbing out of the cove and not really penetrating into the island.

"When was this castle built?" she asked her taciturn guide, curiosity overriding her anger with him.

"Fifteenth century, or so legend says. It was a stronghold of the MacDonalds. Now, like so many things, it's nothing but ruins."

He sounded disgusted and Fiona wondered how much of it was caused by his own situation. Like the castle, he thought his life was in ruins. It was that loss that drove him. If only she could help him.

Immediately, she chided herself. She wasn't here to help him change his life. She was here because he held her prisoner as bait to lure her brother to his death.

It was only a quarter-mile to the trickling stream. It splashed and gurgled over rocks and around bends, its clear water sparkling in the sunlight. A twist and a plunge later, the water settled into a pond that twinkled like diamonds.

Stopping, Niall undid her ropes. Sensation returned slowly to her hands, and her fingers stung as if pierced by needles.

Before she knew what he was up to, he caught both her hands and started gently massaging her raw, aching flesh. Heat flashed through her and in seconds her hands were warm and no longer pained. But her breathing faltered.

He was so close and so powerful and so . . . so mesmerizing. One minute he shoved her captive state into her face, treating her like a prisoner of war. The next second, he was gentle and considerate. He was never the same man twice.

Even as she grappled with the dichotomy that he was, his deep voice said in a husky whisper, "That pond's for your bath."

Chapter Five

Fiona's gaze focused on the shimmering water. Nowhere around it was there the tiniest bit of concealment. If she bathed in the pond, he'd be able to see her every movement—not to mention her nudity. She gulped.

His mouth curved upward, as though he read her thoughts. "I won't watch. You don't have anything to tempt me with anyway."

She blinked several times to clear from her mind's eye the picture she'd painted to herself of being naked to his gaze, before looking back at him. It hurt that he didn't even find her attractive enough to be a temptation. Never mind that she didn't like him or even want him to be attracted to her.

"It's obvious you're no gentleman." He quirked one black brow at her. "A gentleman would have stopped speaking after promising not to look."

The upward curve of his long mouth became a grin. But instead of speaking, he handed her the bag and

then strode to a broad, flat rock where he sat down
with his back toward her.

Frowning at him, even though she knew he couldn't
see her, gave her a modicum of satisfaction. First, he
insulted her, then he walked away without another
word about the situation he'd put her into. He was an
infuriating devil of a man. Never had she met anyone
like him.

Well, he wouldn't discommode her further. Matching him in nonchalance, Fiona knelt by the side of the
pond and washed the dishes. That done, she stripped
to her chemise and washed herself in the cold water,
rubbing briskly with the soap sliver. It smelled of sandalwood and moss, a heady, masculine scent. Belatedly she realized it reminded her of Niall.

A disturbing sense of warmth, mingled with excitement, suffused her. Her stomach felt topsy-turvy. She
cast him a quick look to see if he sensed the heightened
awareness she had for him. He was looking away from
her. Disappointment was an emotion she refused to
feel where he was concerned. To combat it, Fiona
finished her washing in earnest, scrubbing her skin
until it turned pink.

From his perch on the rock, Niall stared into the
distance, watching clouds chase one another across the
sky. After that, he scowled at the sturdy toe of his
black leather boots. They needed polishing.

The soft sound of a splash reverberated through his
body like the crash of a cannonball. He stiffened. She
was washing herself.

The seconds became minutes, and the minutes
seemed like hours as Niall fought the temptation to

turn around and watch her. He'd promised not to look just as she'd promised not to run away. They were both bound by their words, no matter how difficult it was.

Niall swallowed, his throat working furiously to keep from saying something to her. Something like, "I want to make love to you."

She wasn't the woman for him. She was bait. Her brother had sent him to Newgate, and Niall'd sworn to kill him for that.

But no amount of reasoning doused the fire roaring in his belly or eased the tightness making him jumpy. He knew, no matter how much he denied it, that the only cure for the malaise plaguing him was to take her.

"I'm dressed," she finally said.

Niall expelled the breath he hadn't known he was holding. Pretending to wipe dirt from his hands, he dried his sweaty palms on his breeches. Next time he'd let her come alone, after making her promise to come straight here and to return directly to the ruined castle. Otherwise, next time, he wouldn't be able to keep his hands off her.

Scowling at his weakness, he turned to her. "It took you long enough."

She packed the utensils and carefully wrapped the soap in its linen protection before meeting his ire with disdain. "Spoken like a true Highland barbarian. I don't expect you bathe more than once a year—and then only if you're forced."

Head up, shoulders back, she swept past him. Watching her stalk off, Niall wondered what burr had gotten under her saddle. In the meantime, he would enjoy the sway of her trim hips and the shapely turn of her ankles that were just visible beneath her skirt.

Desire was a shaft of pain in him. Clamping his teeth together, he cursed himself for the stupidity of lusting after her. She was his prisoner, and he needed to keep her in sight for no other reason than that.

Niall followed behind her, confident that he could catch her if she tried to get away. As it was, he was hard pressed not to stop her and avail himself of the promise of pleasure she exuded.

Damn to bloody hell! She wasn't here for him to seduce. She wasn't supposed to be so strong-willed and honorable. He wasn't supposed to even like her, let alone want her.

Suddenly she froze, her shoulders rigid. Alarmed, Niall ran the few steps separating them, drawing a knife from his boot.

"What's wrong?" He moved in front of her, using his body to shield her from danger.

Eyes narrowed, he studied the land around the castle rubble. Someone or something could easily be hiding behind a pile of tumbled rock and he'd never see it.

"It's . . . all right," she said at last in a soft voice. " 'Tis only my imagination getting the better of me."

Just then, the raucous caw of a crow rent the calm air. Niall went to the balls of his feet, his arms hanging limberly at his side, the knife clasped loosely in his hand.

Nothing. He didn't see anyone.

The caw was repeated. It came from a tuft of grass at the bottom of the castle keep where they'd spent the night. Approaching, he saw a black crow, one wing dragging the ground. It hopped and screeched as he neared.

So intent had he been on the bird, he hadn't felt her follow him until her hand touched his elbow.

" 'Tis a bad omen," she said quietly. "A crow on your roof presages death."

He looked at her, seeing the unfocused look of her normally piercing eyes. It was as though a cloud moved across their blue sharpness. "That's superstitious rot." But in spite of his bold words, cold moved down his spine.

She shook herself, her eyes coming once more into focus. "You're right. And the bird is hurt."

Stooping, she held her hand out for the crow to perch if it would. To Niall's surprise, the animal hopped onto her wrist. She carried it into the keep and proceeded to examine its wing.

Niall watched in muted interest as the animal suffered her ministrations without protest. The crow could have pecked her eyes out as easily as submit.

When she was done and the animal resting, he asked, "What happened to you out there?"

She turned to face him, the angles of her face drawn. "It isn't easy to explain."

But he knew, had sensed it in her. "You're *fey.*"

She gave him her back and started to clean up after herself, but her voice carried. "Yes. Sometimes—not always and never completely clearly—I can see or tell something's going to happen. I'm not normally superstitious, but when I saw the animal a part of me reacted without thought." She shrugged. " 'Twas stupid. Nothing more."

He spoke quietly. "A gift few people have, and one many people fear."

Fiona angled around to study him, wanting to see his expression, to see what he thought of her now. She couldn't tell anything except that *he* didn't fear her. The tightness around her heart eased, and she found that she was glad he didn't hold her in loathing as many would and did.

"But *you* don't fear me." She said, hoping he'd tell her what he did feel.

"No, I don't. You're still a woman and the sister of my sworn enemy. Nothing else matters."

"And you're still as blunt and unaccommodating as ever," she retorted, stung by his coldness.

He cut a glance at her. "You're not bound."

Which was true. He hadn't tied her wrists again to keep her from escaping. It was a kindness.

Unwilling to continue this conversation because of the things it made her feel about him—things she didn't want to feel for him—Fiona found some of the dried beef and set it in a small pan of water until it softened. She then fed small pieces of it to the crow, who acted starved, taking everything she gave him.

"Poor thing," she crooned. "I think I'll call you Blackie."

Niall snorted. "Original."

"Apt."

"He'll fly away as soon as his wing's healed."

"That's his nature."

"Just as yours is to defy me and try to escape."

Did she detect a note of admiration in his tone? Glancing at him and seeing the harsh sternness in his countenance, she knew it was a fanciful thought on her part. He loathed her. For some reason, she felt suddenly sad, as she had when she was a child and a gift she'd wanted badly had been denied her. She shook off the unpleasant sensation.

"I do what I must," she said softly.

"I know that. Just as I do."

When the bird would take no more and was drowsy, she scooped him up gently and turned to Niall. "Here," she said holding out the fighting crow. "I need you to hold him still while I check his wing."

Niall shook his head. "I'll not touch that thing. Birds remember. When you're done, he'll like as not blame me and try to peck my eyes out while I sleep."

Fiona stared at him incredulously. Then in mock tones clicked her tongue. "A big, strong man like you afeared of a little crow. I'd never have thought it."

But she had to have his help. He had to hold the bird's body so she could spread the hurt wing and see if it needed splinting.

"Come," she insisted, seriousness erasing her humor. "I need you to do this; otherwise there was no sense in my even feeding him. He'll die."

While she waited for her captor to agree to hold the crow, as she knew he would, she crooned to the frightened animal. It's bright yellow eyes watched her as it struggled.

Niall looked from her to the bird that now fought the confinement of her grip. The crow's beak caught her cuticle, and blood crimsoned her nail. It was the first time the bird had bitten truly hard.

"You're determined, aren't you."

She nodded. With an exasperated shake of his head, Niall took the bird, holding it gently around the back and chest. As its beak sank into the side of one of his fingers, he wished he could muzzle it.

"Damn animal," he growled.

Meanwhile, Fiona carefully grasped the wounded wing and spread it out. The shiny black feathers were long and sleek, and she feared to see that the underlying bones had been broken. She sighed with relief when the light bones appeared to be in one piece.

"It looks like he fell, probably from a tree. But I don't he broke anything that will ground him for life. Three of his flight feathers are split, but he'll grow those back."

Feeling much better, Fiona let the wing go and put her arm out for the crow to perch on it. Instead of going to her when Niall released it, the bird sidled away from both of them, not taking its eyes off the two humans for a second. A safe distance from them, it stopped and glared.

"I told you they remember," Niall said, rising and going to his pallet.

Fiona smiled. "He'll forget."

She got some more of the stewed meat and set it down near the crow, who disdained to eat it for all of five minutes. Then, keeping a wary eye on them, he inched to the beef and pecked and didn't stop until the food was gone. Then he walked back to his spot of safety and tucked his beak into his good wing.

Fiona, satisfied that everything was all right with her patient, settled into the most comfortable position she could, using the wall for a backrest. From the looks of things, her captor intended to spend a number of days here. She was doubly glad at finding the crow; the animal would give her companionship the man would deny her. The bird would also give her something to think about besides the man.

Niall sat across from her, the still-smoldering fire between them. His eyes were hooded as he watched her.

Finally, unable to bear his scrutiny longer, Fiona demanded, "Why are you watching me?"

His mouth crooked in that familiar lifting that was as close as he came to a smile. His eyes gleamed. "You're not like your brother. Where Duncan is tall and lean, you're small and rounded. You don't have the same eyes or the same hair, either. Duncan is dark; you're all flame and sky."

The fleeting poetry of his words sang in her mind, reminding her of his music, bringing back the sense of wonder and poignancy he'd evoked the night before. She couldn't keep from asking, "Where did you learn to play the harp?"

His face drew into planes of anger. His mouth twisted in self-derision. "I learned the *clarsach* at my father's knee."

Curious about a relationship that evoked such pain in a man as hardened as Niall, Fiona asked, "Who is your father?"

"Currie of Balilone, Chief of Clan MacMhuirrich."

"And hereditary bard to the Lord of the Isles," she finished for him. "Now I understand."

"Do you?" His fine mouth formed a sneer that couldn't hide the hurt in his eyes.

"Some. At least I know where your gift comes from." She'd been steeped in Highland genealogy all her life, and while she'd never met a Currie, she'd learned about them. "Your namefather was Muiredach O'Daly from the most famous bardic family in Celtic history. He came to Islay to the court of Donald, Lord of the Isles, where he was honored and given much prestige. Your family is still held in honor by Highlanders and Lowlanders alike."

His sneer magnified. "Which makes it all the more shameful to have a son convicted of murder."

She flinched from the bitter pain in his voice. "You didn't murder that woman. It's not in you."

He surged to his feet and strode to the door. She thought he would leave, but he didn't. Looking out over the moor toward the sea, he asked, "How do you know what I'm capable of? My own father thought I did it."

Without thought, only knowing that she had to help him, Fiona rose and went to him. Laying a hand on his arm, she said, "Your father is wrong. I know it in my heart."

Instead of shaking off her hand as she thought he would, he looked down at her. His eyes pinned her, penetrated to her soul, searching for the truth of her words.

"You believe that, don't you."

Unable to speak for the rapidity of her pulse, she

nodded. Her body thrummed, like a plucked harp string. Vibrations spread from where she touched his arm through her in every widening circles.

"Your brother thought I killed her."

The harsh words crashed in on her, countering the feelings he raised in her. This was the heart of his animosity toward her. Duncan's agreement that he'd murdered the woman.

Yet, in spite of knowing this and the way he'd treated her, she couldn't let him draw away. Instinctively she knew Niall Currie was important to her, not how, but that he was. Her future was inextricably intertwined with his—for good or bad.

"But *I* don't believe it of you. That's what counts."

The sneer returned. "Is it? You won't think so after I kill your brother."

Her face blanched and she took a step away from him, her hand dropping to her side. The sheer magnitude of power emanating from him buffeted her, telling her beyond words that he would do as he threatened.

Fiona went back to her place by Blackie. The crow still slept and she wished she did, too. If only this were nothing but a bad dream. She wished she'd never met Niall Currie.

Later, in short, jerky movements, Niall yanked several books out of one of the bags. He tossed one of them to her. It was a book of poems by Robert Burns. He was one of her favorite poets. Anticipation rippled through her.

"How did you know?" she asked, wonder in her voice.

He scowled at her as he sat once more on the other side of the fire. "Know what?"

She looked up from her examination of the book and smiled at him. His frown intensified.

"How did you know Robert Burns is my favorite?"

"I didn't. These are mine, brought to while away the hours while we wait for Micheil's return."

Left unspoken was her brother's arrival after Micheil's message was delivered. It effectively ended any conversation she might have tried to start over the books. Instead, she turned her attention to the lovely lines Burns had written and tried to forget her reason for being here. If she could forget the man responsible for her kidnaping, that would be even nicer.

But it was hard. She looked up to see him sitting across from her, his brooding gaze on the book in his lap. A shank of hair fell over his forehead, its rich blackness making his suntanned skin pale in comparison. Thick ebony lashes shadowed his eyes, lashes too luxuriant for a man. They made the green of his irises glow like the malachite they resembled.

In repose, he became engrossed in the book in his lap, and his long, defined mouth eased. It was the mouth of a poet or a bard—sensitive. Yet it could be hard, too, as she well knew.

The memory of it pressed against hers brought a rush of heat. Her lips tingled as they had for the brief moments when he'd plundered her, impressing upon her his strength by his kiss. That kiss was a brand on her soul.

Fiona shuddered at the sudden chill. Leaning over, she drew a blanket around her shoulders. Instead of easing her discomfort, it increased it. The wool smelled of sandalwood, another reminder of him.

With a sigh, she laid the book down and concentrated on the crow, who was wakening. She gave him her arm to perch on, not thinking of his claws on her still-raw wrists.

"Oh!" The small gasp of pain escaped before she knew she had said it.

"Wrap the linen rags around your arm. That'll give him something besides your flesh to grip for balance."

Warmth suffused her face. She hadn't realized he was watching her. "That's a good idea," she agreed, wondering why she hadn't thought of it herself. Her mind was muddled.

The bandages on, she once more held her arm out to the bird. He hopped onto her without hesitation, cocking his sleek ebony head to one side and watching her with his obsidian eyes. Greatly daring, she tried to stroke his head with a forefinger. He sidled away, but didn't leave her arm. It was encouragement.

"Don't gentle him," Niall's deep voice said. "That will only make it harder on him when he's free again."

"I know he's a wild animal and must be kept so. I only plan to feed him until his wing is healed; then I'll release him."

Niall nodded, his attention returning to his book. Her curiosity piqued by his consuming interest, Fiona asked, "What are you reading?"

"Scott." He didn't even deign to look at her.

Chagrin warred with delight in Fiona. Scott was her favorite author, after Jane Austen. "Which one?"

He grunted and might just as well have told her to

mind her own business. And Fiona wondered why she was finding it so hard to do just that.

She forced herself to concentrate on the crow, trying once more to stroke his sleek head. This time he let her. She smiled, enjoying the silky feel of his feathers under her finger.

Rebelliously, her mind wondered if Niall Currie's hair would be as sleek to the touch. Would the man crook his neck to let her fingers trail down the back of his head? She shook her head sharply to dislodge the questions that shouldn't even matter.

Setting the bird down, she buried her nose back in her book. Her imagination was better used enjoying Robert Burns' poetry or figuring out an escape.

The sun was low in the sky, but not set, when Niall laid aside his book and built up the fire. Fiona, who'd fallen into a doze, the crow asleep beside her, woke to the sounds of Niall making dinner. She knew it was late by the shadows lengthening on the ground outside the open doorway.

"It must by going on eight," she ventured, standing to stretch the kinks out.

"You slept most of the afternoon and will find it hard to sleep the night," he said by way of answer.

"There wasn't anything else to do," she said, squatting down near him to see what was in the stew that made it smell so good.

"Wild onions and thyme with oats for thickening and softened jerky for flavor," he answered her unasked question.

The hair on her nape rose. It was as though they were in tune to one another. She watched his long fingers, sprinkled lightly with black hairs, as he stirred the stew. His movements were sure and deft and beautiful, even in so mundane a chore as cooking. She wondered how they'd feel on her.

More dangerous thoughts. Chiding herself, she shook her head to clear it. He loathed her and she loved Angus; she intended to go to Edinburgh to win him after she warned Duncan about Niall. In the meantime, she'd fetch their bowls and spoons.

The stew was as good as it smelled, and Fiona ate more than her share, indulging in the oatcakes as well. She set small pieces of each by the crow, who hungrily ate them.

After they finished, Niall took her bowl and spoon and put them in a bucket of water that he must have fetched while she slept. She marveled that he would leave her long enough to do so.

"You left me this afternoon to fetch the water."

He ignored her unspoken question of why, rinsing the dishes and drying them on part of the shirt he'd torn apart to bandage her.

"Why?" she finally asked point-blank, wanting to know the answer, wondering why she wanted to know it.

He put the dishes away and spread the shirt out on a rock to dry in the heat from the fire. "You were exhausted. I didn't think you'd wake up in the five minutes I needed to fetch the water. And you weren't going to get very far if you did."

It had been a considerate act on his part. He could have easily woken her for the trek and let her go back to sleep upon their return. Or he could have just bound her again. It's what he would have done yesterday.

"Thank you," she whispered.

He slanted her a look through narrowed eyes. "Don't read anything into it. It was expedience only. Waking you would have been more trouble than it was worth. I'd have had to listen to your incessant questions."

Irritation at his continual belittlement made her grind her teeth, but she said nothing. Instead, she gathered up her blankets and burrowed into them, trying to ignore the pointed hardness of the rocks beneath her.

Closing her eyes, she concentrated on ways to escape. If she could get away from him and hide, she'd still have to get to the mainland. She'd have to get the boat and sail it herself, but she didn't want to sail the boat. She didn't think she had the stamina to paddle it across the Sound of Sleat. Yet that was her only option, and she'd do it. She really had no other choice. Duncan had to be warned.

First, however, she had to lull Niall Currie into complacency where she was concerned. She had to make him think she'd given up all thought of escape. Maybe she'd already begun to do so since he'd left her alone long enough to fetch the water.

She couldn't suppress a tiny smile of success. She was going to succeed. She knew it.

The first strains of the harp lured her from her thoughts. The brass strings produced notes that reverberated through her body, traveling the pathways of her nerves with sure delight.

It was "The Praise Of Islay." A song of sadness, it told of a man's sorrow at being away from the land he loved. Although Niall didn't sing the words, they played through Fiona's head. It was one of the Gaelic songs she'd collected.

She began to hum along with his playing, unable to ignore the haunting music. Niall's deep baritone joined her, weaving in and out in harmony. When she realized what they were doing, Fiona stopped, turned on her side with her back to him, and closed her ears to the magic.

The fire's heat burned her spine and shoulders. That was the only reason she felt hot, unbearably hot, as she struggled to capture sleep.

Chapter Six

Fiona almost didn't recognize her chance when it came.

It was their fourth night on the island. Darkness enveloped the crumbling keep, the fire down to embers, when something awakened her. Struggling with the sleep that held her body captive, she angled up onto one elbow. Shadows mingled with the meager light of the dying flames. The moon had long since set.

Something had startled her. A noise, a bird scratching, caught her attention. The crow—Blackie—was moving restlessly about, his feet scrabbling on the dirt. But he didn't caw. It was as though he were trying to get her attention without wakening Niall.

Her eyes finally adjusted and she made out Niall's sleeping form on the other side of the fire. He was on his back, one arm flung over his eyes, his chest rising and falling rhythmically. She felt a strange tug at her heart, an urge to touch him that she strongly denied. It was a disturbing sensation that she'd been feeling more and more frequently as the days of their proximity increased.

As she fought the desire to reach across the dying fire and stroke the harsh line of his jaw, she remembered. He hadn't bound her wrists before they slept. Why, she didn't know. Perhaps they'd both been lulled into complacency by the sameness of their days. Perhaps she was destined to escape him after all. It didn't matter.

Rising to her feet, careful to make no sound, she made her decision. This was likely to be her only chance. She had to take it, and the consequences be damned.

Stealthily, she skirted the fire, hugging the wall of the keep as she made her way to the exit. The scrabbling sound that had awakened her started again. She didn't need to see the crow to know he was pacing from side to side, his head bobbing up and down. He wanted her to take him.

Torn, not wanting to retrace her footsteps and risk alerting Niall, she paused. But only for a moment, and then she returned for the bird. She owed him that. They were companions. He would keep her company, perhaps bring her luck, in her flight.

Blackie perched on her shoulder, Fiona sneaked into the night.

Niall woke abruptly. A tightness in his chest, a difficulty in breathing, held him motionless. He listened for any sound that might explain the unusual sensations.

Nothing. No noise from the crow, who sometimes woke at night to pace the room. Not even Fiona's steady breathing as she slept.

His hands fisted. He jerked upward, eyes searching for her. She was gone.

"Damnation!" The expletive burst from him as he jumped to his feet.

He'd left her untied last night, thinking she would sleep through the night as she usually did. He didn't want to bind her again and take the risk that she'd have scars for the rest of her life as he had. She didn't deserve that. Nor could he stand the thought of her soft, ivory skin being disfigured by red scar tissue. Now he'd pay the price for that consideration if he didn't catch her.

Getting to his feet, he took several deep breaths. Apparently Newgate hadn't made him as callous as he'd once thought. It should have.

How many nights did his dreams echo his bellows of anger, brought on by memories of what the guards had done to him? How many days had he spent in chains for fighting them or for refusing to pay them the indecent amounts of money needed to get fresh water and food?

Standing in the cold night air, preparing to hunt Fiona down, he remembered one incident with wrenching clarity. He'd only been in Newgate two days and was still weak from the lengthy time he had been held in the ship's brig. His guard had come into the cell, which was little better than a pig stye, and put irons on his ankles to complement the ones already on his arms. Next another guard, filthier than the first, had gotten on his back. They had intended to use him in place of a woman.

Niall took deep breaths to still the pounding of his heart without success. He'd managed to yank one of his arm chains from the wall and had used that on his assailants until they had fled, locking the door behind themselves. Micheil had come the next day. They had never tried again.

Soaked in sweat, he forced himself to stay motionless until he was in control of his mind and body. The memory of the nightmare was something he had to live with, but he didn't have to let it dominate him. It was in the past. When he was confident that the past was exorcised, Niall moved.

Fiona was still somewhere in the night, on her way to warn her brother of Niall's plan. He would find her.

Niall followed the path to the sea and the boat he'd hidden away. It was the only place she could have gone. It was the only way she could escape the island.

Reaching the beach, he followed the trail of the boat's bottom that was etched in the still-damp sand. The tide was going out, and she was going out on it to the mainland.

All the fury, pain, and humiliation of the last three years swamped him, this time beyond his ability to control. She wouldn't escape. She wouldn't thwart his revenge, the only thing that had kept him alive.

With a string of curses expelling the much-needed air from his lungs, Niall stripped off his shirt and discarded his boots. He launched himself into the icy water.

* * *

Fiona struggled with the oars. She was rowing, as she'd been doing, since launching. Blackie paced the prow, looking east toward the mainland.

Sweat drenched her body, running down the grooves on either side of her spine to soak the waistband of her skirt. The sweat burned her eyes. Her back muscles ached. Her palms stung. Still, she rowed.

He would come after her as soon as he realized she was gone. He would come after her; and if he caught her, he wouldn't punish her with only a devouring kiss and bound wrists. This time, he'd go further. She had sensed his violent nature.

She rowed harder.

A wave slapped the side of the boat, sending water into the flimsy vessel. Fiona fought to right her craft, letting go of the oars in her haste. Large, dark hands rose from the sea and grasped the sides. The tiny boat teetered.

Fiona screamed.

The crow cried raucously.

Niall hoisted himself into the boat, dripping seawater.

Fear washed over Fiona as she stared at him, caught by his magnificence and his fury. Dawn lit the sky and haloed his form. His black hair swept back from his face in wet strands that hung to his shoulders. Moisture glistened on the broad muscles of his chest. His eyes blazed.

She gulped.

Feet spread apart, he balanced precariously. His

shoulders were taut, the muscles corded and straining. Curling black hairs were plastered to his torso in a triangle that narrowed down his flat belly to disappear beneath the waistband of his breeches. The leather of his only clothing clung to his hips and thighs, more revealing than nakedness.

Fiona licked dry lips.

The boat rocked dangerously, forcing him to his knees, and still he towered over her. Fury emanated from him in waves that beat at her.

She inched away from him.

The crow screeched, catching Niall's attention. It was a brief respite, but enough for Fiona to regain her defiance. Stiffening her weak spine, she met his look squarely when he turned back to her.

"I'm not afraid of you," she said, disgusted by the hoarseness in her voice.

"You should be."

It was a flat statement, a promise of things to come. Fiona blanched, feeling the cold for the first time since sneaking from her prison.

"You can't do anything to me worse than what you plan for my brother," she said, willing herself to defy him, knowing that in the end he'd do what he wanted regardless.

His harsh laugh rode the waves. Without a word, he turned the small boat back toward Skye. Even fighting the tide, he made the boat speed toward shore. Before Fiona had time to truly contemplate her fate, the bottom of the boat grated the sandy shore.

Niall jumped out, the water at his calves, and pulled the boat ashore. Fiona, not resigned to a fate she saw coming, let him get the boat close enough in for her to be able to hop out without swamping her long skirts in the waves crashing to shore. When he was ankle-deep, she gathered her skirts up to her thighs, leaped out the opposite side, and ran.

The cold water splashed up her legs; the sand shifted under her feet. She sped on.

Niall flipped the boat over; the crow took wing in a limp parody of flight. Its raucous scream carried on the wind as it landed on a rocky outcropping.

Blood pumped through Niall, flushing away restraint. His bare feet gripped the sand, pushing off in bounds that brought him close to her in seconds. Arms spread wide, he launched himself at her legs, then crashed to the beach with her.

Fiona felt the band of his arms around her lower legs. Thrashing her feet, she struggled to escape while he inched up her body.

"Let me go!" she gasped, pushing at the shoulders that were now level with the midportion of her back. "Let me go. You can't do this."

His breathing was harsh as he levered above her, his chest pushing down on her back. She spat out sand.

"I warned you," he said, his voice dangerously low, his breath hot against her nape.

Fiona, the blood pounding in her ears, wriggled beneath him, her fingers scrabbling at the shifting sand. She screamed when he rose off her enough to flip her onto her back. Panting, she stared up at him.

In that instant, she knew him capable of anything.

His narrowed eyes bored into her, their green depths colder than the North Sea. His mouth, so finely formed, was a thin line. His hair hung in tangled strands. He looked wild . . . and dangerous.

She squeezed her eyes closed to shut out this image of him only to snap them open when she felt the pressure of his chest on hers increase. His eyes, still hard as malachite, were lit with an emotion she dared not name for fear that once named, it would engulf her. Then his lips took hers and all rational thought fled.

His mouth slanted over hers, forcefully taking what she suddenly realized she would give willingly. His tongue probed her closed lips and delved into the moist satin of her mouth. Passion, raging like a Highland river, overwhelmed Fiona, thrusting all caution before it.

Her fingers, covered with the sand she'd tried seconds before to find purchase in, flexed against his chest. Her nails dug into him in an effort to hold onto something solid in the midst of the storm he created.

His mouth tore from hers to trail down her neck to the hollow just above her breastbone. Raising on one elbow, his free hand undid the ties holding her blouse closed before slipping under the rough cotton to skim over the silk of her chemise.

Through slumberous eyes, Fiona watched him as his fingers slid beneath her chemise, the rough calluses of his fingers grazing her nipple. He rose above her, the muscles of his neck corded, his eyes shut, his lips drawn against his teeth. Whatever else drove him, she knew desire was foremost.

And his touch. She wanted his touch more than anything else on earth. She wanted his weight pressing her into the yielding moist sand. She wanted him to be intimate with her.

Her hands roamed his chest, kneading and stroking, trying to evoke in him the same aching need he was creating in her. His low groan told she was succeeding.

Lifting up her head, she pressed a kiss on the aureole of one male breast. Niall's sharp intake of breath rewarded her.

Rolling to his back, he took her with him. His hands framed her face; his eyes looked deeply into hers.

"I'm going to *love* you," he whispered, "and there's nothing you can do to stop me."

Shivers pulsed her spine.

He pulled her face to his. His kiss was deep and mind-drugging. His tongue slipped between her teeth, and his hands slipped her blouse off her shoulders and down to her waist. Her chemise followed.

The chill morning breeze caressed her bare flesh only to be chased away by the warm touch of his hands moving down her back to her waist and back up to her shoulders. Shifting her forward on his chest, he took one breast into his hand and massaged it, sending lightning bolts of pleasure shooting through Fiona. Never in her wildest dreams had she imagined this much delight could come from a man.

When he replaced his hand with his mouth, her back arched and she gasped. Her fingers dug into him.

His hands left her waist and moved to where her skirts billowed around his loins, her legs bent on either side of him. Lifting the heavy, wet material, he delved beneath, bringing heat with his touch. He lifted her so that she hovered inches above him.

Tiny gasps of surprise and pleasure escaped her in rhythm with his fingers. She forgot about his mouth on her breast and the sand beneath her knees. What he was making her feel was like nothing in her experience.

His thumb found a small kernel of flesh between her thighs, eliciting a moan from Fiona. Sensation stormed over her like gale winds. She was lost in a raging storm of Niall's creation and didn't care if she wrecked.

Her moans blended with his deeper ones. His hands left her, and she felt him undoing his breeches. His flesh, turgid and demanding, pressed into her. He lifted her hips and set her on him.

"Oh, my God," he groaned, thrusting upward, his eyes shut tight.

Pain, followed quickly by fullness, caught Fiona's breath, making it impossible to breathe as he moved into her. Eyes wide in shock, she looked down at him.

His body arched up from the sand, the muscles straining. The lines of his face were sharp and etched like boldly cut glass. And then he began to move, and it no longer mattered how he looked . . . only how he felt inside her.

Tiny implosions shook her body. Her nails dug into his chest as his fingers hooked her bottom and moved her to his rhythm. He coiled beneath her, and Fiona went up in flames.

Gasping for breath, she collapsed onto him and rode the final wave of his release. His body thrashed as he strove for the peak before stiffening in the final ecstasy.

It was over. Lying on Niall, rising with each breath

he took and listening to each beat of his heart, Fiona felt reborn. She'd fled from him a child; he'd caught her and made her a woman.

She felt a part of him. It wasn't possession, but rather the intensity he'd evoked in her—the fear of his pursuit and the excitement of his seduction. In the last hours, she'd experienced more emotional living than in her entire life.

Through the ultimate act of union, her world had exploded and reformed. Everything else in her life before this was as nothing. Surely it was the same for him. Surely nothing else would matter to him, not even his revenge, after this tumultuous joining.

Turning to look at him, lying so close, she sought his eyes. His were unchanged, as cold and as hard as they'd ever been. What had happened between them meant nothing to him. He'd used her.

Her blood froze. Her chest tightened painfully.

"It won't happen again," he said flatly, rising to his feet.

In his anger, he'd taken her to ease his fury and appease his body. Their joining—that wonderful experience that had shattered her world before re-building it—was no more to him than a tumble in the sand with a whore.

Shame crimsoned her cheeks, followed quickly by indignation and lastly by anger. Her teeth ground together.

Hurriedly, with fumbling fingers, Fiona put herself to rights, ignoring the penetrating sand. She'd be damned if she'd show discomfort to him, just as she'd rot in hell before she told him what their joining meant to her.

Standing, she tossed her copper hair over her shoulder and raised her chin haughtily. "What won't happen again? I can't remember anything out of the ordinary happening that's worth repeating."

His face flushed deeply; his eyes burned. He grabbed her wrist and yanked her to him. Her breasts flattened against his chest so that she could feel the heavy pounding of his heart.

"You know what I meant. You were a virgin; I felt your skin break." His mouth curved into a cruel smile. "I have your blood on me."

It was all Fiona could do not to spit in his face. Words slipped out before she could think. "What a fool I was to think this would help heal you of your wounds!"

He flung her from him. She landed in the soft, yielding sand; her hands spread to keep her from falling to her face. Instead of cowering, she turned to look him full in the face.

"Get up and come with me," he said.

She wanted to taunt him, to ask what he'd do if she refused. The darkness contorting his features made her pause. She'd pushed him too far.

Following, she paused only long enough to fetch Blackie from the rock where he still perched.

Later she tossed fitfully on her blanket, exhausted by her attempted escape and the reprisal that had followed. The day had been a tense standoff as he ignored her and she tried to do the same to him. Now, with night darkening the sky, she dreaded sleep. He'd been in her dreams since the kidnapping; she didn't want him there after this morning.

Groaning, she turned to her other side, determined to sleep without dreaming. Beside her, the fire sputtered, running out of wood. There was no more in the crumbling keep, but Niall would not fetch any. After what they'd done, she knew he would neither take her with him nor leave her here bound. He wouldn't touch her.

Desperate for rest, she tried to make her mind a blank. She almost wished he would play his harp. Anything to give her something else to think about besides his hands on her, his body in hers—and her response to him.

As though he heard her thoughts and agreed with them, she heard him strum the brass strings of his instrument. But when he finally played, the sound was a mash of discordant notes. She almost looked at him, wondering what fresh pain was gnawing at him to so mutilate his music, but she didn't. He didn't want her; he certainly wouldn't want her curiosity or sympathy.

He stopped with a cacophony of sound and a muttered curse. She heard him moving about and realized he was putting his harp away in its oiled cloth to protect it from the vagaries of the weather. She chanced a quick look at him when she knew his back was to her.

He was hunched over one of his ever-present packs, his shoulders bunched tightly. The black waves of his hair, much too long for fashion, but wildly attractive on him, grazed the bottom of his shirt collar.

He was the antithesis of Angus, the man she'd left Colonsay to pursue. Now she couldn't even remember what Angus looked like. Every memory of him was superimposed by an image of Niall Currie. It was a hard realization to acknowledge, but Fiona was used to facing knowledge that was unpleasant. Her gift required her to do so or be destroyed.

So she looked her feelings squarely in the eye and didn't like them. Not only had Niall Currie taken her body on the beach, he'd taken her heart. Now she had to keep him from taking her soul.

Chapter Seven

"Niall," a man's light tenor came from outside the keep, replacing Fiona's unpleasant retrospection with an even less pleasant sense of chilling doom. Micheil was here at last. He would tell Niall that Duncan was on his way. Shudders shook her shoulders and made her fingers tremble.

"Niall," Micheil's voice came again as he entered the keep, "he's not there."

Niall lunged to his feet. "What?" he thundered.

Panting as though he'd run from the beach, Micheil said, "Macfie's been made captain of HMS *Valiant.* He won't be in port for four weeks or more."

Fiona sagged with relief. Duncan was safe. *Niall would release her now. He didn't need her anymore.*

She felt like she'd eaten something bad, sharp pains twisting her stomach. Micheil's news was a mixed blessing; her brother would be all right, but the man she was falling in love with would now send her away. She was only a tool to Niall Currie. He didn't love her, and she'd never get the chance to win his love. Not now.

The last wasn't easy to admit to herself, but she refused to turn from the truth no matter how painful. She'd learned long ago that ignoring something only made it worse when it caught up with you. She'd run away from Edinburgh and the sight of Angus pursuing another woman only to discover that being home didn't stop the emotions driving her. As the days passed, her longing for Angus had increased until it took the joy from each day.

But she'd been a child then, with a child's perception of love and a child's inability to realize her error. Niall and his harsh voice and scarred hands had shown her what life was about. And now she would lose him before she even had him.

She bit her lip to keep from sobbing aloud. She was no maudlin doll to let her world fall apart because a man didn't want her. And there was Duncan. She couldn't be anything but grateful that her brother would not have to meet this dangerous, powerful man.

"A captain," Niall's bitter voice said, interrupting her ruminations. "He made captain while I rotted in Newgate. It should have been me. I had seniority."

He twisted away, his back to Fiona and Micheil. There was such pain in his voice and in the tight curve of his spine that her heart went out to him. To see someone else get something you had worked for and to know that that person was instrumental in your not getting it was hard to accept.

"Niall, I'm sorry." Micheil's face was filled with commiseration. "But you never wanted to go to sea.

Neither of us. Our fathers made us. Remember that."

He took a step forward and put his hand on Niall's shoulder. Fiona expected Niall to shake off the contact; and when he didn't, surprise and jealousy overtook her. Had she been the one touching him right now, he'd have flung her away. But she had to be glad for his sake that he had someone he trusted enough to let him near.

Scant minutes later, Niall turned around, dislodging Micheil's hand in the process. Fiona saw that her captor's—lover's—face was set in harsh lines. He'd come to terms with the information.

"This alters my plans," he said in a cold voice. "I can't waste more time here when there are still two others."

Micheil cast a significant look at Fiona. "What about her?"

Even as he glanced at her, Micheil's light blue eyes narrowed and his mouth twisted. He knew. Fiona didn't know how, but she sensed that in that instant Micheil knew everything that had occurred between her and Niall on the beach. And he didn't like it.

Unaware of the undercurrents, Niall followed his friend's gaze. His face was inscrutable as he studied her. "She'll have to come with us."

"What?" Fiona said, jumping to her feet. Her heart pounded. With hope or despair? She wasn't sure. He wanted her with him, but she was too wise to know it was for anything other than to use her again.

"No," Micheil stated flatly.

Ignoring both of them, Niall stalked to the corner where the bags lay and took from them a small leather pouch that jingled as if it held coins. Almost as an afterthought, although Fiona couldn't believe it to be so, he gathered the oiled cloth holding his harp.

"We haven't time to stand around discussing this. My mind's made up. She comes with us. I can't take the chance of her managing to get a message to Macfie while we're in London tracking Winter."

"Tracking Winter?" Micheil asked incredulously. "Let it go, Niall. Can't you see that Macfie's being at sea is an omen. What you plan isn't to be."

Niall's brows snapped together. "You don't have to come, Micheil. I'll understand. You've been through so much already and stood by me no matter what."

"Dammit, Niall." Micheil's light tenor broke on his friend's name. "That's not it, not it at all. You're courting disaster. Death. You're obsessed with this, and it'll destroy you. I can't stand by and let that happen."

The anger, almost disappointment, left Niall's features. His voice softened. "I'm sorry, Micheil. We've had this conversation so many times before that I react before thinking about your feelings." His voice lowered until Fiona could barely make out the words. "I have to do this. It's all I have left. My honor is gone, and my father has disowned me. But I swear that on their deathbed, the three who sat in false judgment of me will recant their decision. I didn't murder that woman."

"Oh, God," Micheil groaned. "I know you didn't."

Hearing the tortured agony in each man's words, Fiona's gift activated and she sensed with horrible clarity that ruin lay ahead of them. And not just for these two. This was a tangled web that she couldn't escape, only hope to survive. She knew in her soul that she was inexplicably tied to the dark, haunted man who played the Highland harp like a Celtic bard . . . and who drew her heart more deeply into his keeping with each passing moment.

It wasn't an easy trip on any of them, Fiona acknowledged as she frowned at Niall Currie's broad back. He rode in front of her, once more on his stallion while she was back with the familiar MacDuff. Coming ashore on the mainland four days earlier, her one joy had been seeing her Highland pony and knowing that he had indeed been well cared for. So much so, the cantankerous animal hadn't wanted to be ridden.

Before leaving Pat's land, she'd asked Niall to have a message sent to her parents telling them she was all right. He'd grudgingly had Pat take a curt note. She'd felt better, hoping that some of the worry she knew her family would be feeling would be eased.

And she'd had to leave Blackie behind on Skye. As Niall had so quickly pointed out, there was no place for a crow on the journey they were about to make. It had helped that Blackie's feathers were stronger and she was able to leave him a large supply of oats and dried meat. She knew in her heart the bird would survive.

But that had been four days ago. Today she was tired and filthy and hungry. And her wrists were bound again. Her mouth twisted wryly. She distinctly remembered feeling this way the last time she'd mounted MacDuff. It seemed to be a quality of existence that went with Niall Currie.

MacDuff slowed to a halt without her command because Niall's stallion and Micheil's gelding were stopped, the two men conferring in voices too low for Fiona to hear. From what she could tell they were in the Borderlands between Scotland and northern England, approaching Carlisle. So far, they'd slept in the open, eating whatever Niall could catch. It'd been mainly rabbits, with a squirrel or two added. Even the ever-present oatmeal had run out at breakfast yesterday.

Fiona nudged MacDuff forward. Butting between the two men, she asked, "Can't we stay at an inn tonight?"

Micheil looked at her with his opaque blue eyes, but said nothing. Gooseflesh broke out on her arms under the covering of her blouse and cloak.

Niall glowered at her, so she glowered back. "Can't we?"

"How do we explain to the landlord about a single woman traveling with two men, neither of whom is her husband or brother?"

Fiona drew herself up imperiously. "We don't."

One side of his long mouth curled, the dimple she'd once thought lurking in his cheek no longer a possibility. "Ah, you don't care if your reputation is ruined as long as you have a tasty meal and a warm bed. I wish I'd known that sooner."

She blanched as though he'd slapped her. Her voice was cold in spite of the emotional hit she'd just received. "Carlisle isn't Edinburgh or London. And a country inn isn't the Pulteney."

Niall's sardonic smile dropped away. He yanked on Prince Charlie's reins, moving the horse out and away from Fiona. "Your blind trust is stupid. You never know whom you'll meet when you least expect it."

She glared at his back, wanting to pummel him with her bound fists. Belatedly, she felt Micheil's eyes on her. He shook his head in disgust before guiding his mount past her.

"You should never have been brought into this," he said loud enough for Niall to hear.

His words were a splash of ice water on her anger. He was right. She wasn't preventing Niall from pursuing his revenge by falling in love with him when he would never love her. Even with her iron will she couldn't keep her shoulders from slumping.

An hour later, they pulled up beside a weathered wooden sign that indicated Carlisle was two miles to the southeast and she heard Niall mutter something about an inn. But even knowing they seemed to be planning on spending the night in Carlisle couldn't lighten Fiona's dark mood. Micheil's words had taken root, reminding her of everything that had gone on in the past weeks.

"For you to have your warm bed and tasty food," Niall said to her, "I'll have to undo your hands. Going into a town with your wrists bound will only draw attention to us, and I don't want any. I don't intend to leave a trail for your father if he comes looking this way." His green eyes bored into her. "But I won't undo your hands and go to an inn without your promise that you won't try to escape."

Fiona contemplated his words. There was nowhere for her to go here even if she could get away. In London, however, she had an aunt she could flee to. "I promise."

His eyes narrowed to slits. "That easily?"

She nodded, meeting his scrutiny boldly. "If it's too easy," she added, the urge to needle him beyond her control, "I can be more difficult."

Niall's mouth thinned. "Hold out your arms."

He didn't bother to try untying the knots. Slipping his knife from his boot, he sliced her bonds in one sure stroke.

Fiona sighed in relief. "I'd thank you, but there's no reason to."

"Correct," he said coldly. "Expediency doesn't deserve gratitude."

A flush of irritation mounted her cheeks, but she refused to back down. As he had said, he hadn't released her because he wanted to.

They rode into Carlisle and stopped at the first clean inn they came to. Niall went in while Fiona and Micheil waited outside. He wasn't long.

Taking the traveling bags off Prince Charlie, he said, "They've rooms for the night."

Already Fiona could feel a soft mattress under her aching bones. The smell of roast beef came from the open door, and her stomach growled.

"Not a minute too soon," Niall said, reaching for her waist and hauling her down without a by-your-leave.

It was a quick, powerful act with no time to ponder and regret the tingle caused by his hands on her. Fiona lowered her eyes to keep herself from searching his for some emotion, some awareness of her as a person . . . the woman he'd taken with a wild abandon that she'd matched. She was a big enough fool as it was.

"Cover your wrists," he ordered. "If they see the sores they'll wonder, and we don't want them to remember us," he said, his voice deeper and huskier than normal. She attributed pitch and tone to his ire with her.

Micheil slipped between them. "Let's go. I'm tired and hungry."

Fiona stepped away, not wanting the other man's proximity. No matter how she tried to fight it, he made her uncomfortable.

Inside, Niall nodded imperiously to the innkeeper as they hurried by. The man pulled his forelock in acknowledgment of Niall's gesture, but his eyes were on Fiona. She looked back, and he bustled off to the kitchen. Never having gotten that reaction from a man before, she frowned as she followed her captors. Something wasn't right.

They climbed to the first story and turned left. The hallway was dark, but from what she could see it appeared to be clean, just as the tavern below had been. Hopefully there wouldn't be lice in her bed.

Niall handed Micheil a key and gestured to the first door. Taking that as meaning the room wasn't hers, Fiona kept behind him as he continued down the corridor. Two doors later, Niall inserted the key and pushed the door open, standing aside for her to enter.

She expected him to imprison her and be gone. He followed her in.

Her pulse jumped. "What are you doing?"

Closing the door, he locked it. The key went into the money pouch he carried around his neck. Fiona ground her teeth at his deliberation.

His eyes met hers without showing any expression. "We're husband and wife, Mr. and Mrs. McMurdo traveling to London." A wicked gleam entered his eyes. "You're not feeling well and have tried several times to slit your wrists, which is why they're bandaged and why I can tie you up again if I must. I'm taking you to London town to see if the doctors at Bedlam can help you."

Fiona saw red. "What?" Her hands fisted. "I'm deranged? What about you? Who in *their* right mind would believe such a story?"

He shrugged and walked past her to examine the bed. "The innkeeper for one," he said, pressing one palm into the mattress to test its softness. "You may have the bed tonight; you need your rest. I'll take the chair."

Only then did she realize that he'd gotten them the best room in the inn. They didn't just have a full-sized bed, they had a table and two chairs. There was even a fireplace. It didn't ameliorate her irritation with him.

"Don't patronize me," she said through clenched teeth. "I'm no fool and I don't need you treating me as such. Nor will I allow you to sleep in this room with me, whether you're on the chair or on the floor."

He faced her, hands on hips, feet apart. "How are you going to stop me? Tell the landlord I'm a liar? He won't believe you because he already knows you're crazy."

Her breath sucked in with a hiss. He had it all worked out, and there was nothing she could do about it. But she didn't want him in the same room with her. It'd been bad enough sleeping in the open with a fire to separate their blankets and Micheil to chaperon them. In this tiny space with four enclosing walls, there was nothing to keep them apart but his loathing of her and her denial of the desire he evoked in her.

"Damn you," she said softly but potently. "Damn you."

Niall watched her turn away, the glorious fire of her hair catching a stray sunbeam that managed to filter through the tiny window. He had to clamp down on his legs to keep from going to her and stroking the soft curve of her cheek.

Was she as reluctant as he to spend the night together in this tiny room where there was no one to see what their weaknesses might bring them to? It was both a heady and a disquieting thought. He had to get away.

"Stay here," he said more harshly than he'd intended. "I'll have supper sent up to you."

Before she could speak or turn her glorious blue eyes on him in fury, he left, pulling the door sharply closed behind him. Inserting the key in the lock, he turned it. He might have her promise not to try to escape; but now that she knew he'd be spending the night in the same room, he no longer trusted her.

His mouth twisted. He didn't blame her. It wasn't going to be an easy night.

Entering the inn's small tavern, he searched for Micheil. He found him hunched over a plate of food with one hand wrapped around a tankard of ale. Niall motioned the innkeeper to him and gave him the order to be taken to Fiona and one for himself to eat here. That done, he turned his attention to his friend.

Micheil looked at him, his light-blue eyes appearing washed out thanks to the red lines of exhaustion and too much ale that riddled the whites. "You're sharing a room with her, aren't you?" he asked in accusing tones.

Niall's knuckles turned white as he fisted his hands. Calmly he met Micheil's gaze. "Yes. 'Twas the only way I could explain her presence with us. Even a blind fool would know we're no kin."

"You could have said she was your ward or your brother's wife." Micheil picked at a piece of beef but didn't eat it. "You could have found a way to get her a separate room if you'd wanted."

Niall kept his voice reasonable. "If she had a separate room, how could I ensure she didn't escape?"

"And why shouldn't she?" Micheil slammed his fork down. "You don't need her. She can't warn Macfie. He's at sea." He leaned toward Niall. His eyes narrowed into pale, blue slashes. "You want her. That's why she's with us. You lust after her. I tell you, she's trouble. You'll pay for bedding her."

How did Micheil know? Niall kept his face blank with an effort. "You're imagining things."

"No, I'm not. I've eyes and I've seen the way you look at her. I've never seen you look at a woman as you look at her. It means trouble." As though he were a chameleon, Micheil suddenly lounged back in his seat. He gave Niall a sly look. "And besides, you intend to kill her brother. Do you think she'll enjoy your caresses after that?"

For the first time since he and Micheil had become friends so many years ago, anger at his companion flared in Niall. "Do you think I don't know that? Bloody hell, Micheil, leave off it."

The serving wench laid Niall's supper in front of him. He was glad of the interruption. The hurt look on Micheil's face was worse than if he'd punched him. He took a deep breath to calm himself, knowing that further anger would only heighten Micheil's sense of ill-usage.

"See," Micheil hissed, the ease gone from his muscles and his mouth pulled back against his teeth, the hurt replaced by disgust. "The serving wench practically dropped her breasts onto your plate, and you didn't even notice."

Niall sighed in exasperation. "Leave off, Micheil. We've talked this subject to death."

In an effort to divert Micheil's thoughts, Niall gave the serving woman a once-over as she sauntered away. She was comely and well-endowed, but not worth the effort. Fiona was worth the effort. Her scorching response to his caresses traveled along his nerves to remind him of that even now.

"I'm sure the woman'd be as accommodating for you," Niall told his friend.

Micheil paled. "No thanks. I'd rather find my own conveniences."

It was a relief to Niall when Micheil shut up after

that. He was hungry and he was tired, and he was determined not to go to his room until he was sure Fiona slept.

Micheil finished and left without speaking again. Niall sighed and called after his friend, "We leave at sunrise."

Micheil didn't answer, but Niall knew him well enough to know that the lifting of his shoulders indicated he'd heard. With a sigh of relief at having his recalcitrant friend depart, Niall lounged back as comfortably as he could in the ladderback chair and drank another tankard of ale.

The serving girl flashed him a smile and leaned over a little too far when she brought him his fourth tankard. He gave her a lazy smile of appreciation, but shook his head no. The only woman he wanted to bed was upstairs—barred to him. He downed the fresh ale in one long gulp.

Pushing out of the chair, he made his way slowly to the stairs and up to the room. Fleetingly, he wondered what the landlord had thought when he'd taken Fiona her food and found the room locked. Then he remembered that the man thought Fiona was crazy. He smiled derisively. If anyone were crazy, it was him for desiring the sister of a man he'd vowed to kill.

He turned the key and entered, relocking the door behind himself. The fire was dead, or had never been lit, and the only light came from the moon shining in through the small, bare window. He followed the direction of the silver beam with his eyes. It alighted on Fiona.

He groaned. Just his luck that it would highlight the one object in the room he didn't want to see.

She lay peacefully, her face ethereal in the the cool light. Even her hair was muted. Instead of glowing like flames, it shimmered like molten copper where it rippled over the pillow. The urge to touch her was primordial in its intensity.

His feet carried him reluctantly to the bed.

Fiona felt Niall's fingers on her cheek, and it was all she could do to remain motionless. Shivers of delight flowed from his touch all the way to her toes. If only he loved her, things would be all right.

His fingers skimmed over her skin to her mouth, which he touched as lightly as a feather. The pressure tickled, and her flesh tingled. An ache so strong it brought tears to her closed eyes engulfed her.

Before she could weaken and reach out for him, he left her side. She heard him trying to get comfortable in the chair. It was a fruitless battle, and she knew he'd be sore in the morning and likely to take his discomfort out on her.

Long after he'd settled in, Fiona lay awake. Niall's deep breathing filled the air, as did his spicy male scent. Her fingers dug into the mattress.

She missed him, the closeness they'd shared on the Isle of Skye. She even missed his acerbic comments and the vigilant eye that kept her from escaping. But more than all of that combined, she missed the haunting melody and emotion-rich playing of his harp. He hadn't played since they'd made love.

The bittersweet memory of their joining, kept at bay during daylight and during the cold nights of their journey, claimed her. She could feel his hands on her, his mouth devouring hers as his body consumed hers. A sob escaped her, then another.

But she wouldn't succumb to self-pity. Neither would she yearn for a man who thought of her as an object to an end. No, she wouldn't.

Niall didn't love her; he was using her. She wouldn't love him either, not even if it meant walling her heart in ice. She wouldn't love him.

Nor would she worry that her menses was late.

Chapter Eight

Fiona groaned in misery, saw Niall's shoulders twitch as he heard her, and bit her tongue to keep the next groan in. She didn't require much for comfort—a warm bed, enough to eat—but she hadn't had either since they'd left Carlisle. Even the horses dragged their hooves.

They were on the outskirts of London after a journey she'd spend the rest of her life trying to forget. Both Niall and his friend had been surly, Micheil giving no hint that he remembered cutting her bonds on the Isle of Skye. But she had the distinct impression he wouldn't be sorry to wake up and find her gone.

Even worse had been Niall's refusal to do more than glance at her or grunt an answer to anything she said. That had been compounded by the cessation of his harp-playing. Not having the music impressed upon her how much she'd enjoyed it and how much it had soothed her at night, enabling her to sleep in spite of the precarious nature of her situation. And it had been a release for him that he was now denying himself.

Looking at the crowded London streets and the soot-blackened walls of the older buildings they passed, she feared London would be worse. She would have to escape to her aunt as soon as possible. There was no future for her with Niall.

After traveling several more miles into the center of town, they pulled up in front of a clean building. It resembled a boardinghouse. It wasn't in the fashionable West End.

Niall dismounted and went inside. When he returned, he said, "We've got rooms here for as long as we need them. There's a stable around back."

"What about me?" Fiona asked, determined to assert herself this time and not end up in the same room with Niall again.

He gave her a noncommittal look. "What about you?"

"Am I still headed for Bedlam?" she asked, her voice laced with sarcasm.

Instead of answering, he reached up and lifted her down without asking, a habit he'd gotten into that no amount of cold looks had been able to end. That chore done, he gathered up the bags and left Micheil to make sure she got inside.

They found him talking to a thin woman with iron-gray hair and heavily wrinkled skin. In spite of her weathered appearance, the woman smiled at them and bid them welcome with a good cheer. Fiona took her to be the proprietress and wondered anew what Niall had told her since the woman didn't look away from her and didn't treat her like a fallen woman.

"Mrs. McMurdo," the woman greeted Fiona, answering the question, "your husband tells me you suffer from consumption and have come to London to see a doctor. I hope your journey has a happy ending."

Fiona managed to smile around her clenched teeth. After all, it wasn't the woman's fault Niall was a facile liar. "Thank you."

A large hand gripped Fiona's elbow, and she knew without looking it belonged to Niall. Heat and an awareness that went beyond touch confirmed his presence. He pulled her away.

"Our rooms are this way," he said firmly, making sure she kept beside him when she balked.

"I can walk on my own."

"True," he answered. "The problem is that you won't walk where I want you to."

Careful to make sure they were out of earshot, she demanded, "Why do you continue to do this? I'm not your wife."

He cut her a cold glance. "Can this wait until we're alone?"

Only then did she remember that Micheil followed. In her irritation with Niall for continuing to claim her as wife when it was the last thing he wanted her to be, she'd forgotten about the man behind them. Silently, they went up two flights of stairs. Micheil had the set of rooms next to theirs.

Entering the room before Niall as he indicated, Fiona waited only until the door was closed. "I refuse to go through this farce again. Let me go. You don't need me, and I have an aunt here to whom I can go."

His eyes narrowed to dangerous green slits. "You

have a what here? Why didn't you say something before?"

Chin out, she said, "I have an aunt, and I didn't tell you because it was none of your business. She moves in fashionable circles—places *you* won't be frequenting."

"Damn it to hell!" He slammed the bags on the floor and strode across the room, his boots ringing on the uncarpeted portions of the wood floor. "You're one problem after another."

"Then let me go." She matched him force for force. "I didn't ask to be kidnapped. I didn't ask to be passed off as your wife." She was grateful for the anger that masked the hurt caused by the knowledge that while he might claim her as wife for expediency, he would never wed her. Something she now realized she wanted badly. It was the ache in her chest that she had been telling herself was only the beginning of a cold.

Pivoting on the balls of his feet, he stared her down. "I can't let you go."

Fiona caught her breath. His eyes were dark and haunted, hinting at untold misery and conflicting desires. For the first time, she began to wonder if he truly wanted to go through with his vow to kill the three men who'd sat on his court-martial board. Just as quickly, she told herself she was seeing what she wanted to see and not what he felt—just as she'd first told herself he made love to her on the beach because he cared for her. She should know by now that lying to herself only caused more grief.

Still, her heart went out to him for the agony that was making him miserable. She knew how it hurt to be uncertain or regretful, and she couldn't bear to see him so. But neither could she weaken in her determination to leave him. She couldn't save him, but there was still the possibility that if she got away she could save her brother.

"Then you'd better put a guard on me, because I intend to get free of you."

Niall's shoulders tensed beneath the unfashionable leather jacket he wore. "Why make this harder than you must?"

Sadness entered her heart at his determination. "Because you plan to kill my brother. Duncan would have never convicted you unless he believed you guilty. No matter what was done to you, two wrongs don't make a right. Take Micheil's advice: Let it go."

His hand fisted and his mouth thinned. "Damn you."

Before she realized what he intended, he caught her up and tossed her on the bed. Without a glimmer of remorse, he yanked the hated rope from his pocket and bound her.

Fury coursed through her. "You'd better gag me then, for I'll yell this house down."

"Then I'll have to tell the landlady that you're really here for Bedlam."

The rigidity of his muscles told her as surely as his words that he would carry out his threat. Her anger evaporated. It was useless to fight him when he held all the cards and was ready for her to try something. Like on Skye, she'd do better to try and lull him into complacency.

"I promise not to try and escape while you're gone.

Is that good enough for you to undo my wrists?" She met his look squarely, willing him to see the truth in her words.

"Your word as a Macfie?" he countered, his brows furrowed.

"Yes," she said quietly. "My word. I don't want to spend hours bound to this bed. We're several stories above the street, and the door is too stout for me to break through."

His mouth curved sardonically. "You give your word because it doesn't make sense to try and escape under the current circumstances. You're a practical woman."

"I try to be," she said as he undid her.

He left immediately, locking her in.

Fiona wished things were different between them. She wished she could turn him from his destructive course. She wished she could make him love her. Her mouth twisted sadly. If wishes were gold, she'd be a rich woman.

Still . . . it was something to consider. She rose from the bed and went to the window overlooking the front part of the building.

Below her, a young girl cried out, "Chestnuts, lovely hot chestnuts."

The hope in the young voice mirrored the stubborn hope in Fiona's heart.

Why did she have to be Macfie's sister, Niall asked himself, stalking down the hall to Micheil's door. No other woman would have tied him in knots. But with her, he felt an affinity so strong he almost thought he should stop fighting it and make love to her again. It almost made him want to abandon his vengeance so that he could claim her.

Damn her for weakening him.

Micheil opened his door before Niall could knock. "I heard you stomping all the way here. You two must've had another fight."

Unable to make light of the situation, Niall frowned. "Let's get going. I want to go to White's and Brooks's to see if I can learn Winter's whereabouts. The sooner this is done, the sooner we can leave."

Micheil, fashionably dressed in a blue coat that was only slightly wrinkled from being carried throughout Scotland, looked his friend over. "You'd have better luck getting information if you fitted in with the men you'll be questioning. The English aristocracy is notoriously closed."

Impatient as he was to get started, Niall had to agree. Dressed properly, he'd get his answers quickly. Dressed like a barbarian, he'd get ridicule. "Weston might have something he can fit me into, for the right recompense."

Closing his door and brandishing a gold-topped cane, Micheil followed Niall down the stairs and outside. "I'm sure with all the bounty you won while in His Majesty's Service that you'll be able to come up with the blunt."

Out on the busy street, Niall took his bearings before heading to the Bank of England on the corner of Prince's and Threadneedle Streets.

"Do I detect a note of regret?" he asked Micheil.

"A little," the other admitted. "I wasn't good with investing mine and, as you know, have to rely on my father for an allowance."

"Since you're his heir, he's more than generous to you."

It was a fact of his friend's life that Niall accepted without jealousy. Micheil was his father's only son and greatly loved. Niall was his father's fourth son and had been loved, perhaps, while he'd met his father's expectations. But when he'd been cashiered from the Navy and brought disgrace on the Currie name, his father had been quick to disown him. It was a bitter pain that Niall strove to resign himself to. As it was, most of Niall's bounty from the Navy was invested, the revenues going to the Currie clan which, like many Highland clans, was impoverished. Even so, his father still refused to acknowledge his existence.

They arrived at the Bank of England where they were shown into a private office by one of the twenty-four directors. Shortly after, all the funds Niall needed were put at his disposal and they left for Weston's, where Niall was quickly fitted in the current fashion.

Bond Street and White's were crowded, but both men, scions of Scotland's aristocracy, were members of the exclusive club and soon found themselves in the gaming room. Niall quickly had the direction of Winter's townhouse.

Stepping back into Bond Street, Niall said, "I'll go on alone from here."

Micheil put a restraining hand on Niall's arm. "I'll go with you."

The irritation Niall found himself feeling for Micheil of late resurfaced, and he had to take several moments to subjugate it. Micheil was his friend, his only friend. Micheil had stood by him when no one else would.

"Thank you, but I don't want you tainted with my revenge. You've done enough for me; I won't repay you that way."

Before Micheil could persist, Niall hailed a passing hackney coach and hopped inside. Knowing Micheil had Winter's direction, too, Niall leaned out the window and told the driver to hurry. They careened around corners and zigzagged through traffic.

The coach pulled to a halt, the horses puffing. Niall exited and gave the driver a bonus, telling him not to wait.

Winter lived in a fashionable part of London, and his residence was impressive. Niall wasn't surprised. When he had known Winter, the man had been heir presumptive to a cousin who was a viscount. Apparently, he'd come into the title.

Knocking on the door, Niall waited patiently for the butler to answer. Patience was a commodity he'd hoarded in prison for this time. Challenging three men to a duel when all three lived in different parts of Britain required time and flexibility.

But Fiona had put a kink in his complacent plans. He hadn't expected her.

She was a firebrand that threatened to consume him with her heat and thwart his plan if he weren't careful. Somehow, he had to get rid of her without jeopardizing his challenge of her brother. And he had to do it soon—before he lost himself and made love to her again.

Brows furrowed, he was mildly surprised when the butler finally opened the door, having momentarily forgotten where he was. Like Winter, his servant was tall and thin, with a long patrician nose that he managed to look down even though Niall was several inches taller.

"I'm here to see Winter," Niall stated.

"Whom may I say is calling?" the butler asked, his frosty gaze skimming over Niall's fashionable, but hastily acquired, attire.

"Niall McMurdo Currie of Balilone."

"I see," the man said sonorously, opening the door wider for Niall to enter. "If you'll follow me, sir."

The butler led Niall into a small room off the foyer. Only a table and several chairs occupied the center. Obviously, the servant wasn't sure of his visitor's status.

"I shall tell his lordship that you are here."

Niall nodded curtly to the man. Now that the moment was upon him, Niall's hard-won patience deserted him. As soon as the door shut, Niall paced to the window and gazed out onto the street. It was getting dark, and the gaslights were being lit. Several carriages, their lanterns glowing yellowly, hurried by, carrying their well-to-do passengers to the evening's entertainments. With Parliament in session for the winter, the Little Season was starting. Thank goodness Winter attended the House of Lords or he'd be on his estate instead of in town and more difficult to locate.

The door opened and Winter's remembered voice said, "What do you want?"

Niall turned slowly, a hard smile showing his teeth. "As gracious as ever."

Winter closed the door behind himself and moved into the room. "The last I heard of you, Newgate was filling your head with new ways to commit murder."

The urge to hit Winter was intense. Niall resisted it and kept his voice cold and level. "Then you won't be surprised by this." Niall took two strides, taking his gloves off as he moved. He slapped them across Winter's startled countenance. "I challenge you to a duel to the death for my honor and your part in sending me to jail."

Winter stumbled back, knocking over the small table as he struggled to retain his balance. He didn't stop moving until he had one of the chairs between him and Niall. It seemed to renew his courage as he clung to it.

"You're crazy," he said, the print of Niall's gloves livid on his cheek. "I'll no more meet you in a duel than I believe you have any honor to avenge."

Niall took a deep breath to keep himself from jumping over the chair and throttling Winter. "You judge me by your own standards. Any man too cowardly to accept a duel justly given is cowardly enough to commit the type of murder you found me guilty of."

Even the insult did nothing. Winter backed hastily to the door, which he threw wide. "Get out of my house, Currie, or I'll have you thrown out."

The temptation to refuse was great; but even with his blood pounding in fury, Niall knew causing a fracas in Winter's house wouldn't accomplish his mission. Stalking past his adversary, Niall said dangerously, the words a promise, "You will meet me, Winter. Never doubt it."

Winter didn't say a word, but Niall felt the man's eyes staring holes into his back as he went out the front door the butler held open. He wasn't done a second too soon. Micheil stepped out of a hired coach just as Niall descended the last step of Winter's porch.

The irritation at Micheil that seemed to hover constantly below the surface exploded in Niall, exacerbated by his frustration over Winter's refusal to meet him. "I told you not to come."

Micheil, in the process of paying the driver, blanched and dropped the coins.

"T'at be al'right, guv," the driver said, jumping down. "I'll get 'em meself."

Micheil walked away from the coach. "You can't leave me out of this, Niall. I won't let you."

Furious at Micheil's persistence and knowing that short of fighting with his friend he could do nothing about it, Niall pivoted and strode away. He heard Micheil's footsteps hurrying to catch up. He wanted to strike Micheil. Was he going insane? God, he didn't know.

But the idea dissipated some of his unreasonable anger. Slowing down, he allowed Micheil to reach him. "I'm going to walk back to the room."

Micheil fell into step beside him. "Did he agree to meet you?" he asked.

Looking at the ground, Niall kicked a rock. "No. The bloody coward."

Micheil let out a gust of relief. "I can't say I'm sorry. If you killed him, you'd have to flee the country or go to prison again. Trying to appease your honor isn't worth it. And Winter isn't going to recant his decision of your guilt, even if you put a bullet through his heart or a sword to his throat. He's too much of a prig."

"He'd say anything I made him say. He's a·coward," Niall growled. "It's Macfie I'll have to kill. He's got as much honor as I do, if not more."

Micheil sniffed. "Macfie's too high in the instep for the younger son of an impoverished earl."

The hint of jealousy was so like Micheil. Niall couldn't help a snort of amusement, easing some of the fury that had been driving him for the past weeks. No, if he were honest, the anger had been with him for the last three years. It was only in the last couple weeks that he'd begun to realize it was anger driving him and not just a need to revenge his name. The idea that the awareness might be due to Fiona flitted across his mind, but he banished it.

"You've nothing to be jealous of," Niall told Micheil. "You're the heir to a rich viscount, and that outranks the younger son of an impoverished earl any day. If you went about in Society, you'd have all the chits trying to hoodwink you into marriage."

Micheil missed a step. "That's not one of my goals," he mumbled.

"No," Niall sighed, the moment of lightness gone. "You insist on hanging with me."

Realizing he'd given Micheil another opportunity to admonish him about the duels, Niall was relieved to see their boardinghouse just ahead. He sped up so that

Micheil was hard pressed to keep up and unable to speak. Niall entered and took the steps three at a time.

Fiona heard Niall's tread in the hallway before he unlocked the door and entered. Her head throbbed from lack of food, and she was bored. Spending an afternoon confined in a barren room wasn't her idea of entertainment.

When he came into view, she shot a venomous look at him. "It's about time you returned. I'm hungry and I'm sore."

He glanced at her, his face darkening. "And no more pleasant than when I left."

Without giving her a chance to say more, he left the room. Fifteen minutes later, he returned with a tray laden with meat and cheese. He set the meal on the table.

Approaching the food, she absentmindedly scratched her wrists. They were beginning to heal and itched. "I'm famished."

Before he could reply, she sat in one of the chairs and helped herself to the food. There was even a pot of strong tea which she laced with sugar and cream.

He sank into the other chair and stretched his feet out. Leisurely, he helped himself to a bit of everything.

She noticed for the first time that he was dressed differently. Apprehension stilled her hand as she lifted the teacup to her lips. "Why are you in a fashionable coat and breeches?"

He chewed slowly on a piece of sausage. "Why do you think?"

Her eyes narrowed, and she set the tea down. "You found him, the man you're going to kill, didn't you?"

Her chest tightened as she read the answer in his face.

"Yes, and the bastard refused to meet me. But I'll dog him until he agrees."

All her anger with him fled in the face of what he was determined to do to himself. Fiona sank to her knees in front of him, her hands grabbing hold of his.

"Don't do this, Niall. Don't destroy yourself this way."

His eyes became hooded, their green depths alight with passions she could only guess at. "Why do you care? He isn't your brother."

She drew back at the flat coldness in his voice. "He's a human being, and this revenge is destroying you."

He sneered, the pain he kept hidden so well twisting his features. She ached for him.

"I'm already ruined . . . or have you forgotten? I've been convicted of killing a woman." His voice lowered to a harsh whisper. "They say I slit her throat and sodomized her. What can I do that's worse than that?"

Fiona closed her eyes to keep him from seeing the pity she couldn't deny. It was more horrible than she'd imagined, and it was tearing him apart.

Taking a deep breath to steady herself, she looked back at him. "I don't believe you did that. You might be capable of killing a man to defend yourself or even in a duel of honor, but you'd never do those other things to anyone—especially not to a woman."

His laugh was harsh and guttural. "You and Micheil are the only ones who believe that. Even my father thinks I did it."

There it was. The final disillusionment that haunted this tormented man—his father's disownment of him.

It caused such pain and for something Niall could never have done. Coming from a loving family, it was impossible for Fiona to understand a father disowning his own son.

"Doesn't your father know you couldn't have committed so heinous a crime?"

For the first time since entering the room, his eyes turned away from her. "It doesn't matter. I've disgraced the family name. You're a Highlander. You know our honor is all many of us have. The Curries are no different."

"No," she contradicted him softly, "your father is no different and it takes away from him the honor he accuses you of tarnishing."

His gaze came back to her, his eyes the brilliant, intense color of malachite. Dark green striations radiated outward from the black depths of his dilated pupils.

Fiona caught her breath.

He untangled his fingers from hers and brought them up to cup her face. "Don't do this," he said, his voice deep and agonized. "Don't show understanding and warmth for me. Don't believe in me. It'll only destroy you."

She shook her head, making his hands move with her. Pressing her lips to one of his callused palms, she spoke with certainty. "This won't destroy me. Nothing you do will destroy me."

Her belief in him was melting the coldness around his heart, and when it was done completely perhaps he would be healed. Her chest swelled, and the tiny bud of hope that had taken root listening to the young girl below the window burgeoned.

Niall studied her face. He saw character and determination in the upward slant of her glorious blue eyes and the determined firmness of her full mouth. Even her nose, with its retroussé tip was determined. And it was because she believed in him.

That belief was a more powerful aphrodisiac than any potion. It raged through his blood and engorged his loins. In this instant, this moment in time, he wanted this woman more than he'd ever wanted anything in his life . . . even his honor.

A groan tore from him. "Fiona, look at me." When she did, gazing at him fearlessly, he said, "I want to make love to you. I've wanted to do it since the first time I saw you, defiantly sitting astride MacDuff, daring me to reveal myself to you." A tiny, rueful smile tugged at one corner of his mouth.

"You have made love to me," she whispered, her lower lip trembling.

Another groan escaped him and he bowed his head, only to raise it up so that his mouth was inches from hers. "As God is my witness, that wasn't enough."

Tendrils of excitement unfolded in Fiona's stomach and spread to her toes. She gripped his knees, wanting to reach for him but willing herself to wait and let him make the first move. It had to come from him or it would mean nothing.

He bent to her so that his lips brushed hers, his warm breath caressed her face. "I want to love you until nothing else matters but the feel of you in my arms, beneath me."

Tingles ran down her nerves. She longed to feel him again, to have him pressed close to her, his heart beating rapidly next to hers. Oh, God, she wanted him to love her.

"Then love me," she said, her voice catching on the last word.

He searched her face for one long moment as though seeking truth. His chest rose and fell.

Fiona thought she would die if he turned away from her now. Unable to watch him as he decided, she closed her eyes.

His mouth settled gently on hers, asking a question she answered by opening to him. He held her still as he deepened the kiss, his tongue delving deeply, his lips moving with leisurely desire over hers. Fiona's knees gave way, and she sank to the floor. He followed her down.

Releasing her face, he wrapped his arms around her waist and shoulders to support her while he bent over her, his kiss consuming her. Vaguely, she felt the large gold buttons of his coat pressing into her breasts. But the slight discomfort was superseded by the pleasure his mouth gave.

Just when she thought they would tumble onto the floor, he lowered her, making sure she was on the small oval rug that was the room's only luxury. Releasing her mouth, he loomed above her, his gaze traveling over her face to her neck and lower. Heat moved in her.

"You're beautiful," he said huskily, stroking the loosened hair from her face. "You can't know how many times I've pictured you like this, lying beneath me, the sun's rays lighting your hair."

She smiled before reaching up and pulling him to her. Their lips met and she tightened her hold so that his chest pressed into hers, exciting her breasts into swollen orbs of tension. She wanted so badly for him to caress her it was an ache that would be assuaged by his kiss alone.

Breaking away from his mouth, she asked, "Please, Niall, touch me."

Her plea inflamed him. Desire shot through him. "Vixen," he whispered into the red flames of her hair, "I'll do better than that."

He wound his fingers into the silken strands that fanned on the rug beneath her and held her motionless as his mouth skimmed over her jaw and down the side of her neck. Nuzzling away the neckline of her bodice, he licked the sensitive skin of her shoulder.

Small gasps of delight escaped Fiona's parted lips.

He lifted his head to gaze at her, his eyes dark and smoldering. "That's it. Tell me how much you like it."

Her response was incredible. She gave her body to him as wholly as she gave him her belief. And in the giving, she gave him back his soul. Nothing else mattered to Niall but the woman in his arms.

She reached for the buttons on his coat and undid them. Pushing it from his shoulders, she watched as he shrugged it off completely. He untangled his hands from her hair and in several swift, jerky moves flung the coat away and yanked off his shirt.

Fiona marveled at the expanse of his chest, the muscles rippling with each deep breath he took. He was hers.

She laid her palm on him where his heart beat strongly. Moving slowly, she buried her fingers in the thick growth of curly black hair that spread from nipple to nipple and snaked to his flat belly. She felt sensuous and decadent and desirable.

His sharp intake of breath made her feel wicked.

"Don't go lower," he warned, his voice deep. "I want you to enjoy this, too."

Her smiled widened as she did exactly what he told her not to do. Watching him, she undid the fastenings of his breeches and pushed them down his lean hips. The widening, then narrowing of his eyes excited her, made her stomach turn and her toes curl in their sturdy shoes.

"Vixen," he said softly, rolling to one side and removing his pants.

Immensely satisfied with herself, Fiona ran one rosy nail around and around his right aureole until the nipple stood in rock-hard relief against the tanned skin of his chest. That accomplished, her finger trailed lower.

A sense of power flooded her as she grasped his hard length in her hand and gently stroked him. He bucked against her, his teeth digging into his lower lip. He was hers, and she reveled in the knowledge.

"I should have known better than to tell you not to do something," he said, his voice strained,

She chuckled with delight. "You're like satin here." Her fingers squeezed and he groaned.

"And you're a vixen," he replied, steeling himself to

keep from spreading her legs and taking her then and there.

Determined to do to her exactly what she was doing to him, to take her soul into his keeping along with her body, Niall clasped her wrist and carefully pried her away from him. Pinioning both her hands above her head, he undressed her.

As he untied the laces at her neck, his tongue laved the exposed flesh. He suckled the curve of her bone and nuzzled the small hollow at the base of her throat. She purred beneath him, making it harder to keep from taking her, he ached so badly.

Inserting his hand beneath her blouse and chemise, he pushed both up above her chest, releasing her hands long enough to pull the clothing over her head. Her mouth met his in a kiss intended to tease, but one that developed into a deep, consuming communion.

Sinking back to the floor, their mouths entwined, he lay on her, the hair of his chest tickling her swollen breasts. Settling into her soft curves, Niall inserted his legs between hers, rucking her skirts up to her hips.

When he had to come up for air, he undid her skirt and slid it off. His hands rubbed down her legs, pushing her sturdy cotton hose down her calves. With an economy of motion, he slid off her pattens and hose. Then with exquisite slowness, her traced the lines of her leg muscles back up to her thighs—and higher.

"You're like milk and wild honey," he breathed, his fingers teasing her swollen flesh. He gazed down at the creamy whiteness of her flesh and the golden red tangle that beckoned him to enter. His eyes darkened, and his fingers dipped into her molten sweetness.

Fiona gasped with pleasure as he stroked the sensitive skin between her thighs. Only a man who cared made sure his partner enjoyed this act. "And you're like the devil himself, with knowing fingers and dangerous looks."

And he was hers. For this hour in time, she would possess him even as he possessed her.

Fiercely determined to woo him to her, she drew his torso back down, her fingers digging into the muscles of his shoulders. When he lay on her, his weight a satisfying burden that pressed her into the unyielding rug beneath, she undulated her hips in unison with his questing fingers.

He moaned. "If I'm the devil, you're the temptation that doomed me to hell."

Fiona's heart skipped a beat, her motions ceased. His words were too darkly prophetic for comfort.

Putting a finger to his lips, she cautioned, "Don't say such things, not even in jest."

His lips stiffened beneath her touch, and he pulled away. A sharp cry of despair left her even as her hands slipped to his waist to hold him tight.

"No," she said, "don't leave. Not now. Now when we're this close. Forget I said anything."

To enforce her plea, she took his lips with hers and demanded entrance with her tongue. Her fingers curved into the hard strength of his buttocks to pull him back into the shelter of her thighs. Wrapping her legs around his loins, she circled his shaft with one hand and positioned him.

"Oh, God," he said, tearing away from her mouth,

his face contorted with desire and denial. "I'll destroy you."

"You won't," she said, thrusting upward, imprisoning him with her woman's might.

A groan ripped from him as she sheathed him in her tight warmth. Shudders wracked him, and against his volition his back arched to push him deeper.

Fiona joined him with a sharp scream as he plunged to her depths. "Love me, Niall. Love me."

Her words reverberated through him. He could no more leave her now than he could tear out his heart.

"Oh, Vixen," he gasped, "we've gone too far."

Her legs tightened around him, her warmth massaging him. She dug her nails into him and rose up to meet his mouth. Taking his tongue into her, she moved her hips in rhythm with his.

Tension built in her, starting in her loins and spreading to every limb. Her mind whirled out of control, subject only to the intense pleasure he generated with each pumping motion of his hips. She thought she would die.

Rising above her, using his hands and arms for leverage, Niall watched her through slitted eyes. Her face was radiant, her breasts swollen with nipples like ripe cherries. Looking lower, he saw where their bodies joined, where black hair met russet. The hot blood pounding in his loins exploded.

He plunged into her, felt her begin to contract around him. It was his last conscious thought before he catapulted over the edge.

His shout of release mingled with her soft gasps of completion.

Later, limbs entangled, they lay quiescent. The sun had long set and the room was cooling off, making the sweat of their exertions chilly.

Fiona, unwilling to pull away from him and sever their connection, where that most satisfying part of him still resided in her, sighed in repletion. Stroking a strand of ebony hair back from his forehead, she smiled dreamily at him.

"That was wonderful, Niall."

His eyes focused on her face and an emotion she didn't want to name flitted across their depths. "It was a mistake," he said flatly.

Unspoken were the words that it was only sex with no feeling and no love on his part, but she knew he thought them. Fiona rolled away, too devastated to even be defiant. Her dreams had been a fantasy. He was still the hard, vengeful man who'd kidnaped her. And it seemed that nothing she did could change that.

Gathering up her clothing, she hastily yanked the garments on.

Before she was finished, there was a knock on the door. "Niall." Micheil's voice came through the wooden barrier, "I've thought of a plan. Let me in."

Fiona, fighting the tears threatening to fall that would complete her shame, took refuge in anger. "He's always in the nick of time, isn't he?"

Niall, scrambling to get into his breeches, muttered, "Bloody hell." All the irritation fomenting in him surfaced, and he spoke harshly. "Dammit, Micheil, couldn't this wait till tomorrow?"

"No," Micheil said distinctly.

Niall finished dressing and gave Fiona a once-over.

"Don't wait up for me," he said, moving to the door. "This doesn't change our situation."

Fiona bit her lip to keep from railing at him as he left. Damn him. Damn him to hell.

Chapter Nine

Niall faced Micheil. His friend gave him one comprehensive, reproachful look and headed for the stairs. Niall followed, dreading what he knew was coming, but unable to prevent it short of walking off on Micheil as he'd just done Fiona. It wasn't in him to hurt both of them so deeply so close together.

Silently he followed Micheil to a nearby tavern and took a seat opposite him.

"You just finished bedding her," Micheil said, his accusing tone accepting no denials.

Niall opened his mouth to deny it anyway and stopped. He wasn't going to compound his perfidy by lying.

When Niall didn't answer, Micheil said, "At least you're not going to tell me it didn't happen when a blind man could see it has. You have that wild look in your eyes, and your clothes look like you took her with them still on your limbs." He paused, and his voice fell. "And you smell of her."

It was nearly too much for Niall. His shoulders tensed. "You're going too far," he said.

Micheil sniffed. "You don't need to use her for your revenge."

It was a gut punch. Not only his honor, but his sense of fairness proscribed that he not make love to Fiona. It was his body that was weak.

"I'm not using her," Niall said. "And what happens between her and me is none of your business, Micheil." He deliberately relaxed his shoulders. "And I won't say it to you again. Now, what is your plan?"

Micheil took his time, ordering ale and supper. "Winter can't refuse your challenge if you make it in public."

Niall suppressed his exasperation at so obvious a conclusion. Micheil was only trying to help, and the least he could do was go along with him. Besides, guilt at his impatience with his friend made it impossible for him to do otherwise. Micheil deserved better of him.

"That's true, so how do you propose that I get him in public and what reason shall I use for challenging him?"

Micheil rubbed his hands together. "While you were talking to people at White's about Winter's residence, I was talking to one of the servants about Winter's habits." A sly grin showed his teeth, one canine slightly crooked, giving him the look of an urchin if one ignored the fine quality of his clothing. "He gambles every Wednesday night while the rest of London's aristocracy is cavorting at Almacks'."

Niall immediately regretted his earlier shortness

with Micheil. "That's an interesting piece of information."

"Isn't it just?" Micheil said, satisfaction lighting his blue eyes.

The serving wench chose that moment to bring the food and drink that Micheil had ordered for both of them. This woman was thin, but with ample bosom and bottom. Any other time, she would have tempted Niall, but no longer. Even when she put his plate down so that her blouse gapped open and her heavy breasts brushed his arm, nothing happened. He didn't even feel a mild spurt of desire.

"She's willing," Micheil said with a conspiratorial glance as the woman sauntered away. "There was a time when you could bed three wenches in one night. Don't tell me that's not possible anymore." His gaze held Niall.

The attempt to goad him into proving his manhood was so blatant that Niall didn't have it in him to get angry. Instead, he began to feel sorry for Micheil, who obviously feared Fiona's influence and was doing everything in his power to negate it. Niall wished he could help his friend, but he knew with a certainty that if he tried to bed the wench he'd fail.

"We're not here to discuss my prowess, but how to trap Winter," he said firmly.

Around a mouthful of mutton and roasted potatoes, Micheil said, "Just go to White's and call him a coward, for it's obvious he is or he'd have accepted your first challenge."

It was absurdly simple, and it would work. He had only to wait four days for Wednesday to arrive. Four days of being in intimate quarters with Fiona. Four days of hell worse than any he'd spent on Skye. Now he knew the explosive desire she evoked in him. He knew how it felt to be buried inside her. The memory hardened him where the serving woman's bold caress had done nothing.

Niall groaned aloud.

Micheil gave him a knowing look. "Enough ale will deaden any woman's witchery."

It was true enough.

Fiona lay awake in bed. In spite of Niall's command not to wait up for him and her own sense of futility immediately after their lovemaking, she couldn't sleep. Somewhere inside him there had to be a kernel of forgiveness that she could reach. In her heart, she knew Niall didn't want to go through with his deadly plans. And she knew that if he decided not to duel with her brother, a very large barrier between them would be gone.

She heard his footsteps in the hallway before he opened the locked door.

"Tomorrow's another day," she heard Micheil say and wondered briefly what new plan they'd concocted. But she didn't ponder it for long.

Niall tripped, releasing a string of curses she'd never heard from him before and which he must have learned in the Navy, they were that explicit. Barely opening one eye, she watched him in the muted light of the half-moon filtering through the window.

His movements were slightly out of synchronization, reminding her of her father and brothers when they'd had a bit too much to drink. The memory brought a smile to her lips. No one in her family was a heavy drinker and when one of the men went on a bout it was usually because of something bad happening, like when Ian had gotten drunk because his new bride refused to share the marriage bed. Perhaps Niall was like her brothers in that aspect, and he was greatly bothered by something.

As she watched, he reverently unwrapped his harp from its oilcloth and stroked the gold leaf-embossed frame. His fingers strummed across the strings, setting a melodious sound in motion. It was the first time since they'd made love on the beach at Skye that he'd played. Relaxation and a sadness she couldn't deny imbued Fiona as she listened to the haunting music.

A discordant twang ended the bittersweet song, jarring Fiona's nerves as effectively as if Niall had come up to the bed and physically whacked her. She repressed a start at the disharmony, determined not to reveal to him that she was awake.

His brows drew into a frown as he wrapped the harp and replaced it. Moving with more coordination than before, he stripped to his drawers, casting her a glance to see that she still slept.

He was stunning. She had to hold her breath to keep from releasing a sigh of pleasure at the beauty of his male body. In all their time together and the hasty unions of their loving, she'd never had the opportunity to look fully at him—and she now regretted it.

Tall and perfect, muscles rippling across his chest and shoulders, he flexed to loosen the kinks in his back. He held his head proudly, the black hair a wild mane that swept from his wide brow. His chin was strong and his neck corded. He was magnificent. All man.

The flannel of his figure-molding drawers showed narrow hips that led to well-formed thighs and calves that needed no padding. Even his feet were perfect, with high arches and narrow insteps. But it was what nestled between his legs that drew her attention more. The flannel was no obstacle to the engorged surge of his manhood.

The breath caught in her throat. He was looking at her, his eyes bright green. He wanted her.

Emotions rioted through her. Desire for him mingled with a need for him to want more from her than her body. The urge to rise and go to him, caress him, and draw him inside her was terrible in its strength.

He turned away.

The tension broke, and Fiona's body sagged into the bed. She closed her eyes to the sight of his firm-muscled back and buttocks.

It was just as well. There was too much between them and nothing to bring them together.

Feigning restlessness, she tossed to her side so that she faced away from him and temptation. She heard him moving about, getting blankets, then the creak of the chairs as he positioned them so that he could recline in one and rest his feet in the other. He should just bed down on the rug; it hadn't been uncomfortable earlier.

That brought back memories and bodily sensations that increased her discomfort. Once more she had to ignore her restlessness. It wasn't going to be easy falling asleep, knowing he was close by. But then it never had been.

It wasn't easy to wake up either when one hadn't slept much, she decided the next morning as she forced herself to rise. Nor did it seem easy for Niall, who scowled at her from where he still sagged between the two chairs.

"You should sleep on the rug," she advised him, rising and going behind the screen that hid their washing facilities.

"I should get you a room of your own," he growled, unwinding himself from the blankets and dressing while she was unable to see his near-nakedness. But it wasn't what he wanted. No, he smiled sourly, he wanted to put her back into the bed and see if they could improve upon the delight of yesterday.

When she came back out, she was fully dressed, as was he.

"Why don't you get me another room?" she asked innocently. "It would simplify matters."

He shot her a cynical glance. "You wouldn't have to suffer my caresses, you mean. I'll do it if you don't mind sleeping tied to the bed, for I'll not leave you alone in a room all night any other way."

"I should have expected that. The only amazing thing is that you left me unbound last night while you went with Micheil."

"You know why," he said darkly.

Yes, she knew. He'd been as disturbed by their loving as she had been. She clung to that.

The knowledge that Niall had wanted her as badly

as she'd wanted him, and that his desire had disturbed him into being careless, wasn't worth much as she watched him leave. They'd been in London five days, and never once had he stayed with her past dressing in the mornings.

Heart heavy, Fiona wandered to the window, which she opened. Leaning out, she took in great gulps of air, the slight metallic taste of coal intriguing to her Scottish nose that was used to peat. Below, the little girl called out, "Chestnuts, lov'ly hot chestnuts for sale."

Fiona smiled, only to have her pleasure fade as she watched a man buy a packet of nuts. Were the girl's parents alive? Or was she one of many children born to a woman with no husband?

Unconsciously, Fiona's hand strayed to her stomach. It'd only been three weeks since that incident on the beach. But she was late for her menses and was beginning to worry. She didn't want a fatherless babe. Neither did she want a husband who would resent her for trapping him, and Niall would resent if she mentioned the possibility of a child to him. She knew that, just as she knew he would marry her anyway.

Unable to consider it further, Fiona sighed and closed the window. She had another day to get through, and thoughts like this would only make the time drag miserably by.

She pressed her knuckles to her mouth. Why was it never easy?

Niall scowled at his reflection in the mirror as he adjusted his cravat. It'd been too many years since he'd last worn one and his fingers were like opponents in a fencing match as he tried unsuccessfully to get the folds just so.

"Bloody popinjays!" he muttered, giving up. He wasn't going to White's to impress the dandies, anyway. His lips curved into the semblance of a hard smile.

Turning from the small mirror, he felt Fiona's eyes on him. He'd felt them on his back the entire time he tried to get the cravat fixed. He'd felt her presence every second of the last week as he'd waited for this night and Winter's regular attendance at White's gaming tables. He was damn glad it was over.

Even when he faced her, she continued to watch him with those luminous blue eyes that had lit up like a Highland sky at sunrise when he'd made love to her. Suddenly, the shirt that had fit perfectly was too tight around the collar. He ran a finger inside it to pull it away from his skin before shrugging into the new, black superfine coat he'd commissioned from Weston for this night.

And still she watched him.

"What's the matter?" he demanded. "Do I have shaving lather on my face or have I nicked it?"

"No. You look perfect," she said, her voice tinged with sadness.

He ignored the tone. If he gave her a chance, she'd start in on him about revenge and destruction. She'd harped incessantly on it the past week.

Rising from the bed, she moved to him, the rough material of her clothing softened from repeated washing so that it flowed around her perfect form like silk.

His stomach churned. It'd been hell sharing this room with her and not making love to her, particularly since he knew the ecstasy he was capable of achieving in her arms.

She reached him, standing a meticulous two feet away. "Don't do this, Niall."

The tension in his neck and shoulders intensified. "Don't start."

Laying a hand on his arm, she said, "Revenge will only ruin you. Even if he does agree to meet you, what are you going to do, kill him? How will that eradicate your time in jail and the fact that you were still convicted? Will it make your father take you back?"

He glared at her, hating her for telling him all the things he couldn't change. "I'll best him in the duel and, to save his life, he'll say in front of his second that he was wrong to convict me. I'll make him say that the evidence was circumstantial."

"It doesn't change the verdict." Her voice was barely audible, but there was a wealth of strength in it . . . and the fatality of truth.

He twisted from her touch, his hands going to his face. "If only I could remember that night. How I got back to the ship. Whether I even went to the woman's bed."

Fiona choked back a cry. Niall had had other women. She'd be a fool if she thought differently. And he was going to have more women after he let her go. It was something she couldn't change no matter how much it hurt. But right now, this moment, he needed her. She couldn't let her pain keep her from helping him.

"Why can't you remember?"

"I bloody well don't know." He straightened up, his eyes haunted with memories. "I don't know. I didn't know then, either."

"Were you drunk?" She prodded him, trying to make him remember, hoping that if he could do so, it would give him the answers he needed to keep him from going to White's.

"Of course I was," he snarled. "But not so drunk that I didn't know what I was doing."

"Then why can't you remember?" She continued to push him mercilessly. To do otherwise would be to allow him to continue unchecked with his plan of revenge and ultimate death.

His lips curled into a cruel smile. "I don't remember every woman I bed. There're too many and most of them not worth more thought than what it takes to enjoy them."

Fiona gasped, hurt by his intentional cruelty, but beginning to understand. "Don't take your anger out on me, Niall."

"Then stop trying to change me from my course. I planned this revenge three years ago, and nothing you do or say will stop me." He picked up his hat and cane before giving her one last penetrating look. "Remember this conversation when I challenge your brother, because I *will* do so."

He spun on his heel and left while Fiona struggled to deal with his last words. They were a threat and a promise. They also told her that he would never believe that her urgings to him to let the revenge go were prompted as much by concern for him as by fear for her brother's safety. Niall would never believe her if she told him she cared about him and didn't want him destroyed by his own actions. He would always think her motivation was simply to spare her brother from his wrath.

Despair at the futile course she was pursuing bowed her shoulders. She sank onto the bed. Her palms flattened on the cover to keep her from crumbling into a ball when she suddenly realized he hadn't bound her. He'd been so angry with her that he'd left her for the night without securing her wrists.

She was on her feet and at the door immediately. If only it weren't locked! Reaching for the handle, she paused.

If she left now, provided she could, it would confirm in Niall's mind that everything she'd done to try and change his course had been for her brother. He would think she'd run away to tell Duncan—and he would be right.

What if she stayed? Could she persuade him not to continue in this disastrous course? She'd failed so far.

But her going would allow Niall to continue on his path without anyone except Micheil caring what happened to him. She couldn't just leave him. She couldn't leave him to the hell he was pursuing. She loved him.

Drawing her shoulders back, searching within herself for the strength to persevere, Fiona returned to the bed. She had barely lain back when the door opened.

Joy suffused her. Niall had come back. He'd decided not to go through with his plan.

"Niall sent me to tie your wrists," Micheil said.

Fiona's happiness disappeared. Chills skittered

down her spine as he approached her. She didn't know why he made her feel uneasy, except that his aura was black shot through with murky red. Her blood ran cold when he was near.

She got off the bed, uncomfortable in that position with him near, and walked to him her hands out. "Can't you stop him?"

He glanced at her before turning his attention to his task. "You know how stubborn he is."

"He didn't kill that woman."

Micheil's right eye started twitching, his fingers frozen on her wrists. "No, he didn't."

"Then why was he convicted? I can't believe Duncan would have voted for Niall's imprisonment if there weren't indisputable evidence that he'd done it. Duncan's scrupulously honest."

He finished tying her and let her go. Fiona stepped back, glad to put distance between them. It didn't matter that Micheil was Niall's closest friend and believed in his innocence as strongly as she did, she couldn't like him. She wasn't comfortable around him.

Micheil went to the door and stopped. Without looking at her, he said, "Didn't he tell you his lucky piece was found gripped in the woman's hand?"

Her voice barely a whisper, she said, "Someone must have put it there to incriminate him."

His pale-blue eyes gazed blandly at her. "That's what I've always thought."

The words said, he slipped out the door. Fiona was sick. To think someone who was close enough to Niall to be able to get a lucky piece was twisted enough to use it to frame him. It made her wonder what else that person was capable of. And he was still at large.

And why couldn't Niall remember that night? She'd seen him drink large amounts of ale without side effects, so surely his being drunk the night of the murder wouldn't have prevented him from remembering. Could he have been drugged?

It was a harrowing possibility. If so, the person had to be intimate enough to be able to feed Niall something with a drug in it. That meant a friend or trusted associate. Her hands felt like ice.

Fiona sank into a chair, drawing her feet up so that her chin rested on her knees. There was a rightness about the conclusion. It was her gift at work, telling her she was correct.

Chapter Ten

Niall surveyed White's gaming room. Cheroot smoke filled the room. Men hunched or lounged, depending on their individual personalities, around green-baize tables. Chandeliers added their light to numerous candelabra.

Winter sat bent over a whist table. Niall's inclination was to challenge him immediately, to get this business over and done with. He didn't.

Instead, he sauntered up and waited until one of the four men rose, saying the betting was too much for him. Niall promptly sat in the vacated chair. Winter, an expression of unpleasant surprise on his angular features, muttered an aside.

Niall, looking for an opportunity, drawled, "What did you say, Winter? I couldn't hear."

His cheeks brick red, Winter said surlily, "Our play is too high for you, I'll wager."

Niall looked Winter over slowly, insolently. "I doubt that." He smiled at his nemesis. It wasn't a nice gesture. "You see, Winter, I invested my bounty well."

Attention seemingly on the deal of the cards, Niall actually concentrated on Winter. The man was sitting stiffly, his eyes fixed on the dealer, but Niall knew his opponent was really worried about what *he* would do.

Whist was a game of skill, and Niall remembered numbers. His partner had reason to be glad of his play. They won, thanks to Niall's expertise.

"I believe I'll double my bid this time," Niall drawled. "What about you, Winter?"

His face drawn in harsh angles, Winter looked thinner than his norm. Yet, in spite of his discomfort at having Niall at the same table, there was the gleam of a gamester challenged in his gray eyes. "I'll match you. Your luck won't hold, Currie."

Niall raised one black brow. "Skill is something that doesn't go away."

He won again. Raking in his winnings, Niall gave Winter a significant glance. The other man's mouth thinned.

An hour later, Niall's partner was all smiles and calling for a sixth bottle of port. The two of them were still winning. Niall's lip curled sardonically as he thought, *lucky at cards, unlucky at love*. The familiar cliché was no comfort. But he didn't need luck in love, he needed to provoke Winter into saying something that would give him justification to challenge him.

He could have challenged him for finding him guilty of murder, but Niall was reluctant to drag the nasty business up here in White's where any comment would become instant gossip. It was his reputation, after all.

As it was, it didn't have to be much of an excuse for him to challenge Winter. The man was being so obnoxious that no one present would wonder when Niall finally confronted him. And if he weren't underestimating Winter's irritation over losing to him, the necessary slur was already in the making.

Concentrating on the play once more, Niall left his considerable winnings on the table. His eyes met Winter's. "That's my next bet."

Winter sneered. "You don't even know what your hand will be."

A slow smile stretched Niall's lips. "I don't need to know. The competition isn't good enough."

The insult hung in the smoky air. Niall lounged back in his seat, his hands folded loosely in his lap while he watched Winter's reaction. Would Winter call him out?

Winter licked his lips, his eyes darting from his partner's face to those of Niall's partner. Both men looked at him steadily. Winter licked his lips again, but said nothing.

Disgust twisted Niall's mouth. The bloody coward. With an economy of motion, Niall picked up the cards, shuffled, and dealt.

Winter grabbed his cards and rapidly put them in order. His eyes sparkled.

Niall exulted. Winter had a good hand—too bad the man couldn't play, but that was to his advantage.

Grinning, Winter leaned over the table, pushing his money into the center, writing out an I.O.U. slip, and putting it on top. "That meets you and raises you."

Leisurely putting his hand in order, Niall glanced up. "How do I know you're good for it?"

Gasps from the two other men at the table told Niall

louder than any words that he'd gone too far this time. Winter would be forced to challenge him; he'd insulted the man's honor.

Winter's mouth tightened. "You have my word as a gentleman. That's enough."

Niall began to despise the man. "Not for me," he said softly, dangerously.

The other two men at the table said nothing, their eyes on Winter.

"You murdering bastard," Winter said, his hands shaking as he held the cards. "You want me to challenge you so you can kill me the way you killed that woman. Well, I won't give you the satisfaction."

"You always were a coward," Niall drawled, throwing down the first card of the game. "But I suppose that as a gentleman, I shall have to play this game."

Both of the men caught in the middle glanced from Winter to Niall before following suit. However, Niall knew that by tomorrow Winter's refusal to call him out over so blatant an insult would be all over London, as would the tale of his murder conviction. His smile was hard as he picked up the trick he'd just won.

The game progressed much as Niall had expected. Winter might play frequently, but he couldn't remember all the cards that had been played.

On the last hand, Winter led with the ace of spades, a smile of satisfaction on his face. Niall's partner played, a smaller spade. At Niall's turn, he looked Winter in the eye and put down the two of hearts, the only trump not played. Winter's partner played a club. Niall won.

"Jolly good playing," Niall's partner said, seconded by Winter's partner.

"Thank you," Niall said, raking in the wager.

"Where'd you get that heart?" Winter broke into the congratulations, his face feverish. "I'd swear all the trumps had been played."

Niall stopped in mid-rake. His eyes as hard as malachite, it was all he could do not to shout his triumph. This was his chance, the one he'd waited all night to get.

"I believe you're calling me a cheater," Niall said loudly enough for the players at nearby tables to hear.

A hush fell over the room as the import of the words spread. Every man waited to see what Winter would do. Not just the man's honor, but his entire standing in the London hierarchy was at stake. He either accepted Niall's challenge or he retired to the country, his reputation and honor as tarnished as Niall's.

Niall almost felt sorry for the bastard. The man had lost a fortune to him tonight, while Niall played him like a fish to get him to this impasse. Winter always had been less than smart.

While Winter gaped at him, Niall continued, "My second will call on yours."

Before Winter could say a word or refuse the challenge, Niall rose and, taking his earnings, started away. Pausing, he looked back at Winter, who was changing from red to white as he realized that he was fated to meet Niall.

"I'll collect on your voucher at the time of our duel."

Niall left the words hanging in the air as he made his

way to the door. Micheil hastily left his game of faro
and followed his friend from the room.

"You really put him on the spot," Micheil said,
grabbing his beaver hat and cane from the waiting
servant. "You didn't give him a chance, and you
added insult to injury with the comment about his
voucher."

Exultation coursed through Niall as he walked past
the servant holding out his hat. Nothing mattered except that he'd finally gotten Winter in a spot out of
which the man couldn't maneuver. He exited White's
and took deep, invigorating gulps of the cold night air.
His mind was crystal clear and totally absorbed in
what he'd just done.

"Call on Winter first thing in the morning and find
out who his second is. I want this finished as soon as
possible," he said to Micheil.

Micheil matched his step to Niall's brisk ones. "You
don't want to take a chance something will happen to
prevent it, huh?"

"That's right," Niall stated, picking up his pace.
Now that things were falling into place, the impatience
he'd held tightly in check over the years seemed about
to explode in him.

"Let's get a hackney," Micheil said, puffing as he
kept up.

Niall glanced at his friend, noting Micheil's red
cheeks. "Go ahead. But I'm going to walk. I need the
exercise."

Micheil's mouth thinned, but he didn't argue. Waving down a coach, he clambered in with only a backward glance. Niall knew he'd angered Micheil. The

two of them got on each other's nerves lately. Funny, he couldn't remember such irritation with Micheil in all their years as boys or later in the Navy, where they'd served on the same ships.

Only since Fiona's arrival had the two of them seemed on edge with one another. Fiona, the source of so much pleasure mixed with so much anguish. He needed to get this duel over with and the three of them out of London and on the road where they could sleep in the open. He needed to get out of the same room with her before he lost his control and made love to her again.

Every time he saw her, he wanted her. But wanting her wasn't enough. Every time he touched her, he put another dent in his honor. She was the daughter of an earl, and he'd ruined her and couldn't even offer marriage. He wouldn't tie her to him, the man who would probably kill her brother. He wouldn't wed a woman and have her bear his children while she hated him for the rest of their lives.

But damn, she was like the finest whiskey. The sight of her burned him, just as whiskey burns when it goes down before exploding in the gut. She was exactly like that.

He stepped up his pace. These thoughts weren't serving any purpose but to make it imperative that he work off his energy before getting back to the room he shared with her. Otherwise, the sight of her lying in bed would be too tempting.

* * *

Fiona heard the door open. She didn't bother to feign sleep; she had to know if he'd been successful. Sitting up in bed, she lit a candle.

By its flickering light she saw the increased tension in his face, drawing his lips flat. He'd succeeded. If he hadn't done what he'd set out to do, he'd be scowling.

Her gift flickered. Grief knotted her stomach. Her vision blurred to murky shades of vapor. Something terrible was going to happen. She knew it.

She staggered to her feet and moved in the direction she'd last seen Niall. The corner of the rug caught her bare foot and she stumbled. His hands closed around her upper arms, keeping her from falling.

"It's a good thing you left the candle on the table," his deep voice said next to her ear. "What's wrong with you?"

She still couldn't see him clearly. It happened like this sometimes—when something was going to happen—and there was nothing she could do to stop it. She supposed that by not showing her, her gift saved her the futility of trying to prevent the inevitable.

Her fingers groped for his chest. Before she could orient herself, he scooped her up and carried her to the bed. He laid her down and sat beside her, his weight denting in the mattress so that her hip rolled against his. Heat from his body scorched her and gave her something to focus on besides the horror of knowing something dreadful was about to happen—or was happening this moment—and there was nothing she could do about it.

"Are you sick?" he asked in a worried voice.

He smoothed the hair back from her face. Was it her

imagination, a longing for tenderness from him, that made her think his fingers lingered in their task? She tried to ignore the wish, knowing it for just that.

"No, I'm not sick," she said hoarsely, wanting to reassure him. "Just . . . just disoriented."

He rose and went to wet a cloth in the washbasin. Sitting back beside her, he wiped her brow and down her neck to where her nightdress met her collarbone. He stopped, his eyes boring into hers.

Heat flushed through her. The blurred vision of her gift dissipated so that she saw desire dilate Niall's pupils. He wanted her, and—God help her—she wanted him. Even in the aftermath of learning something horrible was about to happen, her body ached for him. She wanted to feel the strength of his arms around her.

Before she could clasp him, he pulled away, taking the damp cloth with him. A safe distance from the bed, he frowned down at her. He yanked at his cravat with his free hand and tugged the long scarf off, tossing it irritably to the chair.

"Now," he said, his voice deeper than minutes before, "what happened to you if you weren't sick? You looked ready to faint."

She smiled wanly at him, enthralled by the knitting of his brows. She knew his anger was as much directed at himself as at her. He didn't want to succumb to the attraction between them. The last of her lingering dizziness fled.

Pushing up to her elbows, she asked, "May I have a drink? Please." When his frown increased and it looked as though he'd deny her, she added, "I'll tell you as soon as I'm not on the verge of throwing up."

He moved to the table near the chairs where he slept and poured her two fingers of Scotch. It would burn going down, but it would also steady her nerves.

Hooking the chair with his foot, he dragged it back to the bed where he handed her the glass. While she sipped the liquor, relishing the heat it returned to her body, he sat down facing her.

"Well?" he demanded the second she quit drinking.

Fiona took a deep breath and studied him. She'd told him about her gift before, but they'd never discussed it and he'd never said whether he believed in precognition or not. Until now, she hadn't thought the situation would arise where she'd have to tell him about an incident.

She certainly hadn't planned to let him know how she'd felt the first time she'd seen him and then Micheil. She'd learned long ago to keep such information to herself. It caused nothing but heartache and solved little. Either they didn't believe her or they hated her for telling them things they couldn't change or didn't like.

So she picked her words carefully. "You got Winter to agree to a duel, didn't you?" He nodded, opening his mouth to tell her not to change the subject, she knew. "I'm not changing the subject," she said, smiling slightly. "That's the starting point. I knew from the tension in your body—the way you held yourself, the slant of your lips—that the tightness in you was from success not failure."

"You're a witch," he muttered, pouring himself a

generous portion of the whiskey he'd brought from Skye.

Fiona couldn't help a look of reproach. "I never told you I was normal. And I'd like some more, too, if you don't mind."

He cut her a quick, hard glance before returning to the table and refilling her glass. He set it on the stand next to the bed without touching her hand.

"Go on," he said, sitting down and taking a large swallow. His eyes closed and he visibly relaxed before opening them again.

Fiona wished her tension could be as easily relieved. But worry was beginning to gnaw at her. What would Niall do when he heard her story? He'd listened to her claim to be fey on Skye, but now she was going to tell him about an actual vision. Would he shun her? Angus would.

Angus. She hadn't thought of him in weeks—not since Niall had made love to her on the beach at Skye. It was a disturbing and saddening thought. She'd been so young and so naive in her wish to return to Edinburgh and win back the man she'd thought herself in love with. She knew better now.

"Well," Niall demanded brusquely.

Returning her attention to the man she truly loved, Fiona started. "Ever since I was a child I've had the gift to see the future—sort of. Mostly I get feelings. Impressions of things. Emotions. Once I had a vision. I was three and saw my favorite bitch dying in birth. I was so upset that I cried for days." She smiled ruefully at the memory. "Not only was I worried about my pet, I was scared sick."

He nodded, taking another drink. "I can understand that."

"Can you really?" she asked, believing him in spite of her question. He looked too sincere to be lying.

"Yes. Your 'gift' isn't unknown, only rare."

It was her turn to nod. "True. Only I've never known anyone else who has it or has known someone with it." She paused, wondering what would happen if two people with the same ability came together. Would they see the same things? Or see totally different situations? She'd probably never find out.

"Chances are that you'll never meet someone else like you," Niall said as though he understood what she was feeling. "So, stop wondering about it and tell me what set you off this time."

Nonplused, she stared at him. "Just like that? You believe me just like that? Why, I haven't even told you anything you can verify and you believe me."

Very softly, his eyes never leaving hers, he said, "I was raised in the Scottish isles. My family comes from a long line of royal Celtic bards."

"And you make magic with your fingers." She breathed the words. "Yes, I was foolish to think you wouldn't comprehend what I'm saying. You live with the unusual every time you pick up your harp."

He gave her a crooked smile. On the right side of his mouth, where his lips rose higher than on the left, a dimple teased her. It was the smile she thought she'd seen once on Skye. It was a smile of great warmth that made her want to go to him and pour her heart out.

Abruptly, he stood and finished his drink in one gulp. "What did your gift show you when I came in?"

Taken aback by his precipitate action, Fiona blurted, "That something terrible is going to happen because of this duel, but I don't know what." Agony tore at her. "I never know—not that it would make a difference. I've only been able to change things once. That was with my dog, and I was probably meant to make a difference since I knew exactly what was happening. After that, I was never able to prevent anything I foresaw. Nothing. Ever." She took a deep calming breath. "I finally stopped *seeing* the future and now only *sense* when something is going to happen. It's easier this way."

He paced away from her. "That doesn't help with this."

She looked sadly at him. *"You* can help with *this* by not fighting Winter. I didn't get this feeling until you succeeded in arranging a duel."

He twisted back to look at her. "Never. This is the only thing that kept me sane in Newgate."

Anger at him and the destructive path he refused to deviate from galvanized her. Leaping from the bed, she stood feet apart, hands on hips. "You're a stubborn fool," she said. "You made it through Newgate because you're a survivor, not because you lived for revenge."

He moved toward her, his muscles rippling like those of a stalking cat. "What do you know of survival? You're a woman."

She stared him down, refusing to allow the overpowering presence of his height and strength to intimidate her. "I know plenty about survival. You taught me."

Her words stopped him in midstride. His chest rose and fell, his frustration and determination making breathing difficult. Confusion and anger contorted his face.

When he spoke, it was in a tight, constrained voice. "And you've taught me. In the weeks I've had you, I've learned to be wary of you and what you do to my body and my resolve."

Fiona's heart started pounding. Their conversation was taking a turn she would have never thought possible. She hardly dared to ask, but she had to. "What do you mean?"

"I mean this," he said, holding out his hands. His fingers trembled. "I want you so badly that you do this to me, even though I know this ardor is wrong. I'm going to kill your brother. There's no future for us. I won't continue to make love to you. I won't marry you."

Fiona, hurt beyond imagining, drew herself up. "I never asked you to."

He stepped back, his hands dropping to his side. His mouth twisted. "No, you didn't. All you ever asked for was my soul. You want me to stop pursuing the men responsible for the last three years of my life. It may not mean much to you, but I've made my plans and what you want isn't part of them."

It was the final twist of the knife. "Then do as you damn well please," Fiona said. "Go to hell with my blessing, but don't expect me to help you."

Twirling around, she threw herself on the bed and burrowed under the covers. If only she could escape him! Somehow she would.

We've got your authors!

If you seek out the latest historical romances by today's bestselling authors, our new reader's service, KENSINGTON CHOICE, is the club for you.

KENSINGTON CHOICE is the only club where you can find authors like Janelle Taylor, Shannon Drake, Rosanne Bittner, Sylvie Sommerfield, Penelope Neri and Phoebe Conn all in one place...

...and the only service that will deliver their romances direct to your home as soon as they are published—even before they reach the bookstores.

KENSINGTON CHOICE is also the only service that will give you a substantial guaranteed discount off the publisher's prices on every one of those romances.

That's right: Every month, the Editors at Zebra and Pinnacle select four of the newest novels by our bestselling authors and rush them straight to you, even *before they reach the bookstores*. The publisher's prices for these romances range from $4.99 to $5.99—but they are always yours for the guaranteed low price of just *$3.95!*

That means you'll always save over $1.00...often as much as $2.00...off the publisher's prices on every new novel you get from KENSINGTON CHOICE!

All books are sent on a 10-day free examination basis, and there is no minimum number of books to buy. (A postage and handling charge of $1.50 is added to each shipment.)

As your introduction to the convenience and value of this new service, we invite you to accept

4 BOOKS FREE

The 4 books, worth up to $23.96, are our welcoming gift. You pay only $1 to help cover postage and handling.

To start your subscription to KENSINGTON CHOICE and receive your introductory package of 4 FREE romances, detach and mail the postpaid card at right *today*.

We have 4 FREE BOOKS for you as your introduction to KENSINGTON CHOICE o get your FREE BOOKS, worth up to $23.96, mail card below.

FREE BOOK CERTIFICATE

As my introduction to your new KENSINGTON CHOICE reader's service, please send me 4 FREE historical romances (worth up to $23.96), billing me just $1 to help cover postage and handling. As a KENSINGTON CHOICE subscriber, I will then receive 4 brand-new romances to preview each month for 10 days FREE. I can return any books I decide not to keep and owe nothing. The publisher's prices for the KENSINGTON CHOICE romances range from $4.99 to $5.99, but as a subscriber I will be entitled to get them for just $3.95 per book. There is no minimum number of books to buy, and I can cancel my subscription at any time. A $1.50 postage and handling charge is added to each shipment.

Name _____

Address _____ Apt. # _____

City _____ State _____ Zip _____

Telephone (___) _____

Signature _____

(If under 18, parent or guardian must sign)

Subscription subject to acceptance

KC 0994

We have
4
FREE
Historical
Romances
for you!

Details inside!

KENSINGTON CHOICE
Reader's Service
120 Brighton Road
P.O. Box 5214
Clifton, NJ 07015-5214

Chapter Eleven

The next day Niall let Fiona leave the room. He took her to a nearby tavern for breakfast. Fiona considered it a mixed blessing after the night before. She felt extremely uncomfortable around him. Not even knowing he desired her helped because he'd made it plain last night that desire was something he didn't want and wouldn't let affect him.

Her musings were interrupted by Micheil, who sat down at the table and ordered kidneys and ham with a pint of ale.

"I wondered where you were when no one answered my knock," he said, slanting a look at Fiona.

"You found us easily enough," Niall said laconically, taking a bite of his ham. "When's the duel?"

Micheil's gaze rested pointedly on Fiona before going to Niall. "There's a lady present."

Niall cut determinedly into the ham. "She already knows all there is to know about this. Hearing when the actual event will take place is immaterial."

"I guess so," Micheil said sullenly. "It's three days from now. Dawn at Hampstead Heath."

"That long?" Niall asked, slamming his fork down. "Bloody coward. Is he hoping I'll cry off or something will happen to me? Does he think I'll forget?"

The cynical tone of his last sentence wasn't lost on Fiona. Without a word of explanation to Micheil, Niall was telling her exactly what he thought of her attempts to dissuade him from dueling.

Stomach churning, she cut in. "Perhaps he's making plans for something to happen to you. It would explain my feelings."

Disgust contorted Niall's features. "If I can make it through Newgate Prison, I can make it through whatever Winter might try."

Micheil's pale eyes focused on her. "The only danger Niall faces from Winter is if Winter gets lucky and shoots better."

"So," Niall said, relaxing some, "he's chosen pistols. I didn't know he was that good a shot."

Micheil shrugged. "Better than he is at fencing. I used to watch him practicing onboard ship. He was awful—couldn't get his hands and feet to work together."

Fiona had had enough. Palms on the table, she stood up and leaned over them. "You're both talking as if this were no more dangerous than a stroll in the park. I tell you, something awful is going to happen and it's because of this duel."

"Enough," Niall said, grabbing her wrist and forcing her to sit back down. "It's not your affair to meddle in. We'll handle this the way we choose, and there's nothing for you to like or dislike about it."

Seething, Fiona gave him a glare that would kill, but she remained seated. There was nothing else she could do. He wouldn't let her go and she couldn't escape—yet.

Niall left early the next day. At first Fiona thought he was going for food because he hadn't bound her, but Micheil's knock within five minutes told her differently.

"Niall told me to stay with you," Micheil said, entering the room and sitting without asking her permission. He looked around. "Your room's no different from mine. Wish Niall could be convinced to move us into the Pulteney."

"He can't afford the Pulteney," she automatically defended him.

Propping his feet on the fireplace grate, Micheil said, "He can afford any place he wants. He's rich." He slanted her a sly look. "Didn't you know that?"

Not deigning to answer his insinuating question, Fiona turned her back to him. She hadn't known. But it made no difference. She loved him for what he was, not what he had.

"Yes, he could deck you out in style if he wanted," Micheil said, his tone implying that Niall didn't think her worth it.

Fiona, uncomfortable with Micheil to begin with, decided to ignore his nasty comments. She took one of the chairs and moved it toward the window, saying,

"Please excuse me, but I find the activity outside entertaining. I feel as though I know some of the people, particularly the child who sells hot chestnuts. She's there every day. Recently, she's started wearing a red, wool scarf which I imagine is a present." Or so she liked to think—that someone cared enough about the girl to give her such a gift.

He gave her a quizzical look which made her realize she was running on. It wasn't like her, but his presence disturbed her. She wanted Niall.

"Why did Niall send you? He could have just tied me up and been done with it." She would have preferred that.

Micheil fussed with the sleeve of his blue superfine coat as though he were trying to give himself time while he decided what to tell her. When he finally looked at her, his eyes were cold. "He didn't want to do that to you."

"Oh." It was all she could think of to say in the face of the hostility he made no effort to hide. If she didn't know better, she'd think him jealous of her.

He jerked viciously at a loose string. "His life's been rotten. He doesn't need you to make it worse by seducing him and making him feel guilty. He might have been in jail, but he has honor." His eyes met hers. "He knows you'll hate him in the end."

Taken aback by his vehemence, her mouth fell open before she could gather her composure. Snapping her lips together, she lifted her chin. "Our relationship is none of your business. And if you're so worried about him, why don't you find a way to stop him from dueling Winter instead of aiding him by being his second?"

He turned away and muttered something under his breath that she couldn't catch. It added to the ire building in her as a result of the entire situation—her captivity, her worry over Niall, and her dislike of this man. She rose and stalked over to him, not stopping till she towered above his seated form.

"And where is he that he sends you to do his dirty work? If you had a backbone, you wouldn't do his biding without a fight, especially since you know that revenge will only ruin him further."

"He's gone to Manton's to buy dueling pistols."

His mouth twisted and his eyes turned opaque. He had the look of a man watching something he both hates and fears. His intensity was like a blow. Instinctively, Fiona took a step backward.

Even as she moved, her vision blurred. Her stomach gyrated. The pulse pounded in her temples, and her entire body began to shake.

"Oh, God," she moaned, reaching for something to steady her. There wasn't anything and she stumbled back, barely keeping her balance.

In front of her, Micheil's fuzzy image moved to help her. She shrank from him. Her vision cleared. Blood dripped from his fingers.

"No, no . . ." she whispered, wanting to scream instead. "Don't touch me."

The back of her knees hit the footboard of the bed and she tumbled onto it, one hand pressed to her mouth, her eyes wide. Blood as red as a fiery sunset fell in large, tearshaped globules from his hands.

Then the vision was gone. Micheil, his hands fashionably white, reached for her. He bent over her, a look of concern replacing the hatred of minutes before.

"What's wrong?" he asked, a look of unease in his pale-blue gaze. "Are you sick?"

Hysteria bubbled up in Fiona. Niall had asked those very same questions not more than two nights ago. The answer was the same.

Now that her vision was righted and her stomach was no longer threatening to travel up her throat, she realized the blood had been a vision. A more powerful evocation of her gift than she'd had since she was three. But she was certain it was no less prophetic.

Somehow, someway, Micheil would do something to bloody his hands . . . and she didn't think it would be a simple act like cutting his finger. No, the immensity of her reaction and the nausea it had caused told her that whatever Micheil intended to do would be deadly.

Gritting her teeth, she managed to push herself up and away from him so that she was on the opposite side of the bed. "I'm fine," she said, chagrined with herself for the tremble in the last word. "I just got a sudden dizzy spell. It happens some times."

His eyes narrowed before his gaze lowered to her flat belly. But he said nothing.

Slipping off the mattress, Fiona moved further away from the bed to put more distance between them. She didn't know what he was going to do, but she wouldn't be surprised if it were murder.

He stared long and hard at her, as though he were trying to decided whether or not she were telling the truth. His right eyelid twitched. "I wouldn't have thought a sister of Duncan's would get queasy easily. He's a hard man."

Fiona met his stare with one of her own. She didn't intimidate easily; and while the direction of his gaze led her to the conclusion that he might be wondering if she were pregnant, she wasn't going to say a word to confirm or deny it. She didn't know herself—for sure.

When she didn't speak, he went back to the chair and gazed into the empty fireplace. For all the attention he gave her after that, she might as well have not existed. He didn't even glance at her when she resumed her position by the window. Fiona wasn't sure it made her feel better.

When Niall returned several hours later, it didn't matter that he had gone to get dueling pistols. She felt safe with him. Even the rich-red mahogany box he held under his arm—the box that contained the finest weapons Manton's could make, which were the best in England, didn't keep her from jumping up and going to him.

She grasped his arm with both her hands and moved close. He gave her a quizzical glance.

"Niall," she said, striving to calm her voice, "I thought you'd never get back."

Micheil shot her a lethal look. "I hope you got the best," he said, taking the box from Niall and opening it.

Inside reposed two matching pistols, their polished wood highlighted by plain burnished-gold handles. The elegant simplicity of their lines made them a work of art, albeit a deadly one.

"Nice," Micheil said, taking one out and weighing

it for balance. He sighted down the barrel, his eyes fixed on her as he pointed the pistol toward her head.

Fiona felt the queasiness returning. She felt helpless. It was a sensation she didn't like. Stiffening her spine, she reached out and pushed the gun so that it was aimed at the window.

"I'll thank you not to point that in my direction," she said coldly.

Micheil grinned. "It's not loaded."

"I don't care."

No longer elated at Niall's return, that emotion submerged by fear, Fiona released her grip on Niall and moved away from the two men. Their words moved over and around her as she leaned against the window frame and gazed unseeing into the street below.

She wished Micheil would leave; she wanted to tell Niall about her vision. She was sure Micheil was going to do something, . . . something bloody . . . something related to her vision of two nights ago. But all she had to go on was intuition, and she doubted that Niall would condemn his friend on her word alone. Niall held Micheil in high esteem, and Niall was loyal to his friends.

She was caught in a conundrum with no solution that she could see.

"Chestnuts, hot chestnuts." The cry came from beneath the sill, the young girl's high-pitched voice penetrating Fiona's awareness.

Opening the window, Fiona leaned out for the first time and yelled, "I wish you luck." *I wish myself luck.*

The child's heart-shaped face with its pointed chin looked up. A smile eased the lines of a harsh life from the pinched features. Fiona wished she'd called out to her before.

Before she could close the window, Niall was at her side. The heat from his body warmed her even though he didn't touch her. As she turned to him, his arm moved past her and she saw a golden boy sail out the window and down to the girl's open palm.

"Thank 'e," the child said, her eyes sparkling. She bit the piece to be sure of its authenticity before pocketing it.

"That was very generous," Fiona said, her heart swelling with warmth for this man who could be so harsh and yet in an instant so giving. She'd sensed the dichotomy in his music.

He shut the window securely. "She works hard at honest labor. She deserves it."

The words were curt, telling her not to make any more of it. Fiona scanned the room to make sure that her sense of Micheil's having left was valid.

"Niall," she said, reaching for him only to have him sidestep her hand. "Something happened while you were gone."

The words were barely out of her mouth when his face turned thunderous. "What do you mean?"

Nonplused by his quick anger, she moved slightly away. Her irritation and anxiety escalated. "What are you angry about? I'm the one who should be angry, not you."

He glared at her, the dueling pistols forgotten on the table where he'd set them after Micheil had left. For some inexplicable reason, her words had conjured in him an image of her in Micheil's arms, her eyes closed in ecstasy. God, he wanted to wring her neck and then throttle his friend. Niall took a deep breath. He was going crazy. "Nothing. I'm not angry, just tired. What happened?"

But Fiona wasn't going to let it go. "Why were you angry?"

He sighed, irritated with her and with himself. "Did Micheil touch you?"

It took all his strength of will to get the words out. If she said yes, he'd have to confront Micheil. But if it were true, it would explain his friend's repeated attempts to make him get rid of her. It would mean Micheil wanted her for himself. It wasn't a pleasant thought.

She looked at him as though he'd lost his mind. "No. He tried, but that was when I almost fainted."

Her words chased one fear away only to replace it with another. "Why did you almost faint?"

Her eyes caught and held his, beseeching him. "I . . . I saw blood. Blood all over his hands, dripping from his fingers. It was . . . horrible."

She buried her face in her hands and turned away from him. Her shoulders shook. He realized without her saying more just how terrified she had been. Without considering his actions, he put his arms around her and drew her to his chest.

"Shh," he said softly, stroking her back. "It's all right. It was your imagination. Micheil wouldn't hurt a dog, let alone do something to make blood run off his fingers."

Until the actual telling, Fiona had thought she'd gotten over the fear caused by the vision. Now she knew she hadn't. She burrowed into the warmth and security of Niall's embrace, hearing his words but refusing to consider their import. All she wanted was for him to hold her.

When he released her, it took all her strength not to cling to him. But she wasn't going to force herself on this man who'd made love to her without loving her and in the process taken her heart.

Stepping away, she smoothed her hair back and ran her damp palms down her skirts. "I know you don't want to believe this, but I saw it. It was my gift. I know it was. Micheil is going to do something awful."

His eyes darkened. "Not you, too." It was a flat statement of the facts as he saw them. "First Micheil tries to tell me you're only going to bring trouble and to get rid of you. Now you're saying the same of him. What's gotten into the two of you?"

Fiona wasn't surprised that Micheil had tried to persuade Niall to release her. After all, Micheil was the one who'd cut her bonds on Skye so she could escape. Why shouldn't he continue to try and get rid of her? But that didn't explain her vision or make it less probable.

Talking calmly, knowing how Niall felt about his friend, she said, "I know what I saw. I don't know what's going to happen, but it's related to the duel. Everything is tied into that."

He pivoted, his boots hammering into the wooden floor as he stalked away from her. "You're like a harpy. I tell you to leave off it." He rounded on her, his eyes blazing, his mouth a thin slash. "If you don't, I'll gag you. I won't hear any more."

She blanched. She'd thought he'd doubt her, but she'd never expected him to resort to such measures. Not when he had conceded that her gift was real and that he believed in it.

In that moment, looking at the fury he made no effort to hide, Fiona knew she'd never win him over. He wouldn't hear bad of Micheil. It was both infuriating and admirable. She turned away from him.

Somehow *she* would have to stop Micheil.

Chapter Twelve

Niall was downstairs and Fiona had been alone since yesterday. Her revelations about Micheil had her on edge. When the knock came—sharp, loud and impatient—she whirled around.

"Who's there?" she called.

"Wilbers, a Bow Street runner, ma'am. And the magistrate, Sir Thompson," a gruff, uncultured voice stated.

Why would a Bow Street Runner and a magistrate be at her door? Fiona wished Niall were here. London was rife with crime, and she didn't trust strange men who came knocking for no apparent reason. No matter who they claimed to be.

"What do you want?" she asked, unmoving.

There was a dead silence while she counted to twenty. She heard muffled voices as though the two men were trying to decide what to tell her. Determination not to open the door stiffened her back.

She'd just decided to prop one of the chairs against

the knob when she heard Niall's voice demanding, "Who are you?"

Shamelessly, Fiona put her ear to the door. Wilbers responded in low tones. She frowned.

"Milord—"

"I'm no lord," Niall cut across the Bow Street runner.

"Sir," the man tried again. "Sir Thompson and meself are here to question you about Lord Winter, and I reckon you'd like to talk with us where others ain't gonna hear."

"What about Winter?" Niall's harsh voice penetrated the stout door more clearly than the runner's.

"Ahem, Mr. Currie," Sir Thompson interposed, "this is a grave matter that could result in your being returned to Newgate."

Fiona gasped. They knew about Niall's past and were threatening him with it.

Niall's footsteps gave her enough warning to back away from the door before he flung it open. He gave her a look that said, "Be quiet." She nodded, but decided that if she had to disobey him for his sake she would.

The two men entered behind him.

"Ma'am," the shorter man said, tipping his beaten hat. "I'm Wilbers. This be Sir Thompson."

Fiona inclined her head, taking each man's measure. The runner was not much taller than she, but heavily muscled. His hair was a sandy brown and his eyes were a piercing gray. His clothes were serviceable and clean. The man beside him was tall and elegantly turned out. He was older than the runner, and his hair was silver. A still-black mustache emphasized the thin perfection of his lips and the hawk-like angle of his nose. His eyes were brown and no less shrewd than the runner's.

She didn't like this.

"Now, Mr. Currie," Sir Thompson said, "we're here at the insistence of Lord Winter's family. Several of his friends saw you contrive to put him in a position at White's where he had to agree to a duel with you. According to his butler, you'd come to the house a week before and challenged him but Winter refused. Is that correct?"

Niall's face hardened. "What are you getting at?"

The Bow Street runner tensed, his muscles bunching under his clothing. Fiona thought for sure that she could see the outline of a pistol under the coat near his waist.

Wilbers spoke up. "Mayhap yer not aware that Lord Winter was found dead this morning."

"Oh no," Fiona gasped, barely keeping back the words *I knew something was going to happen.*

Niall's eyes widened for an instant before narrowing to slits. "How did he die?"

Wilbers cast an apprehensive look at Fiona. She held her ground saying, "I won't leave and I've every reason to hear this."

The runner looked at Sir Thompson, who shrugged. Niall, however, demanded, "Let her go. She doesn't need to be subjected to this."

"No," Fiona said firmly. "I'm not leaving, so if you want an answer to your question, Niall, this man will have to tell you in front of me."

Niall's mouth thinned. "Go ahead."

"Winter's throat was slit and he was sodomized."

Bile rose in Fiona's throat. Once again Niall had been framed.

Niall, his face white, said, "And you're here because you think I did it."

Wilbers nodded as Sir Thompson said, "We're here to question you about your whereabouts. You're the primary suspect and the only person who seems to have a grudge against the man. It's well known that you forced the duel on him."

Niall, never one to suffer fools, stated flatly, "Don't be greater idiots than you have to be. If I'd intended to kill the man outright, do you think I'd have gone to the trouble of maneuvering him into a position where he had to meet me in a duel? As you indicate, this has set me up as the logical suspect. I'm not stupid."

Fiona almost groaned. No matter how logical his arrogance was, he wasn't helping himself with it.

Sir Thompson drew himself up. "You're the only man we know of who wanted Lord Winter dead. Now, you can cooperate with us or we can arrest you and put you in Newgate until your trial."

"And after I've answered all your questions, you'll put me there anyway," Niall said, all but snarling.

"You was there once before—for murder," the runner interjected darkly.

"I didn't kill that woman," Niall ground out between tight jaws. "Just as I didn't kill Winter. I haven't been near the man since we met in White's."

"That's as may be," Wilbers said, "but that's only your word."

"The word of a convicted killer," Niall said sarcastically.

"Yessir."

Fiona looked from Niall to the two men. Things weren't going well. Niall was irritating them and they had the power to throw him back in jail. But what could she say? Nothing.

"Okay." Niall unclenched his fists. "What do you want to ask me?"

"Why did you challenge Lord Winter to a duel?" Sir Thompson asked.

Niall looked at the man. "A matter of honor."

Sir Thompson said quietly, "According to the family, he sat on a court-martial board that convicted you for murdering a woman in Boston, Massachusetts. They think you wanted to kill him for that."

Niall didn't look away from the man's piercing eyes. "I wanted to force him to retract that. I planned to best him in a duel and, in lieu of killing him, make him state that the evidence against me was circumstantial and not enough to convict me. They only found me guilty because they couldn't find another man without an alibi. And we had to appease the Americans because of the political situation. I was a scapegoat."

"They found your lucky piece in the woman's hand."

"Well, there, you know it all," Niall said, sarcasm dripping from every word. "Why are you even bothering to question me when you've already found me guilty?"

He held out his hands, an arrogant move that pulled

the sleeves of his coat up to show the scars from Newgate's irons. The two men ignored his gesture.

Wilbers was the first to speak. "Where were you last night?"

Niall's mouth curled. "That's the crux of this, isn't it? I was here."

"Is there someone who can vouch for that?" the runner asked, his gaze sliding to Fiona.

"No," Niall stated before Fiona could speak. "I was here by myself."

"What about the lady?" Wilbers insisted.

"Leave her out of this," Niall said dangerously.

But Fiona had had enough. Stepping between Niall and the men, she said firmly, "I was here all night . . . So was he."

Now Sir Thompson spoke, "And what is your name?"

"Leave her the bloody hell alone," Niall said, pushing her behind him. "I won't let you drag her into this cesspool."

Fiona tried to pry his fingers loose, but they were around her wrist like iron. "You dragged me into this, Niall. Now let me finish what you started," she stated, finally managing to step around him.

Her bitter words were acid to Niall only because he knew she was right. He let her go.

"He was with me all night. He didn't kill Winter. He's been with me since the time he issued the challenge—except for an hour when he went to Manton's for pistols, and that was two days ago."

Sir Thompson gave her a once-over. "And who are you that we should believe your word."

Affronted by his insult, Fiona drew herself up to her full five feet. "I'm Lady Fiona Macfie."

"I've never heard of a Lady Fiona Macfie. Is there someone besides Currie who can vouch for your identity?" Sir Thompson spoke coldly.

On her mettle, Fiona snapped, "Lady Rachel Douglas, the Honorable Joshua Douglas' wife, is my aunt."

"Joshua Douglas is a respected and powerful member of the House of Commons," Sir Thompson said. "I hope you know the liberty you're taking if you're lying."

Fiona's skin flushed with rage. "How dare you doubt my word, sirruh?"

Niall couldn't help but admire her. She had spunk and she had pride.

Instead of answering her, Sir Thompson said to the runner, "Stay with them while I pay a call on Douglas and his wife."

When Niall made a move to follow Sir Thompson, Wilbers drew the pistol Fiona had thought she'd seen under his coat. "Sorry, sir, but me job's as good as gone if I let you go now. Might as well make yerselves comfor'ble."

The runner took one of the two chairs and positioned it by the door so that he could see the entire room. Niall sprawled insolently in the other. Fiona, not wanting to sit on the soft bed where she'd feel compromised, moved to stand by the window. Unfortunately, the lively street did nothing to make her feel better.

Her reputation was in shreds, and she still might not

have saved Niall from another bout in Newgate. It was a bitter pill to swallow.

The only consolation, and that not much, was that while in Newgate Niall couldn't kill her brother. Her mouth twisted. She closed her eyes on the scene below and waited.

The sun was setting in the autumn sky when the door opened again. Sir Thompson stood in the threshold; behind him in the dimly lit corridor were two people Fiona could barely distinguish.

Immediately, Sir Thompson was pushed aside and a regal woman of older years sailed past him. She was dressed in the latest fashion; a maroon cape trimmed in ermine flowed from her shoulders to her feet. A turban of silver with three ostrich feathers died pink sat on her elegantly coifed head. They were bold colors to wear for a woman with flaming-red hair and turquoise-bright eyes, but the former Rachel Macfie carried them like royalty.

"Aunt Rachel," Fiona said, going to her father's younger sister.

Lady Rachel, after a scathing look at Sir Thompson, folded Fiona into her arms. "There, there child," she said. "Whatever are you doing in this slum and—if Thompson hasn't lost his wits—living with a man accused of murder?"

"Easy on the girl, Rachel," a man said, his voice mellow and rich.

Looking past her aunt, Fiona saw her uncle. He was several years older than his wife, and his blond hair was silvering at the temples. He wasn't handsome, but he was distinguished. And his reputation was impeccable. He could have had a peerage for his work in India on behalf of Britain, but had turned it down to remain in the House of Commons. Fiona had always admired him.

Fiona went from her aunt to him. "Uncle Joshua, I'm so glad to see you."

He smiled wryly at her as he took her into his arms. "Child, you're lucky Parliament is still in session, but I expect you knew that when you told Thompson to seek us out."

"True." He had always seen right to the workings of her mind.

"Well, it seems you are who you claim to be," Sir Thompson said dryly. "The only question is your integrity. She says Niall Currie, the man we suspect of killing Lord Winter, was with her all last night."

Fiona stiffened within the circle of her uncle's arms.

Quietly, but definitely, Joshua Douglas said, "Fiona's word is unquestionable." Releasing her, he turned to Niall. "So, you're Malcolm's youngest. You have the look of him."

It wasn't a compliment Niall appreciated. "Yes, I'm Niall McMurdo Currie, late of His Majesty's Navy."

"And still smarting from the ignominy." Joshua Douglas extended his hand to Niall. "Well, can't say as I blame you, for you must be innocent or my niece wouldn't be defending you."

Fiona smiled gratefully and moved closer to her aunt. Lady Rachel put an arm around her niece's shoulders and drew her near. Fiona was glad for the warmth.

Niall took Joshua Douglas' hand, the defiant glint

in his eyes dissipating. "Thank you, sir, but I have to refute Lady Fiona's testimony. She didn't spend the night here with me."

Fiona gasped indignantly. "Don't go casting aspersions on my integrity. I was here, and that's all there is to it."

Douglas looked from one to the other, his shrewd eyes seeing more than was spoken. "I'm sorry, lad," he said to Niall, "but Fiona's word is as good as another person's vow. It always has been—had to be because of her gift. I can't gainsay her now."

Turning his attention to the Bow Street runner and the magistrate, Joshua Douglas said, "I believe Niall Currie was in this room when Lord Winter was murdered, and I'll stake my reputation on it."

His steely eyes met the irritated gaze of Sir Thompson, who was the first to look away.

The Bow Street runner put on his hat. "We'll just leave him in yer custody, sir," he said. "Iffn Lord Winter's family has any problems, we'll know where to find Currie." Nodding, he took his leave.

Sir Thompson was slow to follow. "I hope you don't regret this, Joshua. Saving a convicted killer at the cost of your niece's reputation isn't a trade I'd make." Shaking his head, he left, his words hanging in the air.

Rachel Douglas strode to Niall and her husband. "The man's right, Joshua. Fiona's ruined. No man will have her now, and no hostess will receive her." She turned her formidable gaze on Niall and sized him up. "You may be a convicted killer, as Thompson was so quick to point out, but you're the best we have. You'll have to marry her."

Without batting an eye, Niall looked coldly at Fiona. "I know my duty, Lady Rachel."

Fiona couldn't believe they were making such plans. She bristled. "I won't have it. I won't marry a man because my reputation is ruined." She sniffed. "Besides, no one but the four of us and those odious toadies ever needs to know about this."

Joshua Douglas shook his head. "You're living in a fantasy world if you think this won't spread, child. Thompson has to tell Winter's family or they'll insist on having Niall arrested."

"Oh dear," Lady Rachel sighed. "Winter's mother is the biggest gossip. By tomorrow the tale of your sharing lodgings with this young man will be all over London. No, Fiona," she said sternly, "you will marry him and I won't hear another word about it. The only pity is that your mother and my brother won't be here to see it. Though, on second thought, perhaps—under the circumstances—that is a blessing."

Exasperated, but knowing better than to defy her aunt when she was set on something, Fiona gave up. Later, she'd talk with her uncle. He was more reasonable.

"Now," Lady Rachel said briskly, "let's get you sorted out—although there doesn't appear to be much to pack—and get you out of this hovel."

"Pardon me," Niall said almost deferentially, "but I have a friend in the room next door and I'd like to tell him where I'm going."

Giving him a penetrating look, she said, "Ask him to come with you. We've plenty of room."

Fiona rolled her eyes. It was so typical of her aunt to invite everyone to her house, determined to make right everything that was wrong. Her uncle was similar, only more realistic. He knew when to leave well enough alone.

Early the next morning, Fiona knocked on the door of her uncle's library. She knew Aunt Rachel would sleep for several more hours, and she wanted this time to persuade Joshua Douglas that a marriage between her and Niall would be a bigger mistake than the ruin of her reputation. Uncle Joshua was a reasonable man and would understand.

She'd always been able to talk to him about anything. When she'd been six, they'd come to spend the Christmas holidays at Colonsay and she'd been instantly impressed with the tall, angular man married to her Aunt Rachel. He'd found her huddled into a tight ball at the foot of one of Colonsay Castle's many stone steps. She'd felt a premonition of pain and grief, causing her to turn in on herself because by then she'd known there was nothing she could do to prevent the future. Uncle Joshua had held her and let her cry it out.

She'd loved him unreservedly ever since.

His voice bidding her enter put an end to the memory, but the warmth stayed with her as she walked into the room.

"Have a seat, m'dear," he said. "What can I do for

you?" While he waited for her to speak, he carefully tamped down tobacco in a well-worn pipe and lit it, taking a puff.

Fiona looked around the room. She'd never been in her aunt and uncle's London townhouse, seeing them only when they returned to their Highland estate for the winter when Parliament wasn't in session. This place had the same warmth as their home on the mainland of Scotland. Her sense of comfort increased.

"Uncle Joshua, I need your help." When he smiled gently, his gaze on her lap, Fiona realized she was wringing her hands. She couldn't help a rueful smile. "Badly."

"You want me to intervene with your aunt and prevent your marriage to Currie." He took another puff of his pipe.

She shook her head in admiration. "No wonder you're so formidable in the Commons."

"Compliments will soften me, child, but they won't win me to your side." He set the pipe down and leaned forward, his eyes holding hers. "This time your aunt is right."

"No." Fiona jumped up from her seat and paced, jaw clamped tightly. "No, she isn't." She stopped and looked her uncle straight in the eye. "He doesn't love me."

A smile curved one side of his mouth, reminding her of Niall. It tore at her heart.

"That's as may be, Fiona, but I believe this marriage is for the best. Young Currie is a deeply troubled man and has been condemned of a most heinous crime, but I believe he's innocent. He comes of good stock, the Currie's of Balilone, even if his father isn't always what one would wish in a Scotsman."

"But he kidnapped me. He plans to kill Duncan," Fiona said the words in a desperate rush. "Does that count for nothing?"

Joshua Reynolds raised one hand to silence her. "As I said, he's a deeply troubled young man, but he isn't bad." A twinkle entered his gray eyes. "And he doesn't seem to have harmed you."

She gaped at him. "You're making excuses for him."

Sighing, he rose and went to her, putting a hand on her shoulder. "Yes, I am. Your aunt and I talked about this last night. With your parents at Colonsay, we're responsible for you. We love you like the daughter we've never had, and we don't want harm to come to you."

"Uncle Joshua," Fiona whispered the words, her heart full.

"Your aunt feels your happiness resides with young Currie." A wry smile curved his lips. "And I've often thought that a little bit of your gift lives in Rachel. I trust her judgment in this, just as I ask you to trust us."

Fiona dropped her head, unwilling to meet his clear gaze as she pondered his words. Marriage to Niall was what she'd longed for these past weeks. She just hadn't thought it possible. Now it was.

As though he understood her doubts, her uncle spoke. "Faint heart never won anything. You stood bravely by him when he was being accused of murder; stand by him now."

Her brows knitted with the enormity of the decision

facing her. Her chest tightened painfully. What if she made the wrong decision? What if her aunt were wrong?

Her uncle's next words, however, took the choice out of her hands. "I'm not your father," he said slowly, considering every word, "or better yet, your mother—but I have to speak to you as they would. Is he your lover?"

She flushed. In a tiny voice, she said, "He has been."

"Then there's the chance of a babe."

The air whooshed out of her. Her hand strayed to her abdomen. It was too early for her to show. A rueful, bittersweet smile twisted her mouth. "A chance, yes. Please don't tell Niall."

Joshua Douglas put a finger under her chin and forced her to look at him. "I won't, Fiona, but you've no choice. You must marry him for the babe's sake."

He was right. She knew he was. But she wanted Niall to love her.

Chapter Thirteen

Niall stood stiffly in Joshua Douglas' library, Fiona's choice of location for their civil marriage. He wore the same black superfine jacket and pantaloons he'd worn the night he'd challenged Winter to the duel. The duel that never happened.

His thoughts spun, had been spinning since yesterday and the accusation that he'd killed Winter. He still had no answer, just a gut instinct that the same man who killed the woman in Boston killed Winter. It wasn't a pleasant conclusion because it didn't leave many people who could have done it. At least not that he knew of. It could be anyone who had been on the same ship as he, and it didn't have to be an officer. That possibility was easier for him to accept. He'd make his way to the London docks and see if he could discover anything to help his case.

"Here she comes," Micheil said, jabbing Niall in the side.

Niall suppressed the flare of temper caused by Micheil's unnecessarily sharp poke. Micheil's confrontational behavior about Fiona had increased sharply the second he learned of the change in plans. A marriage between Niall and Fiona seemed to be Micheil's worst nightmare. Well, Niall didn't like it either.

Thank God it wouldn't last long.

Resisting the urge to stalk from the room, Niall turned toward the door and forced himself to look at his bride-to-be. The floor dropped out from under him.

Lady Rachel had bullied her modiste into hastily making what she termed "a suitable gown" for Fiona. Niall understood what she'd meant.

He thought the material was muslin because that's what all the women were wearing, but it was so thin it appeared to be transparent. High-waisted, it fell to her ankles in waves of pristine whiteness. As she walked toward him, it flowed around the contours of her body. Niall swallowed hard and dragged his attention upward.

Her hair was piled in curls on top of her head except for wisps that teased him from the edge of her eyes and the graceful curve of her neck. Her eyes were clear like flawless aquamarines, so clear he could see into the depths of her soul where she reproached him for this sham of a marriage. She hadn't looked at him once since yesterday's accusations by the runner and magistrate, as though she didn't want any part of him.

His hands fisted at his sides. She didn't want him and he couldn't blame her but she knew, as did he, that she must take him or forfeit her reputation. The daughter of an earl didn't live with a man to whom she wasn't wed. As it was, there would be plenty of talk.

He would let her go as soon as possible. No woman wanted to be married to the man responsible for her brother's death.

Fiona watched Niall as she approached him. His eyes were the bright color of malachite that she associated with anger or desire. She knew it wasn't desire he felt for her right now. He didn't want to marry her.

But there was the babe. The babe she wouldn't tell him about until absolutely necessary. Her mouth twisted in a wry smile. She still hoped to win his love and to keep him from self-destruction. She wanted him to be the father of her baby in heart as well as body. And she would do everything in her power to accomplish that.

"You look lovely," Aunt Rachel said, floating regally to Fiona and giving her a warm kiss. "But you're as pale as a moonflower."

She pinched Fiona's cheeks to bring some color into them. Fiona grimaced, but stood still for the ministrations.

"Leave her be, love," Joshua Douglas admonished his wife with a fond smile. "You were a pale bride also."

Fiona gave him a grateful look and rested her hand on the arm he held out. He would give her away in lieu of her father. Her chest tightened. All her life she'd dreamed of being married at Castle Colonsay with her mother and Gran helping her prepare and her bluff, large-hearted father giving her to the man she would love all her life.

They reached Niall, and her uncle put her hand in the younger man's. Niall's skin was hot and dry, the calluses on his palms were rough. His fingers tightened on hers, and she felt giddy with the urge to go fully into his arms. No matter what happened from here on, he was her love . . . and always would be.

The ceremony was brief.

Afterwards, Niall led her into the dining room. Fiona's aunt and uncle followed them with Micheil bringing up the rear.

They sat down to a lavish dinner with sparkling silver and crystal. The chandelier gave more light than Fiona wanted because it showed clearly the lines of dissatisfaction marring Niall's rugged face. Whenever she glanced his way, his gaze rested on her with a brooding darkness that made the hairs on her nape raise.

Micheil's scrutiny was no better. His washed-out blue eyes were opaque as they watched her every move with an intensity that was frightening. His right eyelid twitched.

Looking at her aunt and uncle, she admitted to herself that they were the only ones truly happy with the situation. Both of them felt this marriage was good. She wished she could agree. Her gaze fell to her still-full plate.

"Ahem," her uncle said, standing with his wineglass extended. "I propose a toast to the wedded couple. May their life together be long and fruitful."

Lady Rachel clinked her glass against her husband's. "And may they find true happiness as we have, my dear."

There was so much love and respect in the glance they exchanged that Fiona's eyes blurred. She dashed a white-gloved hand across her face in an attempt to stop the pending tears before Niall saw them. He'd only despise her for such a weakness.

Slowly, as though reluctant to make a toast to something he didn't want to happen, Micheil extended his glass as well. But he remained silent.

Niall frowned at Micheil so that the tension between the two became so thick Fiona swore she could cut it with the knife the butler was handing her to use on the wedding cake. With a sigh, she stood and forced a smile. Things had to get better; they couldn't get worse.

"Thank you, Aunt Rachel, Uncle Joshua . . . and Micheil."

Niall stood beside her, saying nothing. His arm and shoulder grazed hers. Heat sparked through her, and she had to resist the powerful urge to lean against him. She was sure that if she did, he'd move away.

Without more ado, she sliced the small, elegant cake. Made in two tiers, it was covered in white icing and delicate red rosebuds.

While she cut, her uncle signaled the butler to fill everyone's glass with champagne. Fiona watched with half her attention, thinking she'd already had more liquor than her norm. But she needed all the false courage she could consume. She knew her wedding night would not be happy.

With a flourish of bravado, she placed the first slice of cake on the plate Niall held out for her. It was the piece they would share.

Niall looked down at her, his eyes mocking her. The anger she'd held in check throughout the past weeks, submerging it beneath concern for him and later for her unborn child, flared up. How dare he treat her so cavalierly, insulting her when this marriage was his fault. If he hadn't kidnapped her and dragged her to London against her will and then challenged Winter to a duel, they wouldn't be in this situation.

When he lowered his head for the bite she was to feed him, she jammed the entire piece into his mouth with a ferocity that bared her teeth. *There,* she thought as he choked down the sweet concoction. His eyes narrowed dangerously. In their depths, she saw a promise of equal treatment.

Her smile widened as she cut another piece, much smaller than the last. "Coward," he murmured as he fed it to her. She'd won a skirmish, but knew the battle was still to be fought.

They sat back down and Fiona sipped her champagne. Soon they would have to leave the table and go to her room. Their room.

Would he touch her? Would he make their marriage a true union? Or would he continue to ignore her?

Her stomach tensed and her throat was suddenly dry. She gulped more champagne.

Instead of following them to the room, as they might have done under happier circumstances, Fiona's aunt and uncle stopped at the foot of the stairs. Fiona forced herself to smile at them. It was an awful situation, but not of their making, and she wouldn't put the burden of it on them by acting less than gracious.

Micheil, on the other hand, deserved a stern look for the daggers he was sending her.

"Remember," he said loudly enough for everyone

to hear, "the night is followed by the day and weakness is always repented for at leisure."

Anger flared in her, but she knew better than to pursue it. Determined not to add to the unease that Micheil's remark had made worse, Fiona turned on her heel and went up the stairs. Let Niall follow if he wanted. Right now, she didn't care what he did, she was so angry.

Entering her room, Fiona walked to the bed and turned around, her hands clasped in front of her, her head held high. When Niall followed her, she let out a sigh of relief she hadn't been aware of holding. But her anger at Micheil and the entire situation wasn't ameliorated.

"Your friend has the manners of a boar."

He stopped short, his coat trailing from his hand. "Micheil is his own person. Don't take your dislike of him out on me."

Fiona bristled. "There was no call for his remark."

Niall undid the cravat at his neck and tossed it to a chair in which he immediately sat and began pulling off his boots. His eyes met hers coldly. "I told you once before not to speak badly of him to me."

Affronted and hurt at his callous dismissal of her feelings, Fiona turned away from him, her back stiff and straight. She should have known he wouldn't care.

In an effort to calm herself, she traced the pattern of leaves in the coverlet on the bed. The material was a heavy wool damask done in shades of green and rose, feminine, yet substantial. The rest of the room had a similar cast.

When she had herself under control and was sure

her voice wouldn't tremble, she faced him. He was buttoning the black-leather breeches he'd worn before their arrival in London. The white-lawn shirt that he'd worn for the wedding was open at the neck, showing a tuft of black hairs that she knew angled down his flat belly to . . .

Fiona pulled herself up sharply. "Why did you change?"

He gave her a hard look. "I've business to attend to."

Apprehension gnawed at her. Where was he going and why? But more importantly, would he return?

She swallowed and forced her voice to stay level. "It's our wedding night."

He sneered as he pulled on his leather jacket. "What does that matter?"

Hurt, she could only gape at him as she pulled her wits about her. The words slipped from her lips before she realized she intended to say them. "Are you coming back?"

It was such a pitiful question. Fiona felt the hot blood flood her face and would have given the world to call back the words. But she couldn't, so she lifted her chin and met his eyes defiantly.

"For now," he stated flatly, heading for the door.

Involuntarily, she took a step forward before catching herself. She wouldn't disgrace herself further by going after him. She'd take him at his word and wait for his return.

She watched the door close behind him, her eyes blurring. She didn't have any other choice. He didn't have to return; he'd already given her his name. He could leave her now.

Breathing became difficult, and she scrubbed the back of her hand over her moist cheek.

Niall cursed Fiona under his breath as he made his way down the servant's stairs and out the back door. She was tearing him apart. He wanted her with a ferocity that made him ache. But he wouldn't take her: That way led only to greater sorrow.

Tomorrow he would leave for Edinburgh and his rendezvous with Sculthorpe, the second man who'd sat on his court-martial board. Tonight he intended to comb the London docks for information about Winter's murder.

Four hours later frustration ate at him like acid. The memory of the American woman refused to be obliterated. Ever since the runner and the magistrate had accused him of killing Winter, the woman's image had resurfaced and remained firmly fixed in his mind. Her murder had been vile and cruel. And now Winter had died the same way. It made his stomach knot.

He had to find out who was behind this hideous plot to defame him.

In an effort to erase the recollection, he beckoned to the barmaid to bring him another pint of ale. When she laid it on the table, swaying close enough to give him a more than adequate look at her charms, he asked, "Is there anyone in here who's only been in town a couple days?"

"Coor, guv." She dimpled at him. "There's plenty o'

that. Comin's and goin's likes ta make yer 'ead spin."

Niall fished a shilling from his pocket. "Point out a couple."

With dirty fingers, she indicated several men scattered around the dark, smoky room. Niall flipped the coin to her, and she caught it in midair with a deft flick of her wrist.

"T'anks, guv." She gave him a saucy smile and sauntered into the crowd, hips gyrating with unspoken invitation to any takers.

Unmoved by her display, Niall studied the men she'd indicated. Men could change a lot in three years—*he* had—but he didn't recognize any of this lot.

He took a long drink and forced himself to study each one more slowly. The big fat one might be Jimbo, but Jimbo sported a knife scar the length of his right cheek and neck from an encounter with a pirate. This man didn't. The next one appeared to be of medium height and solid build. He could be any one of a number of sailors on his old ship, but Niall didn't think so. The last was similar in shape to the second and equally indistinguishable from anyone else.

Niall downed the rest of his ale. He'd combed the docks, spoken with sailors and whores, and still had no leads to a man who'd once served on HMS *Valiant*. He didn't think he'd learn anything else here.

Rising, he left without a backward glance. Perhaps Winter's death was just a coincidence, a random murder. He wanted to believe that. Short of hiring every Bow Street runner in London, he didn't see how he could prove otherwise. Even then, he'd probably never find out the truth.

Unbidden, Fiona's words about Micheil echoed in his ears. Blood dripping from his friend's fingers. Fiona with the gift of foreseeing.

He shook his head to clear it of the disturbing and erroneous idea. She might be fey, but she wasn't infallible. She and Micheil had disliked each other from the first. Where he was concerned, it would be easy for her to see evil where none existed.

Exhaustion weighted every muscle in his body as he made his way back to Joshua Reynolds' London townhouse. He needed a good night's rest. With any luck Fiona would be sound asleep.

She was affecting everything he did, and not for the better. She insisted he stop his quest for revenge as she insinuated her way into his affections. The sooner their farce of a marriage was over, the better for them both. They weren't good for each other.

He took a deep breath of the cold night air, the smell of salt and fish and seaweed strong. It was a familiar scent. But it brought no distraction from the problems facing him.

Fiona sat up, wondering what had woken her from a sleep she hadn't intended to take. A sound came from the door. Glancing at the window, she saw it was still dark out. Niall was the only person who'd come to this room at night.

He entered, a deeper shadow in the shadows cloaking the room. As she watched, he prowled the area, taking off his coat as he went.

"Where have you been?" she asked quietly, unable to stop herself.

He paused in the act of pulling his shirt over his head. "You're still awake."

It was a statement that did nothing to conceal his irritation with her. It set her back up. "It's our wedding night."

He sat down and pulled his boots off. "You've said that before. That doesn't mean you needed to wait up for me like a watchdog."

His callousness hurt. It was tempting to say something equally cutting to him, but she'd had time to think while he was gone. Starting their marriage with anger and lies would only condemn it to failure.

So, taking a deep breath, she told him the truth. "I was afraid you wouldn't come back."

His second boot hit the floor with a thud. There was a long silence before he spoke. "Not yet."

The succinct statement set off bells in her head. "What do you mean, 'not yet'?"

He moved through the moonlight-dappled room to the settee positioned near the window. "Just what it sounds like. Not yet, as in 'someday I won't come back.' "

Fiona sat on the edge of the bed, her toes not touching the green-carpeted floor. "We're married now. You have to come back." But she knew he didn't.

"I don't have to do anything," he stated, sitting on the settee. "Particularly when this marriage is one of convenience that I intend to have annulled as soon as I meet your brother."

Fiona managed to stifle a gasp of shock. All her

dreams of making this union work began to crumble around her. "Annulled?" she whispered, her heart pounding so loudly she could barely hear herself speak.

When he didn't answer, she slid to the floor. Her toes curled against the cold wood beneath them as she made her way to Niall.

"We can't get an annulment," she said. "We've already made love."

The moonlight from the window made him appear sinister. The hawk-like narrowness of his nose and the high prominence of his cheekbones were silvered, the lines of a statue. Hard. A frisson chased down Fiona's spine.

He opened one eye and gave her a sardonic look. "You'd prefer a divorce? That takes an act of the House of Lords and will ruin everything we tried to prevent by this marriage."

"But our marriage has been consummated," she said, doggedly pursuing that one thought. "We can't get an annulment, and neither one of us will benefit from a divorce."

Wearily, he closed his eye and propped his hands under his head. "Our marriage hasn't been consummated. We were lovers out of wedlock." Sarcasm laced his words. "There *is* a difference."

He was going to leave her. He was going to leave her and the babe she carried.

What about her unborn babe? If she told him about the child, he'd stay with her. His own father's disownment of him had cut too deeply for him to do the same to his child. But she didn't want him on sufferance.

Fiona stood in the wintry glare of the moon and stared down at him. The cold from the floor beneath her feet radiated up her legs and settled in her chest.

She wanted him for love.

And there was only one other way to keep him. She had to love him enough to make him love her in return. She had to bind him to her, and there was only one way she knew of to do that.

It was an instinctive decision and a desperate act. But short of telling him about the babe, which she refused to do, it was her only recourse.

Taking a deep breath to regain the courage she was known for on Colonsay but which seemed to have deserted her in the time she'd spent with this exasperating man, Fiona closed the distance between them.

Going to her knees by the chaise lounge, ignoring the chill that flowed through her nightrail and up her body, Fiona said silkily, "Niall . . ."

He opened one eye.

She'd never considered herself a seductress, but he was susceptible to her. She knew that from their past encounters. All she had to do was use her imagination, something she had plenty of.

"Niall, I want to love you," she said softly, her eyes searching his face for a reaction to her boldness. He had to respond to her. He had to. This was the only way she knew to bind him to her.

He opened his other eye. His mouth thinned.

Before he could stop her, her hands pulled his lawn shirt out of the waistband of his pantaloons and slid underneath to glide over the hard musculature of his chest and abdomen. He felt hot and dry, like kindling. With one smooth action, she pushed the shirt up and bent down to stroke his nipple with her tongue. His sharp intake of breath told her she was doing the right thing.

She had the shirt worked up and was transferring her attention to his other nipple when he grabbed both her hands and pinned them above his head so that she lay spread on top of him. She looked up at his face. His eyes were bright green.

"What are you doing?" he asked softly, menacingly.

"Making love to you." Knowing that if she allowed him to coerce her into stopping all was lost, Fiona bent back to his chest. She sucked on his nipple and rimmed it with her teeth. She wasn't called a fighter by her family for nothing.

"Stop it," he ordered, pulling her hands tighter so that she inched up his chest until her face was just below his.

"No." Taking advantage of the new position, she traced the line of his jaw to his ear, which she circled with the tip of her tongue. "I'm going to make you want me."

It was a bold statement that called for bold action. Lifting her head the distance needed, she ground her mouth down on his. Her tongue traced the hollow between his lips, insinuating into the warmth moistness of his mouth. He tasted of ale, hops and honey. Fiona drank deeply.

She felt his chest rise and fall beneath her. His heart pounded, his pulse increasing as she greedily helped herself to him. When his fingers loosened their grip, she acted.

Rolling off him, she braced herself against the chaise and undid the fastening of his pantaloons. She reached inside and pulled his turgid shaft out. Sitting back on her haunches, she admired its length and thickness in the pale moonlight that glinted along its length.

A slow smile of triumph lit her face. He wanted her. His words might deny it, but his body proclaimed differently.

"You're aroused," she said softly, running a finger down the length of him.

His answer was to pinion her wrist. "Don't do that."

Her smile increased. The brilliant hardness of his eyes told her he didn't mean it.

"Let me go," she said. "Let me show you exactly how you make me feel."

His gaze never left her face, but he released her. She allowed her hand to lie on his chest for a minute and her fingers to tangle in the growth of black hairs that spread from nipple to nipple before arrowing lower. She followed that path.

He sucked in his breath as her fingers circled him. Tentatively at first, she massaged him. When his hips bucked, she bent over him and took him inside her mouth.

A sharp groan of desire and despair escaped him. Fiona began to move over him, her fingers cupping the tight sacks that proclaimed his need.

Excitement twisted in her belly as he reacted to her against his will. He thrashed beneath her ministra-

tions, his breathing becoming fast and harsh. Moist
warmth curled between her thighs and the longing to
have him inside her grew until she was as aroused as
he.

Just as she thought she must release him long
enough to mount him, his hands closed on her head
and carefully pulled her away. His eyes were glassy
and unfocused.

"Enough," he said hoarsely. "I don't want to climax
and take away your pleasure." He took several deep
breaths, his eyes becoming hooded as he stared at her.
"Take off your clothes," he ordered, his gaze encom-
passing her. "You want to seduce me, then do the
rest."

The blunt order dimmed her ardor, but not enough
to make her stop. Neither did it make her forget her
original reason for this path. He was hers, and she
would prove it.

Standing, she reached behind herself and undid the
laces holding her gown together. The thin material
slipped to her breasts, catching on her aroused nipples.
When she glanced at Niall, his mouth was stretched in
a predatory smile that made her blood heat.

"Come here," he ordered.

She did as he bid, wanting the touch his eyes promised. Kneeling before him, she waited, her loins aching
for him. He rose up and pulled her between his thighs.
His mouth took her nipple, the thin barrier of muslin
the only thing between his heat and her flesh. Pleasure
shot from her breast to her stomach. Her muscles
turned to melted wax, and it was only the support of

his arm around her waist that kept her from falling to the floor.

Just when she thought she could take no more, he changed to her other breast. The nipple he'd sucked into a peak and left alone trembled in the coolness caused by the wet material where his mouth had been. She searched for his hand and placed it on that breast.

He lifted his head and gave her a knowing look as his finger closed on her flesh and began to squeeze in a rhythm she remembered from their lovemaking. Heat washed over her. Her back arched. A low moan escaped her parted lips.

He took her mouth in a kiss that seared to her depths. His hands hooked under the muslin of her bodice and yanked it down her torso to her hips. His fingers caressed her hips as he pushed the gown down. The only thing between her and his touch was her chemise. Soon there was nothing.

Dimly, in the recesses of her conscious mind, Fiona realized that she'd gone from the seducer to the seduced. It didn't matter. Nothing mattered but his mouth on hers, his fingers stroking her, and—soon—his body buried deeply in hers.

She didn't know when he left her long enough to undress himself, but she found herself beside him on the chaise, their legs entangled as he kissed her deeply. His hands kneaded up and down the ridge of muscle on both sides of her spine. His thigh nestled between hers, rubbing the core of her desire. Tiny gasps of pleasure came from her with every stroke of his muscled leg between hers.

She wanted him so badly it was an ache in her heart,

a wound on her soul not to have him. Reaching between their straining, sweating bodies, she grasped him and tried to position him for entry.

"Time enough for that," he said, catching her hands and positioning them on his shoulders. "Right now, I'm going to do to you what you did to me." He flipped her onto her back and smiled. It was a domineering, wolfish expression.

Pulling her to the edge of the chaise, he went to his haunches between her thighs. Fiona couldn't believe he was doing this. Instinctively, she squeezed her legs shut but only succeeded in trapping his fingers near her, a situation he used to his advantage.

"Wet," he said, his voice raspy. "Open up for me, vixen. Leg me give you the pleasure you bestowed on me."

The generous nature of his words was belied by the mocking gleam in his eyes. But Fiona was beyond caring now as his fingers slicked along her swollen folds. She was only half-aware of allowing him access as she slipped down further on the chaise and he positioned her thighs on his shoulders. She was completely open to him.

When his tongue touched her it was as though a thousand cannons exploded in her belly and shot to every part of her body. She trembled uncontrollably. Her nails rent the fabric of the chaise. Small, strangled gulps escaped her.

When his tongue entered her, flicking with unerring precision, her body went rigid. She screamed.

Niall watched her through slitted lids. She made him feel omnipotent by the completeness of her response.

She sent all his good intentions into the depths. Nothing mattered when she was in his arms, taking what he gave and moaning with pleasure. Nothing mattered.

Unable to hold back any longer, he covered her with his body and thrust into the warm depth she opened for him. She fit him to perfection. It was all he could do not to end the encounter then.

Teeth gritted, he pulled out and reached between them with his fingers. Slowly, perspiration breaking on his forehead at the concentration needed not to plunge into her, he delved into her heat and withdrew, his fingers rubbing her all the while. The renewed tension on her face was his reward. He was going to love her until she lay exhausted, no thought in her mind but him and what he did to her.

He increased the tempo.

His body strained against the control he kept on it. The sight of her lips parted and swollen from his kisses, her eyes half-focused on his face as he pushed into her, was too much.

With a shout, he thrust deeply into her, felt her pulse around him as her voice joined his. His release was exquisitely intense, blurring his vision and pulling sensation from the bottom of his spine outward. He was dying.

Later, still between her legs, Niall came back to himself. Fiona lay on her back, her hair spread decadently over the green silk of the chaise. Her eyes were closed, their long auburn lashes like a burning slash in her flushed complexion. Her mouth was slightly parted, the fine white teeth gleaming moistly.

He had to resist the urge to cup her still-swollen

breasts in his palms before running his hands down her ribs to her waist—and lower. They were still joined, the musky scent of lovemaking flared his nostrils. He couldn't stop his hips from thrusting into her, his shaft still firm and eager. She clenched him.

He groaned. "Don't."

Her eyes opened to show him languid pools of aquamarine. Satiation radiated from her in waves of sensuality that threatened to overwhelm his decision to withdraw.

"That was wonderful," she said lazily. "Exciting and pleasurable. Why not do it again?"

And why not? he asked himself. She was willing and he was eager and capable. God, was he ever! He still ached for her.

But he knew why not. She would hate him soon enough. It was only a matter of time before Duncan Macfie's ship came into port.

Meanwhile, he didn't want to get her pregnant and make it impossible for them to get out of this marriage. It wasn't fair to her to tie her to him when their future together was as bleak as the North Sea.

Clamping down on the urge to make love to her again, Niall rose. "This doesn't change anything. I'm still going to get an annulment."

Chapter Fourteen

Unable to sleep after Niall's words, Fiona lay in bed determined not to cry. She'd made a fool of herself over him. Thinking she could seduce him on their wedding night and make him stay with her was the most foolish thing she'd ever done. Oh, he'd taken what she'd offered and torn her world apart in the process, but he'd made it plain he was using her. Just as he'd used her since kidnapping her weeks ago.

It seemed years.

A sound caught her attention. Rising onto her elbows, she squinted into the dark shadows of the room. Movement by the window told her Niall was up and dressed.

She lit a candle. "What are you doing?"

"It's pretty obvious," he said, his back to her while he packed a shirt into one of the saddlebags. Next he wrapped his harp in the oiled cloth it traveled in.

"You aren't leaving?" she asked incredulously.

He turned to her. In the flickering light of the single candle he'd lit to pack by, he looked tired—tired and disillusioned. Her heart wrenched before she hardened it. He was a cold man. Unfortunately, he was also the father of her child.

His mouth twisted. "Your performance earlier leaves me no choice. I don't intend to weaken again, and the best way to ensure that is to go to Edinburgh without you." He ran his fingers through his black hair, increasing its wildness.

He was going to leave her. Just like that. Well, he had another thing coming. She jumped out of bed, anger spurting through her veins. "I'll be damned if you'll walk out on me, Niall Currie."

He turned his back to her and continued stuffing things into the bag. Fiona stomped over to him and poked her fingers into his back.

"Look at me."

He turned around, his eyes dark and inscrutable. "Go back to bed, Fiona. Forget you ever saw me."

"What? We're married—or have you conveniently forgotten that one small detail?" Sarcasm dripped from every word.

He flushed. "No, I haven't. But if you could *conveniently* lie about our lovemaking before we were married, I see no reason why you can't *conveniently* lie about it after our marriage. In other words," he said pointedly, "nothing's changed. Your little performance was pleasurable, but it wasn't worth tying myself to you for life."

She swung at him. The deadly right that had connected frequently with her brother's jaw when they'd argued too heatedly caught Niall on his jaw. His head jerked with the force.

"Don't treat me like a whore," she said, her voice harsh. "You were willing enough." The last was said tartly, her ability to keep the hurt at bay fading.

"That's why I'm leaving. The last thing I want is for you to get pregnant." He stepped around her and headed for the door.

His words were a punch in the stomach; his leaving was worse. Fiona knew that if he went through the door she'd never see him again . . . unless it were at Duncan's funeral. She ran after him.

"If you leave me, I'll be able to tell Duncan what you plan. I'll tell him everything—about Winter, the murder . . . and Micheil's hands. If he knows, he won't meet you."

Niall stopped in his tracks. Turning around slowly, his face a mask of controlled fury, he said, "You won't do anything."

"Try me," she said, meeting his hard glare with bravado. "Remember, you said yourself you should never tell me not to do something because it only ensures that I will."

"Duncan's at sea," he countered.

"I'm his sister. I can go to the Admiralty and get a message to him. Uncle Joshua can see that it's done." The smile she gave him was triumphant.

He sighed wearily. "Go ahead and do it. I know Duncan. Once he finds out about our marriage and that I kidnapped you and seduced you, he'll hunt me to the grave—his or mine."

His capitulation was unnerving. Fiona eyed him, seeing the exhaustion and disillusionment that haunted his face. She knew this was the turning point in their relationship. If she stayed with him, there was a chance for them. There had to be. If she let him go, it was over.

"Give me five minutes," she said, standing her ground, watching him for any reaction.

Instead of turning his back to her as she'd half-expected him to, he nodded. "No more. And—" he stared at her "—don't repeat last night. The first time you do, I'll leave you where we are. I don't want a child from this union."

Fiona took an involuntary step backward, as though physical action could ward off the emotional devastation of his words. How could she continue to force herself on him? How could she not?

Fiona scrambled into the same clothing she'd worn the weeks of their travels. Aunt Rachel would be scandalized if she knew, but that was the least of Fiona's worries. Niall wasn't walking out of her life.

Breathlessly, she said, "I'm ready. But I'd like to leave a note for my aunt and uncle." At his scowl, she hastened to add, "I'll put it on Uncle Joshua's desk in the library."

When he didn't reply, she went to the small writing desk and penned a quick message. In it, she asked her uncle to warn her brother. She knew Duncan well enough to know it would do no good. Niall was right. When Duncan found out about the kidnapping and forced marriage, he'd track Niall to hell. But she had to try.

*   *   *

Dawn pinked the sky. They'd been traveling several hours and were well outside of London. The clean country air, without the metallic taste of burning coal and the stench of human closeness, was a balm to Fiona's frayed nerves.

They stopped near a stream with late-fall grass that the animals could eat growing on its banks. It was an idyllic site, and under different circumstances Fiona would have enjoyed the respite.

But even though Niall hadn't tied her wrists this time, he was still treating her like a prisoner. She looked away from his hard profile. He didn't need to bind her; her love for him was bond enough.

Fiona slid from MacDuff's back and spoke for the first time, determined to break the silence. "Where's Micheil?"

Niall frowned at her, and she thought he wouldn't answer. When he did, he spoke curtly. "He's finishing some business in London."

The memory of Micheil with blood on his fingers resurfaced. "What kind of business?" She had to know.

His mouth thinned. "Winter."

Alarm chilled her palms. "What about Winter?"

Niall sighed and ran his fingers through his long, unruly hair. Fiona longed to smooth it back from his brow but knew he'd resent that.

"He's hiring some Bow Street runners to investigate Winter's death."

Somehow the words didn't ring true. Fiona realized it was her gift. While Niall might think Micheil was doing that, she doubted that Micheil was. But one look at Niall's closed face told her not to tell him her thoughts. He was already exasperated with her and would refuse to listen to any words of disparagement about his friend. She admired his loyalty even as it presented difficulties.

Accepting that there was nothing she could do, Fiona hobbled MacDuff where the pony could reach the grass and water. That done, she knelt by the stream and scooped up the cold liquid. It tasted fresh and clean.

"We haven't got all day." Niall's harsh voice came from directly behind her.

He was right. With a sigh, Fiona splashed some water on her face and rose. Knowing Niall as she had come to, she understood that he'd want to make Edinburgh in record time.

Two weary hours later, Fiona had to bite her tongue to keep from asking him to stop. She could only be thankful she wasn't prone to morning sickness as her mother had been. That would have made this bumpy, rocky journey on MacDuff's uncomfortable back unbearable.

"Why don't we use the toll road?" she asked instead of pleading for rest. "Even on Colonsay we've heard of these roads and how they improve travel. For that matter," she continued, caught up in the idea, "why don't we just get a stage ticket? It can't be any worse than this." Rubbing her lower back, she added, "And it's not as if anyone would recognize us, or care if they did."

The last was her jab at him. As seemed to be the norm when she was with him, she was tired and hungry and miserably cold. But she'd be damned if she'd ask him to stop.

He glanced back at her, but didn't slow Prince Charlie. "I don't like traveling in the stage."

That was it, she thought, fuming. He didn't like stages, so they wouldn't ride in one. Gritting her teeth, she urged MacDuff on.

Niall sensed her temper building. She was uncomfortable and probably cold. When she didn't lash out, he grudgingly admired her stubbornness. He even felt he owed her an explanation.

He pulled back on Prince Charlie's reins until their horses were nose to nose and Fiona's face was level with his shoulder. "I'll put you on the stage if you wish." Now that he had started, he found it hard to tell her the truth.

She gave him a fulminating glance from under her thick copper lashes. "Thank you ever so much. And then you'll promptly lose yourself and I'll never see you again."

His mouth quirked up in spite of himself. "I'd collect you at Edinburgh. But that's not why I won't ride the stage." He took a deep breath and prepared to explain something he didn't fully comprehend himself. "I rode it to Scotland after my release . . . the stage. It was small and dirty and smelly. It was like being in Newgate all over again. I thought I'd go crazy before the trip was over." His voice lowered. "I was never gladder to see anyone than I was to see Micheil in Glasgow with Prince Charlie."

Niall's stallion shied and danced so that Fiona had

to guide MacDuff away. She knew without asking that Niall had yanked on the reins. And she knew why.

The stage reminded him of prison. Her heart went out to him, her anger of minutes before gone in the face of his misery.

"Forget the stage," she said. "I traveled from Scotland to London on MacDuff once before. I can return to Scotland the same way."

She only wished they would rest. She didn't seem to have the energy she used to have. Her mother had told her once that childbearing was hard on the woman, taking her strength, but that it gave much in return with the birth of the child. She was beginning to understand a little of what her mother had meant. Fiona gritted her teeth.

That night, Niall got them room in an inn without Fiona's having to ask. As he closed the door behind them, she said, "Thank you."

He laid their two bags on the single chair the room boasted. "Make the most of it."

It was his way of telling her he didn't intend to do this every night. "Why can't we do this all the time? We're married now—or have you forgotten?"

"I haven't forgotten."

The intense quality of his voice unnerved her. Awareness of him as a man assailed her. He stood near enough that if she reached out she could touch him. Her fingers could stroke his face, or . . . Fiona licked her suddenly dry lips.

He was potently masculine in the tight fitting black-leather garments he wore once more—and he was wild. While in London, he'd had his hair trimmed, but only enough to make him marginally fashionable to the aristocrats who'd been his entrée to Winter. But that had been two weeks ago. Now it fell to his shoulders in heavy waves that accented the hard lines of his cheek and jaw.

She wanted to dig her fingers into his hair and bring his mouth down to hers. She wanted to make love to him. She took an involuntary step toward him.

His green eyes smoldered. "Don't, Fiona."

She froze even as her blood flowed hot. Taking a deep breath, she said, "This is why you don't want to stay in an inn, isn't it?"

He nodded, the knuckles of his hand white as he gripped one of the saddlebags. "Yes. It's much easier to fight this attraction when there isn't a bed big enough for both of us." He took a deep, shuddering breath. "At least when we're out of doors, I can build a fire between us. Here there's only a few feet of hard floor, and I'm human enough to want to sleep in the bed."

"You want more than that," she said softly.

The tension in his face told her more. He was human enough to want to love her. A tiny, triumphant smile curved her mouth.

"Yes, dammit." He threw the bag down and turned on her. "I want more. I want you."

Desire blazed at her from his eyes. His mouth was drawn tight with it. His body throbbed with it.

Fiona waited for him to come to her. She held herself back, knowing that it would be sweeter for him to enfold her in his arms than for her to rush to him.

"But I won't take what you offer," he growled, stalking past her to the door.

Stunned, Fiona twisted around. He stood with one hand on the doorknob, the other clenched at his side. His chest rose in deep breaths that told her he was as disturbed as she.

"Why do you fight it?" she asked, hoping to wear him down.

"You know."

"Yes, I know. You don't want me to conceive because you're going to leave me after your duel with my brother."

Niall watched her head droop and wished things had been different. He wished he could put aside his revenge; but after living with it for three years, he had made vengeance a part of himself. If he stopped pursuing vengeance he was afraid he'd lose his purpose for existing.

In a voice more guttural than he wanted, he said, "I'll get some food. Stay here."

Recognizing defeat when it stared her in the face, Fiona nodded. There was nothing else to do. She loved him and was determined to break through the barrier he held between them.

But it was a miserable night—as were the succeeding nights of the journey to Scotland.

After days of heavy riding and little sleep, Fiona realized they were on the outskirts of Edinburgh. True to his word, Niall hadn't touched her and he hadn't left her behind. She was thankful but no less waspish.

"What do you plan now that we're here?"

He cut her an irritated glance. "Find Sculthorpe."

Fiona bristled at the short reply he made no effort to soften. He'd been speaking to her like that for the duration of their trip. She was feeling particularly argumentative. "And kill him, I suppose."

He twisted in the saddle so that he faced her, his jaw clenched. "Right."

Fiona looked away, unconsciously jabbing her heels into MacDuff's flanks. The pony shied. It was enough to jolt Fiona and make her reconsider the acrimonious words she'd been about to speak. They were both tired and hungry and filthy. Not to mention on edge from Niall's enforced celibacy in spite of the desire that arched between them like lightning in a thunderstorm. It would be easy to pick a fight with him, and it would accomplish nothing.

In more conciliatory tones, she said, "I have a godmother who would take us in. She lives in Charlotte Square in the west end of New Town. I stayed with her when I had my coming out."

"I don't want anyone to know we're here."

It was the answer she'd expected, but she had an argument for it. "I'm sure my uncle has sent word already."

"It won't have beat us here," Niall said, urging his stallion past her.

Fiona sighed in exasperation, her good intentions beginning to fade. She spurred MacDuff to catch up.

"You stubborn mule. It won't be long in coming. Then my godmother will search for us. Why make it hard on everyone, including us, by not going to her first?"

She thought for sure he was going to berate her. To

her surprise, when he looked at her there was a gleam in his green eyes.

"Now I'm a mule. You have a way with words, vixen."

It was the first lightening of his attitude toward her since their marriage. Hope began to unfurl once more in Fiona's heart.

"My godmother is Lady Fennimore. She can get us entrée into Edinburgh society." She paused to let that sink in. "It should ease your hunt for Sculthorpe since I've no doubt he moves in those circles. Provided he isn't in the country."

It was a chance, but Fiona knew that most naval officers came from the gentry or aristocracy. Surely Sculthorpe did, too.

"You've thought of it all, haven't you?" He slowed Prince Charlie to MacDuff's pace. "Sculthorpe's here. He doesn't—or didn't—like the country, and he's a baronet."

Fiona released a sigh of relief. "Then that's settled. We'll stay with my godmother."

It was another thirty minutes before they turned into the fashionable Edinburgh street where Fiona's godmother lived. Jumping from Prince Charlie's back, Niall strode to the imposing front door with its Corinthian columns.

Niall's peremptory knocks brought an aged butler to the door. Stooped over, white hair brushing his bushy eyebrows, the old man gaped at them.

"Lady Fiona," he said, surprise cracking his voice.

Fiona smiled at him. "Ben. Please be so kind as to let Lady Fennimore know we're here." She stepped past him, paused, and added, "Ben, this is Niall Currie, my husband."

The old man's mouth dropped open. As an afterthought, he bowed. "Welcome, sir."

Niall couldn't suppress a wry smile at the old retainer's surprise. "Good day, Ben."

Fiona, impatience goading her now that she was in a familiar house and about to see a woman she loved and trusted, said, "Better yet, Ben, is my godmother in her parlor?"

At his bemused nod, she hurried down the hallway. With only a brief knock, she barged into the room. Niall followed.

Closing the door behind them, Niall watched through narrowed eyes as Fiona rushed headlong into the room. It was much like her and one of the things he found intriguing about her.

She stopped in her tracks, her face radiant with joy. "Mother! What are you doing here?"

"Fiona, child."

A dark-haired woman with bright eyes rose from a chair by the fire and hurried to Fiona. The woman was much the size of her daughter; and although she'd born the Earl of Colonsay three children, she had retained her slim figure. He imagined Fiona would do the same.

Fiona went into the older woman's arms. Niall saw tears glistening on his wife's lashes.

His throat closed painfully for a second. He hadn't realized how much Fiona missed her parents; she hadn't mentioned them after the initial kidnaping. He was glad he'd sent them the message.

Another woman, about the same age as Fiona's mother but plumper and with ash-blond hair, rose slowly from her chair. Only after Fiona and her mother had stepped back from one another did the second woman approach them. Niall surmised she was Lady Fennimore.

"Fiona," Lady Fennimore said, her round face breaking into a smile, "I told your mother you'd be all right. Any man who'd send a message can't be all bad. But she's been inconsolable since arriving this morning."

Fiona embraced her godmother as she said to her mother, "You just got here?"

Mary, Countess of Colonsay, nodded, stepping back to survey her daughter. "Your father went with Coll and Allan to retrace your path up to the point where you were kidnapped, but they couldn't find anything to lead them farther. Your father is beside himself. You know he prefers action."

Fiona smiled and nodded. "Which is why it's surprising that *you've* come to Edinburgh and not he."

Her mother's face clouded over. "Some things have happened recently and he feels it's better for him to stay at Colonsay Castle until they're straightened out. However, he's sent men to London and Glasgow to search for you." She glanced at Niall. "We didn't know what had happened to you; and when no ransom note arrived after the first message saying you were safe, we didn't know what else to do."

Retaining her mother's hand, Fiona said, "I'm so sorry, Mama. I knew you'd fret, but there was nothing I could do." She took a deep breath. "But I'm safe, as you can see, and I've brought my kidnapper with me."

"What?" Mary, Countess of Colonsay asked in a terrible voice.

Before Fiona could say more, her mother turned to face Niall. The woman's eyes blazed like polished swords. Her black brows winged upward to meet the ebony sweep of her hair. Her mouth was a thin slash. She was a formidable woman.

Niall met her scrutiny without flinching. She had every right to hold him in loathing; but while he'd submit to her study, he wouldn't grovel.

"Who are you?" she demanded in a voice accustomed to commanding.

But Niall detected a burr in it as well. It was as though the aristocratic accent was underlaid by a more earthy pronunciation. He knew she was a cottar's daughter whom the earl had married for love.

"I'm Niall McMurdo Currie," he stated clearly.

"The man who kidnapped my daughter?"

"Yes."

"Mary." Lady Fennimore stepped between the two. "He hasn't harmed her. Has he harmed you?" she added, turning to Fiona.

"No," Fiona answered softly.

Niall's attention went to the woman he'd wronged in more ways then he could count. Her eyes met his calmly.

"There," Lady Fennimore said. "That's settled."

"No, it's not," Fiona's mother said. "Why did you take my daughter in the first place and why have you brought her back?"

She was an astute woman, much like her daughter.

In spite of the martial light in her eyes, Niall found himself admiring her and wishing he'd met the woman under more auspicious circumstances.

Before he could speak, Fiona interjected, "It doesn't matter, Mama. Not anymore. Niall and I are married."

"You can't be," Mary, Countess of Colonsay, thundered.

"How delightful," Lady Fennimore said simultaneously.

"When and how?" Fiona's mother demanded, moving to her daughter and putting her arm around Fiona's shoulder.

Niall told her the complete story, from the kidnapping to the marriage, not sparing himself in the telling. However, he kept to himself his plan to challenge her son to a duel and the repercussions of the last challenge he'd made. He would allow the countess to think what she wanted.

When Fiona disengaged herself from her mother and came to stand beside him, he wished she hadn't. He'd done nothing but use her and intended to keep doing so. He didn't want her forsaking her mother for him. When she tried to insert her fingers in his, he kept his fisted. He noted the action wasn't missed by his mother-in-law.

"So," Mary said, "you kidnapped Fiona for revenge and Joshua forced you to marry her. It's not a pretty picture of yourself that you paint, Niall Currie."

He met her look levelly. "No, milady."

For the first time since she'd learned who he was,

Niall saw a glint of admiration for him enter her eyes. She was a most unusual woman to value honesty over respectability. But then, her daughter was unusual, too.

"Well," Lady Fennimore interrupted once more, "no sense in crying over spilt milk. What's done is done, and now we must make the best of it. I imagine you're both tired, so I'll have Ben show you to a room. When you're rested, the four of us will decide how best to undo the harm your hasty marriage has caused Fiona's reputation."

Before Niall could tell them of his intentions to leave Fiona as soon as he could arrange an annulment, the woman had rung for the butler and been answered. As the door closed behind them, Niall heard Fiona's godmother chuckle.

"Wait until Angus Magee hears that Fiona's up and married another man. This will certainly put a crook in the man's handsome nose."

Chapter Fifteen

The room they were shown to was large and opulently decorated. Heavy mahogany furniture filled every wall and spilled into the center. Thick velvet in shades of lilac and pink adorned everything. It was a woman's fantasy and a man's nightmare. Niall wondered if Lady Fennimore was married and, if so, why her husband let her get away with this.

But it was only a ruse he tried to play on himself to keep at bay the anger caused by the lady's parting remarks. He might be planning to let Fiona go, but the thought of another man picking her up was like a knife in his chest. He was being irrational, but he couldn't stop himself.

"Who's Angus Magee?" he demanded. "Was he your lover?"

Fiona gaped at him, his words stopping her in the act of slipping off her worn, ill-fitting shoes. "My lover? You better than anyone should know he wasn't."

His eyes snapped as he took a step toward her.

"There are ways to make love to a woman without taking her virginity."

Fiona stared at him. "Are you jealous?" she asked, hope lifting her voice.

"No." He turned away. Before she could follow up on that, he said, "I'm going out."

Fiona stared at his back. She should have known not to press him, but she was tired and the meeting with her mother had tired her further. It made her an easy prey to the fear caused by Niall's words.

"Are you going to look for Sculthorpe?" At his nod, she added, "Will you come back?"

Emotions warred across his features. Without his saying a word, she knew he didn't want to but that he would.

"Yes."

The bald word answered her spoken question, but it wasn't enough. It wasn't reassurance that he wouldn't leave her another time.

"Why don't you leave me now since you're determined to annul our marriage?" It was a question that had eaten at her from the moment they were wed. It had eroded her confidence as they'd traveled, and it would continue to haunt her until she knew the answer.

He stared at her, his eyes dark and haunted. When he spoke, she knew he lied. "Because I'm not done using you. As you pointed out yourself, my hunt for Sculthorpe will go much more quickly if your godmother takes us about in society."

Sadly, she said, "It's all for your revenge and nothing more."

"Nothing more," he snapped, twisting away from her and slamming the door as he left.

Outside their room, Niall breathed deeply to slow the beating of his heart. It was getting harder and harder to deny Fiona. She made no secret that she wanted him, and he was beginning to believe she might love him. Had things been different, had his life been different, he would rejoice at that knowledge. Now all it did was increase his desire for revenge on the two remaining men who made it impossible for him to accept the gift of her love.

Out on the street, Niall headed in the direction of a coffeehouse he'd frequented when in town. If he remembered correctly, and he'd had three years in Newgate to perfect his memory, Sculthorpe enjoyed coffee. Besides, he'd arranged to meet Micheil there.

While he'd gone to school in England, as had his older brothers, he'd come to Edinburgh enough to be familiar with the city. It didn't take him long to reach the coffeehouse. The inside was aromatic with the scent of cheroots and thick, black coffee. At a table near the back, Micheil sat hunched over a steaming cup.

Sitting beside Micheil, Niall ordered before asking, "Is everything taken care of with the Bow Street runner?"

"Yes," Micheil said without meeting his eyes. "Wilbers will send any findings to me."

Niall put a hand on Micheil's shoulder and

squeezed. "Thanks. You've been a true friend through all of this."

For the first time in the history of their friendship, Micheil shrugged off Niall's hand. Blue eyes met green with a resentment that was corrosive in its intensity. "You could have done it yourself, but no! You had to marry that woman and then bring her here. Even worse, you've used every excuse you can think of to be with her when you should be getting rid of her." His face twisted. "How many times must I tell you she's trouble? She's the sister of your enemy." He stopped and his eyes narrowed. "Unless you've decided not to kill Duncan Macfie after all."

Niall shook his head slowly. Seeing Micheil's dislike for Fiona in the corrosive lines etching his friend's face, Niall realized for the first time just how much Micheil hated her. It didn't help knowing inside himself that Micheil was right when he said Fiona was nothing but trouble. Since Fiona had come into his life, he'd done things to be with her that he'd never done before. He'd lied to himself.

He wasn't staying with her to try and ease her reputation before annulling their marriage. That made about as much sense as marrying her in the first place. He was staying with her because he didn't have the strength to leave her.

"You're in love with her," Micheil said harshly. "Don't deny it."

"I don't know what I feel for her," Niall admitted. "But you're right. Kidnapping her was a mistake. Except that it's ensured that Duncan Macfie will hunt me down."

Having said that much, Niall found he could go no further about his feelings for her. He desired Fiona; he even liked her. But he didn't want to love her.

He took a swig of his coffee. "Damnation!" he growled as the hot liquid burnt his tongue and gullet.

A tight smile lightened Micheil's countenance minimally. "Have you found Sculthorpe yet?"

"No," Niall said, putting the cup down. "We just got into town this afternoon. But I need to find the man soon. It can't be long before Macfie's ship is back, and I'd lay money the Admiralty has an urgent message for him."

Micheil cocked one sandy brow. "You think her uncle gave them a message for Macfie?"

Niall smiled coldly. "I'd stake my life on it. Fiona left Douglas a letter, and I'm sure it included a note for her brother. In fact, I'm counting on it."

"Ah," Micheil drew the word out, the deep lines around his mouth easing. "That's why you've kept her with you. To draw Macfie. Clever."

Niall considered telling Micheil the truth, but he held back. It was obvious to him that Micheil didn't want him to be attracted to Fiona. However, he hadn't kept Fiona with him to draw Macfie. He didn't need to. Her brother would come after him even if Fiona were safe in Colonsay. Niall would if another man abducted her; Duncan Macfie would do no less.

Instead of speaking, Niall took another sip of his coffee, which had cooled. "Fiona's godmother is Lady Fennimore. She plans to introduce us to Edinburgh society. Do you know her?"

"No, but I've heard of her. She's a widow with a penchant for matchmaking."

Niall made himself grin. "Then you'd best keep away. As soon as she finds out I have a friend who's wealthy and heir to a viscount, your days will be numbered."

Micheil laughed dutifully, but his mirth was strained. "I count on you to protect me, since I need to be with you to find Sculthorpe."

Again, the irritation at Micheil that simmered below the surface rose in Niall. "Let me do the hunting. All I ask is that you be my second. There's no stigma to that—or very little."

"There's no stigma to being with you at any time," Micheil said vehemently. "You're the one who's haunted by your past."

It was useless to argue with Micheil on this point. Niall could only be thankful that his friend would stand beside him when needed. But then, Micheil had always done so. Even as boys, when Niall had initiated an adventure that both knew they were forbidden to do, Micheil had gone along and stayed beside Niall throughout whatever punishment was meted out.

Rising, Niall said, "I'd best be getting back. With luck, Lady Fennimore has wrangled us invitations to something tonight and, with even more luck, Sculthorpe will be there." He threw several coins on the table. "I'll send word as soon as I learn more."

Niall arrived back at Lady Fennimore's to a scene of chaos. As late in the day as it was, that formidable lady had managed to coerce a modiste and a hair-dresser to her house.

Watching the tableau from the door to the room he shared with Fiona, Niall's mouth curled. Someone was spending the blunt, and he didn't think it was Mary, Countess of Colonsay. It was said that Macfie had mortgaged himself and his land to the hilt to save his clan from starvation.

Fiona stood in the center of the bustle with only a transparent chemise and a drape of sapphire-blue silk over her pantaloons for modesty. Standing tall and proud, she held an allure for him that he couldn't deny. Niall feasted on the sight of her slender figure.

Her firm breasts strained against her chemise, their pink nipples visible through the thin fabric. He knew what they felt like in his mouth, their silken fullness satisfying and exciting. He knew how they felt pressed to his chest as he made love to her.

Her narrow hips and long, slender thighs encased in pantaloons beckoned his sight lower. The feel of her hips pressed to his, her legs wrapped around him, pulling him into her . . . He became turgid.

"You're back at last," Lady Fennimore said, moving around Fiona and shattering Niall's fantasy.

Only then did Niall realize that a man stood behind Fiona, his fingers buried in her rich copper tresses. His reaction was immediate and primordial. He closed the distance and yanked the man away.

"What do you think you're doing?" he demanded in a dangerous voice.

A good foot shorter than Niall, the man stared up at him with his mouth agape. "Ahem, ah . . . that is

. . . I was . . . was attempting to curl her ladyship's hair."

Niall released the man instantly, self-derision twisting his mouth. What had come over him? He was acting the fool over her for all the world to see. It had to end.

"Don't let me stop you," he said curtly, going to the bed and flinging himself down on it.

Through hooded eyes he watched their ministrations to his wife. Fiona, her face a polite mask, did as told. She turned one way, then another. Meanwhile, the modiste draped and pinned the material. The hairdresser once more buried his fingers in Fiona's hair and tried various styles.

By the time they were done, Niall was so aroused he could have thrown her on the floor and taken her without thought. He wanted to sample the curves the modiste had been fitting so precisely. He wanted to feel the silken strands the hairdresser had been shaping. But most of all, he wanted to lose himself in the ecstasy of her body. He wanted to forget everything but the feel of her around him and the explosion of desire as their bodies came together.

"There," Lady Fennimore declared, satisfied. "Now she's ready. I only hope you have suitable clothing," she added, glancing at Niall.

Once again, Niall found himself having to focus on Fiona's godmother when what he wanted was Fiona. He could only be grateful to the woman. She was saving him from breaking his vow not to make love to his wife, but he still ached with frustration.

"What do I need 'suitable clothing' for, if I may be

so bold as to ask?" Wry amusement with himself and the situation flavored his words.

"Why the musicale we've been invited to this evening." She frowned at him. "Weren't you here when we talked about it?"

Niall shook his head. He could see that dealing with Lady Fennimore would be on her terms. "No, I wasn't. The only presentable clothing I have is what I got married in, and it'll have to be cleaned and pressed."

"Why didn't you say so?" She clapped her hands together briskly. "Where's Ben when I need him? Better yet," she said, eyeing a serving girl. "Jane, take Mr. Currie's clothing and see that it's ready by nine."

"Yes, milady," the girl said, curtsying.

Lady Fennimore continued. "Fiona, turn around so I can see how the demi-train drapes. Lovely, lovely." She breathed a satisfied sigh when Fiona did as directed. "Don't you think the blue sets her eyes off to perfection?" She turned her attention once more to Niall.

He scowled at the picture his wife made. Niall knew he had to break her hold on him. "Who's money are you spending so recklessly?"

"Well, I never!" Lady Fennimore gasped indignantly. "You ill-mannered man. It's my money that's being spent—not yours. Fiona is my only godchild and will inherit my not inconsiderable fortune, so you may keep your unkind remarks to yourself."

Fiona struggled not to show how his words had hurt. She should have expected them. He'd done everything he could to show her he didn't want this marriage; why should she have expected him to like her transformation? But that didn't mean she would let him go unscathed.

"Don't you feel much better having that question answered?" Fiona asked, her gaze critical.

Instead of replying, he got off the bed and sauntered to his bag from which he took the jacket and breeches he'd worn for their wedding. "Your maid forgot these," he said, handing them to Lady Fennimore, who took them with a sniff.

As soon as her godmother was out of the room, Fiona wearily ran her fingers through the curls the hairdresser had spent over an hour arranging. It was an effort to keep her shoulders from sagging.

"Please leave her out of our battle, Niall. She's an old woman who takes pleasure in clothing and society. There's nothing wrong with that and she means no harm. Quite the contrary. She hopes to mend the damage we've done to my reputation by having it put about that we married so hastily because of love." Her mouth twisted cynically on the word.

His eyes told her nothing of his feelings and her gift was silent. But she couldn't let him take his frustration and anger out on Lady Fennimore.

"You're right," he finally said. "I'll apologize to her at dinner."

"Then you'd best practice," she said tartly, "for dinner starts in fifteen minutes. You'll have to change afterward."

Good to his word, Niall apologized the first thing. Taking Lady Fennimore's plump hand in one of his, he lifted it for a light kiss. "Please accept my apologies, my lady. I had no right taking my anger out on you. None of this is your fault."

She blushed and dimpled like a young miss just out of the schoolroom. It was completely out of character with the picture he'd formed of her. She went into dinner on his arm.

The hearty meal was cut short precisely at eight when Lady Fennimore said, "We'd best go or we'll be later than fashionable." When they rose, Niall noticed that Fiona's mother didn't call for her cape. He cocked a brow at Fiona, who merely shrugged.

Once they were settled in the carriage, Niall asked, "Why isn't the countess coming with us?"

Lady Fennimore answered, "Mary isn't feeling well. She arrived just before the two of you and is tired from her trip. Colonsay, while a lovely island, is very out of the way. No roads and no place to sleep."

Niall exchanged a glance with Fiona in the flickering yellow light from the carriage lantern. They were both well aware of the discomforts of traveling near Colonsay.

When they pulled up at the house where the musicale was to be held, Niall was grateful to leave the confines of the carriage that had put him too close to Fiona. Her thigh had pressed his the entire journey and created havoc with his control.

Inside, Lady Fennimore introduced them to everyone she could find. After a while, Niall turned to Fiona and asked, "Is there anyone she doesn't know?"

She smiled at him, but he noticed there were lines under her eyes that weren't normally there. She was tired.

"My godmother has lived in Edinburgh most of her life. She thrives on the interaction, so I guess the answer to your question is no."

"Would you like some punch?" Niall asked, taking her arm and trying to guide her past a large man who was entertaining two young ladies with anecdotes of his last visit to the country. As they came abreast of the threesome, Niall felt Fiona stiffen. Her fingers dug into his upper arm.

Just as he was going to ask what was wrong, the small group turned their way. The man's gaze skimmed past Niall and stopped dead on Fiona.

"Fiona?" he asked in a deep voice with just a trace of burr. "Is that you?"

Niall stared the man down, one eyebrow cocked at the affected accent. The man's perusal traveled over Fiona in a proprietary manner that stiffened Niall's shoulders. He was swamped with the same overwhelming dislike that he'd felt earlier for the hairdresser. Once a fool, always a fool, Niall whipped himself mentally.

"Angus," Fiona said softly, her face void of color.

"Do you know this man?" Niall asked, keeping his voice calm when what he wanted to do was give the man a facer. But he knew the answer. This must be the Angus Magee Lady Fennimore had chuckled over.

"Yes," she said, color returning to her cheeks in an apricot blaze.

"Fiona, it is you," the man called Angus said, his voice warm and welcoming. The two young women he'd been regaling with tales frowned. One even went so far as to put her hand on his arm. He ignored her.

In two strides he had Fiona's hands in his and brought them to his lips. Her blush deepened when he kissed her fingers.

"How are you, Angus?"

"Well. And you? You disappeared before I could say goodbye."

Niall noticed Angus Magee's eyes were a dark, soulful brown and that Fiona seemed to be drowning in them. He felt like a dog competing for a bone, and a losing dog at that. It was a situation he loathed.

"The woman you are making love to with your eyes is my wife," Niall said pointedly. With an economy of motion, he disentangled Fiona's fingers from her previous lover's grasp.

Angus stepped back as though just coming to his senses. "Dreadfully sorry," he murmured, his gaze never leaving Fiona.

The girl who'd tried to hold onto him finally flounced away, her friend in her wake. Niall didn't blame them. The man was a flirt.

"Suzanne just left," Fiona said in a deceptively mild voice. "You'd better hurry, Angus, or you'll lose her and all her thousands."

He turned brick-red. His eyes lost their melting soulfulness. "You always had a sharp tongue, Fiona. I see it hasn't changed."

This time she smiled roguishly at him. "Just as you always had a wandering eye, constantly searching for the latest heiress. Well, I wasn't one three months ago and I'm not one now. So you're only wasting your time."

Without another word, he turned and stalked off.

Niall watched him go. "Why did you tell him you're not an heiress? Lady Fennimore plans to leave her wealth to you."

Fiona sighed and shook her head. "Because that's all Angus wants. A wife with deep purse-strings. And three months ago I didn't know I was her heir."

Niall's eyes narrowed as the import of her words sank in. "Meaning that if you'd known three months ago it would have made a difference."

"Probably," she said, her mouth drooping at the corners. "Thank goodness I didn't know. I'd be his wife now."

The knowledge that she'd felt strongly about another man—possibly loved him—ate at Niall. His reaction was irrational, but knowing that didn't ease the knot in his gut or the tightness in his shoulders.

When he spoke, he was harsher than he'd intended. "Are you ready to go now? Your former lover appears to be engrossed with his latest paramour."

Taken aback by Niall's sharp words, Fiona nodded. Was this another sign of jealousy? Her mouth crooked downward. If it were, it did her no good. He might lash out when another man paid her attention, but he hadn't committed himself to her.

Perhaps he never would.

Chapter Sixteen

Fiona searched for a place to sit. They'd been at this rout for at least an hour. The people were boring, the food mediocre, and her feet ached beyond belief.

This was their fifth day in Edinburgh and their fifth social function. Everything was on a smaller scale then London, but with the holidays approaching there was no lack of entertainment. Her godmother had gotten them entrée everywhere, but thus far Niall hadn't located Sculthorpe.

Finding a seat at last, she sank gratefully onto it. Her feet seemed to swell easily now. Slipping off one velvet slipper, she wriggled her toes and thought it was ecstasy.

"Here you are, Fiona," a rich masculine voice said, preceding Angus Magee's appearance around a Grecian column. "May I join you?"

Fiona surreptitiously stuffed her still-aching foot back into its shoe and managed a smile. She was mildly surprised that he'd seek her out after their last meeting. "If you wish."

As he made himself comfortable by spreading his coattails to keep from wrinkling them when he sat down, she studied him. It was funny how her heart no longer pounded when he was near, yet he was as breathtakingly handsome as ever. His dark brown hair was as thick and wavy as it had ever been. His eyes were as soulful and his lips as fully sensual. But he did nothing for her.

"Has your husband deserted you?"

Fiona sensed undercurrents and paused to see if it were her gift. No, just the tenor of Angus' voice and the angle at which he held his head. He'd always cocked it to one side when something bothered him.

"Niall is playing cards, something you are very familiar with."

"Most men are," he said, leaning forward to murmur in her ear. "But I never left you when I was your escort."

She leaned away from him, uncomfortable with his proximity. "No. Only when it mattered."

His mouth turned down as though she'd wounded him. "You knew I needed to marry an heiress. I never kept that from you."

He was still the same Angus. "No, not after you found out I wasn't one."

"Well, you are an earl's daughter. It stood to reason that you'd inherit wealth. I only did what any man would do who had estates to put in order and no money to do it with." His eyes glowed with sincerity. "And I cared for you. You'll never know how hard it was for me to turn to someone else."

Looking at him, seeing the earnestness he was so

good at projecting, Fiona couldn't help believing him. Perhaps she'd always sensed that he truly cared for her, and it was that instinctive knowledge that had sent her heading back to Edinburgh to win him over a month ago.

"And now I'm married," she murmured.

She almost wished things had turned out differently. Angus was simple and her feelings for him had been uncomplicated. With Niall, nothing was smooth and it was even less certain. Her love for him was mixed up with the child she carried and her determination to keep her husband from killing her brother. It was so confusing.

Angus took one of her hands. "That's why I'm here. There are ugly rumors going around about your husband."

Fiona considered taking her hand back, but found that the warmth of his fingers felt unusually good "What type of rumors?"

He glanced around to make sure no one was close enough to hear. "That he's a murderer."

Bald words to describe a despicable act. Were they talking about the woman or Winter? she wondered. It didn't matter. Her hackles rose. "That's a lie."

Angus shrugged, but the casual act was belied by his grip tightening around her. "Is it? I've heard that even his father has disowned him."

Anger for Niall's sake boiled up in Fiona. "His father is a fool. Niall could no more murder than you or I." She tried to stand, determined to go to Niall, but Angus wouldn't release her. "Is there more?"

"Be careful, Fiona. They say there was a woman in

America, and more recently a man. A man your husband challenged to a duel."

They knew about both of them. News traveled faster than the crow flew. "Gossip for small minds," she said, twisting her fingers free. In spite of her temper, she managed to smile halfheartedly at Angus. "Thank you for telling me."

He stood with her. "We might have had our differences, Fiona, but I don't want to see you hurt."

Meanwhile, Niall, disgusted with his bad luck at cards and in search of his wife to take her home, rounded the column in time to see Angus Magee kiss Fiona's wrist. It was an intimate gesture that bespoke familiarity.

In a low, dangerous voice, Niall said, "My second will call on yours tomorrow, Magee."

Fiona gasped and yanked her hand away. The righteous anger she'd felt on Niall's behalf was immediately turned on him. "Is that your answer to everything?"

Angus, his face paling, said, "As you wish, but I meant her no harm and you no offense."

Niall clenched his fists. This man affected him in violent ways. Every time he laid eyes on Angus Magee he wanted to flatten him. He knew it was because Fiona had once loved this man and might turn to Angus after their marriage was annulled. But knowing didn't lessen his narrow-eyed fury. His shoulders bunched.

"Don't be fools." Fiona stepped between the two men and turned furiously on her husband. "Angus warned me that there are rumors circulating about you—that you're a murderer. Is that the act of a man who's trying to seduce your wife?"

Niall raised one black brow. "Sounds like a good place to start."

"You're right about that," Angus said, "but wrong about my goal. The truth of the matter is that I came to warn Fiona about you. I didn't know she already knew, and I wanted her to be on her guard."

Niall glared at him, both disliking him and admiring his honesty. Angus Magee wasn't the gutless fortune hunter he'd thought. Which only made Angus more likely to get Fiona in the end, after Niall had their marriage annulled. It didn't make Niall happy. His shoulders began to ache.

"Now that you know Angus' reason for seeking me," Fiona said, jutting her chin out, "I expect you to retract that challenge."

Niall looked at her, noting her flashing eyes and heaving bosom. He glanced at Angus Magee, who'd regained his color and nonchalance. Niall had made a fool of himself over her once again.

With a curt bow, he said, "My apologies. I acted in haste because of your past relationship."

Before Angus could take offense at the shortness of the apology, Fiona yanked Niall's arm. "It's time we left."

He followed her, having intended to leave from the start. As they threaded their way through the people, Niall noticed several looking at them. Earlier in the evening he'd dismissed the glances as curiosity about a couple reputed to have married for love—a commodity not often come by in aristocratic circles. Now he realized it was morbid interest in a man convicted of murdering a prostitute and the woman who'd dared to marry him.

Damn them.

He reached for Fiona's hand and put it on his arm, drawing her close. She glanced at him, then around the room. He knew the instant she realized what was going on. Her fingers dug into his arm. But she held her head proudly.

"There's Lady Fennimore," she said in a loud, clear voice, every inch an earl's daughter.

Niall guided her toward her godmother, admiration for his wife growing with every step. She was a brave and remarkable woman.

"La, Fiona. Niall," Lady Fennimore said, waving an ornately painted fan in front of her flushed face. "Have you met Lord and Lady Simmons?" Before Niall could say no, she rushed on, "I didn't think so."

Lady Fennimore made the introductions. Lord and Lady Simmons nodded, their smiles polite but not welcoming.

"Please excuse us," Niall broke in on the trivialities, "but Fiona and I were on our way home. We came to ask if we could borrow your coach, Lady Fennimore, and send it back for you."

Lady Fennimore continued to fan herself as if it were the middle of July and sweltering instead of early November and cold. "Of course. Of course. Just tell Jack to come back."

"Thank you." Niall bowed with courtly flourish, his sardonic gaze resting briefly on Lord and Lady Simmons. A criminal he might be, but he was also the son of a Highland chief with a heritage descending from Irish royalty.

Escorting Fiona to the door, Niall wondered if Lady Fennimore knew what was being said. So no one could hear, he asked, "Does she know?"

"She does," Fiona whispered. "She never fans herself unless she's upset over something."

That moment several couples passed by them. Fiona nodded and smiled. Niall gave them a cool stretching of lips. The women in the group tittered, their eyes moving avidly over Niall. His mouth curled in disdain as he purposely looked away.

It was the cut direct and the women's titters turned to gasps of outrage. On his arm, Fiona giggled.

"Serves those hussies right. While they thought you were at their mercy, they deigned to examine you. When you fought back, they didn't know how to handle it."

She fairly flounced at his side. Niall cut her a sideways glance. "How would you have behaved?"

They were outside now and the cold November air whipped at their cloaks. Fiona pulled hers tightly around herself and huddled against him for warmth as she considered her answer.

"First, I wouldn't have stared. But if I had so forgot myself as to be that rude, I wouldn't have gotten angry when you cut me. Instead, I very likely would have confronted you with the rumor." She grinned wryly. "I have a bad habit of facing things head-on. It comes of having the sight and knowing up front that something is going to happen. I learned not to avoid it."

"You're no shrinking violet," he said, waving to the

coachman, who was just pulling the carriage to a stop. "Don't bother," he added when the postilion prepared to jump down and open the door.

Niall stepped to the curb and opened the door. Fiona was as light as thistledown when he handed her in. He noted, with wry amusement, that she sat on the side of the coach with her back to the driver. It was the worst position.

"Are you afraid I might sit beside you?" he queried, taking a seat opposite her and relaxing back into the pale pink squabs. Lady Fennimore had a definite taste for the color.

Fiona, having been afraid of just that, decided to face it head-on. "Yes."

"You're right to have been afraid," he said darkly.

Fiona's heart skipped a beat. She didn't know whether to be glad or sad that she'd avoided an opportunity to be close to him. He hadn't touched her since their wedding night, and as far as she knew he was still bent on annulling their marriage. She, on the other hand, was as positive that she was pregnant as she could be without showing. Her menses were five weeks late and she'd never been late before.

As it was, the interior of the vehicle was barely lit by one lone lantern, its yellow circle almost exclusively on the door. She and Niall sat in shadows.

Since he sat across from her, she could feel the heat from his legs. He brushed her whenever the coach swayed, which was often enough on the rough road. Musk and sandalwood, masculine scents she associated with him, were strong in her nostrils.

Yes, she'd made a mistake to sit here.

When they arrived at Lady Fennimore's, Fiona waited for Niall to offer her help. He did it with an easy show of grace. It was obvious to her that he wasn't bothered by her proximity the way she was by his.

"Thank you," she muttered when he handed her down.

He released her hand as soon as she was securely on the ground. Disappointment pursed her mouth. But when she glanced up at him, his eyes were a bright malachite with the sheen she associated with desire. Instead of looking away, as she expected him to, he continued to study her upturned face.

Everything around her ceased to exist except for Niall. The cold wind that cut through her clothes to her very bones disappeared. The servants were gone, the coach having been taken to the stables and the front door remaining unopened. Only the two of them—husband and wife—stood on the sidewalk.

The sickle-shaped moon cast its silver glow on them, showing her the sharpness of his face. His eyes darkened, their depths taking on a haunted look. She reached for him, wanting to ease the pain etched in lines around his mouth.

He stepped back. She let her hand drop, the green leather of her glove a streak in the silver moonlight.

"It won't work, Fiona," he said softly. "I want you. I want you so badly it's an ache worse than any I ever received in Newgate. But I won't love you. I won't."

Before she could reply, he strode up the stairs. Instead of knocking, he opened the door himself with a violent push that told her more clearly than any words just how upset he was.

A tiny smile started at the corners of her mouth. As it widened, her heart warmed. He wanted her. In spite of himself, he wanted her. If she persevered, he would love her, too. He had to, or her heart would break.

Slowly, her feet still aching but the pain no longer of real importance, she mounted the steps he'd taken two at a time. Reaching the door, she entered the welcoming light of the foyer. Niall had disappeared.

Her smiled widened. It would be an interesting night.

Fiona made her way leisurely up the stairs and down the hallway to the pink-and-lavender room she shared with her husband. Entering, she noticed that no candles were lit. For a second, she thought he wasn't there, that he'd gone somewhere else. Then she saw him at the chaise by the window—his "bed."

Since her wedding night, she'd been circumspect, his warning about leaving her always uppermost in her mind. But tonight she sensed that he was weak and, if nothing else, she could make him suffer a little bit for all he'd put her through.

Now she smiled broadly. Either of her brothers could have warned Niall had they been present. As it was, he must have sensed something wrong because he stopped his undressing to scowl at her. Fiona ignored him and lit several candles.

"What are you doing?" he asked, his voice flat.

"What does it look like?" she retorted innocently. "I need light by which to undress. I need to see to brush my hair."

She met his frown with a guileless look. Before he could turn his back to her, she started undoing the hooks of her bodice. When she'd gotten as far as she could, she asked, "Will you please do the rest?"

Niall, sitting on the chaise in his shirt and breeches, didn't move. "Call your maid."

"I don't have one. I've been sharing Mama's, and Betsy is asleep by now." She reached up and pulled the pins from her hair so that red waves tumbled down to her shoulders. "Surely, you don't want me to wake the poor woman simply because you're scared to come over here and undo the rest of my bodice."

It was a goad she knew he couldn't resist. It was a direct aspersion on his self-control.

He rose from the chaise in one long, smooth flow of muscle and stalked toward her. "You're playing with fire, little girl."

Excitement pumped the blood through Fiona's limbs so that she felt instantly hot. "Am I?" she asked, turning away from him. "I don't think so."

She heard his snort with a pleasurable rush of success. The next second his fingers were touching her back as he undid her gown. He moved with swift, sure speed. When the last hook was loose, Fiona let her arms fall to her sides so that the bodice of her dress slid to her waist. A wiggle, and the material puddled on the floor in a ripple of green muslin.

She stepped daintily out and picked up the garment. Carefully, she draped it over a chair before checking to see if Niall were watching her. He was.

He stood with his fists clenched at his side, his jaw

rigid. "Fiona, I've had all I'm going to take. Don't tempt me or I'll leave."

Fiona paused in the act of unlacing the small corset she used more for support of her full breasts than to reduce her waist. Her eyes met his. He meant what he said.

With a sigh of resignation, Fiona stopped. But she'd try again another day. She had too much at stake not to.

Niall scowled into his cup of steaming coffee, remembering how Fiona had teased him the night before. It was becoming harder and harder to deny the attraction between them, particularly when she so blatantly offered herself to him.

His scowl deepened. If only he'd met her before Newgate. But he was fatalistic enough to admit that if he hadn't gone to jail and thus been seeking revenge from her brother, he would never have met her. That was fate. And now his fate was to challenge and kill Sculthorpe and then Fiona's brother, Duncan.

His eyes narrowed as he stared across the smoky room of the coffeehouse to where Sculthorpe sat at a table talking with several men.

"Have you decided not to do it?" Micheil asked, his low voice intruding on Niall's dark thoughts.

Instead of answering, Niall kept his attention on Sculthorpe. The man had been hard to track down. He hadn't gone about in society as Niall had expected. Neither had he been in Edinburgh until recently.

Niall took a sip of his drink. "I haven't changed my

mind." He took another sip. If he kept this up, he'd begin to like the bitter brew.

Niall looked at his friend. Gone was the worry Micheil had once shown when confronted with Niall's desire for revenge. He almost looked elated.

"Then what are you waiting for?"

His blue eyes shone with an emotion Niall couldn't name. In a woman he would have called it jealousy. In Micheil, he didn't know what it was.

In a rush of determination, Niall stood, nearly knocking his chair backward in the process. Sculthorpe had been his friend once. That was before the court-martial board. Sculthorpe had voted for his condemnation just as the other two had. Now, the memory of that betrayal drove Niall on.

"Sculthorpe," Niall said, hovering over the table where his adversary sat with three other men. "Remember me?"

Sculthorpe rose slowly to his feet. He stood as tall as Niall. His hair was brown, his eyes hazel. He'd put on weight since his time in the Navy, and his stomach hung over his breeches. But he met Niall's eyes squarely.

"Niall Currie," he said, his voice even. "I'd heard you were in town."

"After three years in Newgate."

Sculthorpe nodded. "I don't imagine it was pleasant."

"I've a score to settle with you," Niall said quietly, wondering if Sculthorpe would refuse as Winter had. That thought brought back what had happened to Winter, making Niall's stomach churn. He told himself it was a coincidence, otherwise Micheil would have heard from the Bow Street runner by now.

"You want to challenge me to a duel," Sculthorpe said, his fingers drumming lightly on the table he stood beside. "I've been expecting it. Winter sent me a message—before he was killed."

He should have anticipated that, Niall told himself, but he hadn't. "That's right. Name your weapon."

"Pistols."

Niall smiled, a predatory stretching of his lips. "You were a crack shot."

"I still am," Sculthorpe said calmly. "Mackinsay here," he gestured to the burly man beside him, "will be my second."

"Micheil Alpin will be mine."

Sculthorpe's gaze traveled past Niall's shoulder to Micheil. "Hello, Alpin. Still standing with him, I see." His hazel eyes returned to Niall. "He always thought you were innocent no matter what the evidence said to the contrary."

Niall's smiled widened. "Unlike some others."

Sculthorpe shrugged. "I did what I had to do. You should understand that."

"I was innocent."

"The evidence said differently."

Around them was a stirring as the other patrons became aware of the tableau. Niall realized numerous sets of eyes were on him that he hadn't felt before. As in London, there would be plenty of witnesses to this challenge.

Micheil stepped between him and Sculthorpe to address Mackinsay. "I'll call on you tomorrow."

Niall was glad of the interruption. Now that he'd done what he'd set out to do, he felt deflated. There was none of the exhilaration he'd experienced with Winter. And he still had to face Fiona.

Turning abruptly, he strode into the cold, damp afternoon. All he wanted was to get away. He would meet Sculthorpe because he had to. It was the only way to avenge his name and the wrong done to him.

But it was a shock to him to realize that he no longer relished fighting Sculthorpe. All his fury and hatred had paled, and in their place was an emptiness.

He shook his head and picked up speed so that he was almost running. This was crazy. Of course he was eager to meet Sculthorpe. Sculthorpe had sat on the court-martial board that sent him to Newgate. He was going to make the bastard recant his vote of guilt or he was going to kill him.

It was as simple as that.

Chapter Seventeen

By the time Niall reached Lady Fennimore's he was in a foul mood. He no longer knew what he wanted . . . except . . .

Ben had the front door open before Niall could knock. It didn't improve his temper. "Thank you," he said automatically.

If Ben heard the surliness Niall did nothing to hide, he didn't show it. The perfect butler, he bowed and took Niall's hat and cane. Niall gave them over without a glance and headed up the stairs to the room he technically shared with Fiona. With any luck, she wouldn't be there.

His luck was out.

She sat in one of the three chairs the room boasted. It was done in lavender velvet and she'd pulled it close to the roaring fire. When she heard him, she looked up from the book she was reading. He recognized it as his copy of Robert Burns' poetry. He remembered her telling him on Skye that Burns was one of her favorite poets.

"Where have you been?" she asked, setting the book down on a nearby Queen Anne cherry table.

"Out."

He crossed the room to the chaise where he slept. Shrugging out of his jacket, he regretted coming here. He should have continued walking until he was calmer.

"Out where?" she persisted, her eyes narrowing as she studied him.

Fed up with her nagging and angry at his self-doubts, Niall said baldly, "Challenging Sculthorpe."

Fiona glared at him. In the two weeks they'd been here, she'd been lulled into complacency because Niall hadn't been able to find Sculthorpe. When she'd heard the man was out of the city, she'd allowed herself to cling to the hope that she would convince Niall to stop this quest for revenge before his second target got back into Edinburgh. Time had run out on her.

While she fumed, Niall retrieved his harp from its resting place beside his "bed." He acted as though his news had been nothing more than telling her about the weather. He made an elaborate show of tuning the bronze strings, then began to play "Sweet Barbara Allen." Immediately, he hit a wrong chord.

"Dammit," he said, setting the instrument down and glowering at her. "Get it over with."

Fiona, taken aback by his vehement attack, fell back against the cushions of the chair. She stuck her chin out. "Get what over with?" she goaded him.

He ranged about the room, then stopped abruptly, towering over her. "Your ranting and raving. Your arguments against this duel. All of it."

When her mouth fell open, Niall realized what he'd done. Once more he'd let her get to him and make him lose control of his temper. She hadn't even had to say a word. He'd imagined it all for her and when she hadn't complied, he'd demanded that she do so. She was driving him to Bedlam.

Fiona's mother chose that moment to barge into the room without knocking. Her face was contorted. Tears glistened in her eyes and stained her cheeks.

"Fiona," the countess said, her voice strained to the cracking point.

"Mama," Fiona cried, brushing past Niall, who stood frozen in place. Fiona reached her mother and flung her arms around her. "What's wrong?"

"I . . . oh, Fiona." The countess put her arms around her daughter and hung on.

Fiona's heart sped up. Something was dreadfully wrong. Her mother never acted like this. Her mother was the calmest, most level-headed person she knew. But right now, her beloved mama was coming apart in her arms.

"Mama," Fiona said, leading the countess to the bed. She sat down and pulled Mary Macfie beside her. "Take a deep breath and tell me what's gotten you so upset."

The woman's voice cracked with pain. "It's Julie." She stopped and took another deep breath. "Julie's dead. Both of them."

"What?" It couldn't be true.

"Julie's dead," her mama said. "So's Ian."

Grief contorted Fiona's features. Her chest was so tight it hurt. "Julie? Ian? Dead? But how?"

"Murdered. She was murdered clearing Ian's name."

The words were muted, but Niall heard them. Another person murdered. His gaze shot to Fiona. It was as he'd thought. She was in hell and trying desperately not to let it show. She wanted to protect her mother.

"What do you mean *clearing Ian's name?*" Fiona asked gently, the control it took her evident in the white knuckles of the hands that still held her mother. "I thought she and Ian were at Colonsay."

The countess pulled herself together with a visible effort that left her shaking, her face pale but composed. Niall admired her courage in the wake of such a loss. He knew from his time serving with Duncan that Ian was the oldest Macfie child, dishonored for not fighting in the Napoleonic Wars. Most Highlanders had gone to battle.

In a voice charged with emotion, Fiona's mother said, "Ian was called to France over a month ago. We were told he died there, betraying Britain to a French spy working for Napoleon's restoration. Julie followed him, determined to clear his name." She took a deep breath, her lip trembling. "I just received a letter from your father. She was killed."

"My God," Fiona whispered. "Why didn't you tell me?"

The countess gave her daughter a watery smile that didn't hide her pain. "You had trouble enough without adding to it yet. I'd planned to tell you soon."

"Oh, Mama, I'm sorry."

Fiona gathered her mother to her bosom. It was the

only comfort she could give. It was the only comfort she could receive.

Niall realized this was a very private moment for the women and knew he should leave them. But he couldn't desert Fiona. He had to be here in case she needed him. She was being so brave and putting her mother's grief before her own, but he knew hers would have to be dealt with sooner or later. He intended to be with her then.

He watched Fiona rock her mother, crooning all the time. She was the child, but she tried to comfort her parent. Niall had always known she was a strong woman, but he hadn't realized just how strong.

Both women wept silently, their torment too great for sound. Knowing the pain Fiona was going through wrenched Niall's heart. But it was nothing compared to the knowledge that he intended to deprive her of her last brother. He was going to cause her even greater pain.

For the first time since setting on his path of revenge, he began to doubt his reasons.

When her mother finally left, Fiona felt numb, drained of all emotion. She turned hollow eyes to Niall, who was waiting in the lavender-velvet chair where she had sat what seemed ages ago, although she knew it couldn't have been more than an hour. He'd sat calmly through the worst time of her life. And he planned to take her other brother from her.

Fury welled up inside her. "You're going to kill Duncan," she accused him. "And what for? Revenge."

Niall jumped from the chair and grabbed her up. Holding her tight, he sat down on the bed and cradled her to his chest. Her body shook against him; shudder after shudder swept over her.

Fiona pushed against his chest, hating the weakness in her that made his warmth welcome. "Damn you," she said, her voice hoarse from crying. "Damn you for what you're going to do."

Then she could fight him no longer. The strength left her limbs and she collapsed onto him. She had no energy to defy him. She had no energy to do anything but keep from falling apart.

Niall dug his fingers into her hair and held her face into his shoulder where her tears soaked his shirt. More than anything he wanted to comfort her, but all he could do was hold her. He felt helpless.

There'd been times before when he'd thought he was helpless, such as when he'd been unable to prove his innocence and been imprisoned. But he'd always been able to fight back. He'd used words in his own defense during the court-martial, and he'd fought with his fists when the Newgate guards had tried to sodomize him.

Now, with this woman sobbing in his arms, no amount of thinking or action on his part would comfort her. He couldn't ease the grief wracking her body because he couldn't bring back the people she loved who were dead. He couldn't do anything—except give her back her last brother.

"Fiona," he said softly, "I'm sorry. And . . . and I want you to know I won't challenge Duncan. I can't do that to you."

The words were easier to say than he'd imagined.

He'd thought revenge was all he lived for, but he'd been wrong. At least in this instance.

A tremor went through her, then she was still. She looked up at him, her eyes swollen, her mouth a red slash of pain. "What are you saying, Niall?"

"I'm saying I won't challenge Duncan. I can't bring back your other brother or your sister-in-law, but I *can* let Duncan live."

Bewilderment showed in her eyes. "Why? I don't understand."

Niall shrugged, keeping her close to him. "I don't understand, either, vixen. I only know I can't shoulder this hurt for you, and that knowledge is twisting my gut. But I can keep you from feeling it for Duncan."

She looked at him, still confused. "You're not going to challenge Duncan?"

He nodded.

Fiona was afraid to believe him. She was too accustomed to his lusting after Duncan's death. This change was too sudden. Particularly now, when her own emotions were so disjointed. It would be too easy for her to believe he was saying something when he actually wasn't. She would wait until she wasn't as bruised, then she'd ask him to tell her again.

His arms tightened around her. His fingers massaged her scalp, and his warmth penetrated the cold that had settled on her with her mama's news. She snuggled against him and greedily took the comfort and strength he offered, shutting everything else out of her mind.

Niall held her, not relaxing until her muscles softened into sleep. He hoped that for her sake she'd sleep till morning.

Much later, Lady Fennimore knocked softly on the door. She'd just left Mary and was worried about Fiona. When no one answered, she peered in. Fiona lay in her husband's arms, both of them asleep. A gentle smile curved that lady's full lips. Perhaps some good would come of this.

Fiona woke in Niall's arms.

With consciousness came memory. All the horror and agony of her mama's words rushed in on her. Grief shook her. But Niall was with her. Niall would protect her. It was unreasonable of her to think so; but instinctively she knew it was true, and instinct had always been her guide.

Opening her eyes, she sought his. His pupils were dilated, a ring of brilliant green cut through with black striations the only color showing in his eyes. His skin was drawn taut over high cheekbones.

He wanted her. She could sense it in the stillness that gripped his muscles. There was an urgency about him, an energy held in abeyance but no less powerful for that restraint. And God help her, she wanted him. She wanted to lose herself in the mindless ecstasy of his embrace.

And they both knew it.

"Fiona," he whispered.

She turned into him. "Please, Niall. Love me so that nothing else matters."

Her arms twined around his neck and pulled him down.

It was a hungry kiss, taking as much as it gave. Always before, passion and anger had mixed in their loving; this time it was passion and fire and a need to forget everything that had happened. Fiona opened to him with a need that was explosive in its intensity.

Niall teased her lips with his tongue. He nipped the corner of her mouth. He tantalized her. Shivers skated down her spine; her fingers threaded through his hair to keep him close.

She flicked her tongue at his, inviting him inside her warmth. He came. It was a surcease of pain. It was ecstasy.

Lying beside her, he ran his hand down her arm and back up to her shoulder. His fingers traced the line of her high-necked bodice and skimmed lower to graze her aching breasts. Through the yellow muslin, he rubbed her nipples with his fingers. Fiona arched into him.

She felt him smile against her lips. "What's amusing you?" she asked, her voice husky.

He pulled far enough away to gaze at her. "You. Only not amusing, pleasing. Your response. When I make love to you, I feel like an omnipotent god. Whatever I do, you enjoy it."

He bent and took her breast into his mouth, the material of her bodice a barrier that heightened Fiona's anticipation by hinting at the exquisite pleasure she knew his tongue would cause on her bare flesh. She moaned and begged for more.

When she was straining against him, he released her

breast from his hot mouth. She fell back, her eyes half-shut, her breath coming quickly. He rose above her and brushed her bosom with his chest. Clothed as they were, Fiona still found his action erotic.

Reaching up, she undid the buttons of his shirt, then pulled the material from the waist of his breeches and ran her hands underneath. Her fingers skimmed his flesh, rubbing over the corded muscles of his stomach and up his ribs to his nipples. She circled them with her palms, reveling in the wiry feel of his hair on her flesh.

He rose above her and pulled his shirt over his head. He flung it to the floor.

Fiona smiled. She felt sultry and wicked, the pain of her loss forgotten in the blazing inferno Niall ignited in her. She never wanted their lovemaking to end.

"Don't look at me that way, vixen," he murmured.

Her smile turned languid.

He groaned.

Rising up, she tried to undo the hooks at the back of her dress. His arms wrapped around her and his fingers replaced hers. Heat flowed from where his flesh touched her. She wasn't free a second too soon.

Sitting, she pushed her bodice down. She was lifting her hips when he said, "Stop."

She looked up at him. "What?"

His lips spread in a sensual grin. His gaze rested on her breasts where they poked through the thin material of her chemise. "I want to look at you," he said, his voice deep.

With one finger, he traced the rosy circle of her nipple. Tingles shot through her. Without conscious thought, she leaned back onto her elbows.

He followed her down. "You're beautiful," he said, taking her nipple into his mouth.

Lying on top of her, her suckled her. The fingers of one hand tangled in her hair, pulling it free of the pins. Still caressing her breast with his mouth, he used his hands to spread her hair on the pillow in a vibrant wave of fire. He left her long enough to admire his handiwork.

"Your hair has always made me think of copper. Now it's like molten strands of fire."

"Beautiful words," she murmured, trying to pull him back to her, "but I want action." Her roguish grin wasn't lost on him.

"Vixen," he murmured. "I'll give you action.

Living up to his words, he tugged her chemise off. When she lifted her hips, he pulled both her skirt and pantalets off in one smooth stroke. Only when hose was all she wore did he stop.

His gaze burned her as it followed the sweep of his hands. The calluses on his palms were deliciously rough against the sensitive skin of her thighs as he stroked down her legs. With exquisite slowness, he eased his fingers under her left stocking and started rolling it down her calf. His hands lingered on her ankles before slipping the gossamer silk off her arched foot.

When he did the same to her right stocking, he ran the tip of his tongue along the arch of her foot and up to her ankle. There he paused to look at her. Sensing him watching her reaction, Fiona blushed, but she returned his heated gaze.

"I'm going to love you until you beg me to stop," he promised.

Fiona felt her stomach quiver with anticipation. When his tongue continued up the inside of her calf to her inner thigh, she bit her tongue to keep from screaming. When he rose still higher, she gave up.

"Niall," she gasped. Her fingers locked into his hair and she yanked him up and away from her.

His eyes were nearly black. His mouth was slick. "Let go, Vixen," he said softly. "You've enjoyed this before."

Warmth curled deep inside her. Yes, she'd enjoyed this before. With a sigh of resignation, she released him. He slid down between her legs, only instead of staying on the bed, he slipped to his knees on the floor beside it. He took her with him so that she lay with her back on the mattress and her legs draped over his shoulders.

Startled, she raised up on her elbows.

"It's all right," he murmured, not taking his sight from the copper nest he intended to plunder. "Just relax, Fiona."

A shudder ripped through her. "That's easy for you to say," she gasped as his tongue touched her. "You're . . . not prone on . . ." another shudder gripped her ". . . this bed." Her body bucked. "Oh, Niall!"

Niall exulted in her shocked, wide-eyed stare, even though he knew she wasn't seeing anything. She was experiencing completely what he was doing to her. He inhaled the musky scent of her womanliness as he strained against the confines of his breeches. He smiled ruefully. He should have gotten out of them before starting this, but he hadn't anticipated this intense a response this quickly.

He was a fool. She always affected him like this.

Kneeling between her satiny thighs, he delighted in her response to his touch. He slicked his tongue along the beads of moisture she weeped and inserted his fingers. She clenched him so tightly, he groaned with arousal—hard and swift and painful.

If he weren't careful, he'd climax before he even undressed himself. He paused to give himself a respite to regain control.

"Niall?"

Her voice was raspy, her fingers dug into his shoulders. It was an intensely satisfying realization that this woman, who'd turned his world upside-down, was as out of control as he.

"Shh," he reassured her. "I'm not going to stop."

And he didn't. With all the skill he had, with every ounce of control he could muster, he made love to her with his mouth and his fingers. He was rewarded by her heavy breathing and the tiny gasps that escaped her swollen lips with each stroke of his tongue or twist of his fingers.

"Niall, oh, Niall."

Her moans rent the heated air of the room. Her body heaved beneath him. It was too much.

Jerking to his feet, Niall ripped the button from his breeches. He had to free himself or die of the need. He sprang to her, turgid and pulsing, ready to plunder the depths he'd been tasting.

Spreading her legs wider, he pulled her to the edge of the bed. Her eyes opened, their slumberous depths a molten blue. He knew she barely registered the change, so far gone in her own pleasure had he taken her. It gave him an incredible surge of exultation to know he could do that to her. He throbbed anew with that knowledge.

Then he could hold back no longer. With one sure thrust, he threw his head back and took her.

He filled her completely. But it wasn't enough. Grabbing her hips, he pulled her to him and anchored her there as he withdrew only to plunge in again.

His eyes shut and his breath came in ragged gulps as he pumped into her. He felt her tightening around him, then begin to spasm.

Her scream filled the air.

He rushed to the top and spilled over the precipice. He exploded inside her, burning to ashes.

He'd taken her and she had welcomed him. She was his.

Later, entangled in the covers for warmth against the cool air of the late afternoon, Fiona forced her eyes to open. Niall lay beside her, the tense lines of his face relaxed. As she watched him, his eyes opened to show her irises the color of malachite. Then he smiled.

It was a slow, lazy action. His teeth gleamed white; and if she looked hard enough, she could see the dimple that was just a hint in his cheek. It was exquisitely beautiful to her because she so rarely saw it.

She took his hands from where they still cupped her engorged breasts and brought them to her face. Gently, reverently, she kissed the scars on his wrists where he'd worn the prison irons for three years.

Looking at him, she whispered, "I love you."

His gut knotted. Threading his fingers into the silken strands of her hair, he brushed the curls back from her face. In the aquamarine depths of her eyes, he saw her sincerity.

He was free to love her now. With his promise to her that he wouldn't fight Duncan, he could love her all he wanted. He could give her his baby. He could make a life for himself with her.

"I love you, too," he murmured, his mouth against hers. "I think I've always loved you."

Chapter Eighteen

He loved her.

Fiona gazed at Niall in wonder. Her hope had been fulfilled. She'd taken the risk of staying with him and it had been worth it. She snuggled closer to him, contentment easing some of the pain that still shrouded her.

But still a doubt niggled at her. Tracing the fullness of his lower lip with her finger, she asked, "Are you sure?"

His mouth quirked into a grin. "Will you always doubt me? Of course I'm sure or I wouldn't have said so."

She released the sigh and worry she'd unconsciously held. "Then you really meant it when you said you wouldn't challenge Duncan? You said it because you love me?"

His eyes narrowed. "I've never lied to you, Fiona."

He was affronted by her doubt. It was reassuring.

Catching the finger that still rimmed his mouth, he held it prisoner. "I only hope you don't live to regret marrying me. It won't be easy wed to a man convicted of one murder and under suspicion for another."

She stretched up and kissed his mouth. "Hush. As long as you love me, I won't regret this."

He let her hand go to circle her waist with his arm. Cupping her to his growing hardness, he murmured, "Prove it to me, vixen."

Fiona willingly obliged.

The next couple of days were difficult. Word was officially put about regarding the death of Fiona's brother Ian and his wife Julie. Thankfully, Ian's name had been cleared, and he and his wife were declared heroes in Britain's fight against France. However, it didn't ease Fiona's grief.

It was the third day after the news, and Fiona sat on the settee in her godmother's parlor smiling wanly at the second set of callers that day. Niall stood behind her, a dark, brooding presence. He hadn't left her side since learning of her brother's death.

His strength and love were what kept her going. She'd sent her mama to bed with laudanum long ago. The day after tomorrow Mary Macfie was returning to Colonsay and the comfort of her beloved husband. Having Niall, Fiona finally realized how much support and care her parents gave to one another.

"My dear Lady Fiona," gushed the stout, middle-aged woman who'd come calling on the pretext of being one of Lady Fennimore's friends. Fiona knew the woman was morbidly curious. "How terrible this has all been for you. And your dear mother, the count-

ess." Her head, covered in silver curls and crowned
with a maroon turban boasting six ostrich feathers,
bobbed like a bird pecking at seeds.

Fiona's smile faltered. She actively disliked this
woman. "Death is never easy."

"So true, so true," she burbled. Her bright bird-eyes
skittered to where Niall stood and just as quickly
darted away. Rouge stood in stark relief on her plump
cheeks.

Fiona knew the woman was suddenly remembering
the rumors about Niall. The obvious discomfort she
felt gave Fiona a spurt of satisfaction. It served the
voyeuristic old crow right.

Sitting beside the woman, his long skinny legs
drawn up nearly to his chest, her son smiled politely,
obviously not interested in the death of Fiona's family
members. His eyes kept straying speculatively to Niall.
But as soon as Niall returned the inspection, the man
looked away. It was as though he were viewing a dangerous animal and didn't want the creature to consider
jumping out of its cage and attacking. Yet the knowledge that it might excited him. Fiona could see it in the
flush that rode his narrow face.

Niall, watching the tableau through hooded eyes,
considered snarling to see the popinjay jump, but one
glance at Fiona's strained countenance told him it
wouldn't be a good idea. However, he refused to stand
passively by any longer and let these thoughtless visi-
tors torture her.

In one powerful surge of muscles, he moved around
her chair. "I'm sure you'll understand if I insist on my

wife's resting. It's been forty minutes as it is, and she's not feeling well."

Pointedly he looked at the woman, who had the grace to blush, and then at her son, who jumped to his feet. Niall suppressed a smile as he watched them scurry from the room, mumbling polite apologies. The door hadn't closed behind them before he scooped Fiona up.

"Niall," she gasped, her fingers grasping his coat's lapels. "What are you doing?"

His arms tightened around her. "Taking you to our room to rest."

"I don't need to," she said, but he was already moving to the door.

He cocked one black brow. "Do you want to make me into a liar?"

She smiled up at him and allowed herself to relax into his embrace. "No, love."

He opened the drawing room door and strode into the hall just as Ben, Lady Fennimore's aged butler, closed the front door behind the unwelcomed guests.

"Ben," Niall said, "see that Lady Fiona and I aren't disturbed."

Without waiting for an answer, Niall mounted the stairs two at a time. Fiona clung to him, her cheeks blazing. His words would have Ben thinking they were making love, something they'd done every afternoon and every night since he'd confessed his love.

Surreptitiously, she looked up at his face. Determination etched lines around his mouth. As though he felt her watching him, he glanced down at her. There was a tenderness in his eyes that she was still not completely used to seeing. Ever since the news of her sister-in-law and brother's deaths, Niall had treated her like a cherished treasure.

It warmed her. For awhile, the cold, harsh man she'd married was gone. In his place was the man she knew Niall could be. Now, if only she could make him call off his duel with Sculthorpe.

Inside their room, Niall put her gently on the bed. His arms lingered around her, causing Fiona's heart to speed up. She twined her hands around his neck and pulled him down to her.

Regretfully, Fiona roused herself and slipped from Niall's arms and out of bed to dress. She'd promised to help her mother pack this afternoon. Mama was returning to Colonsay tomorrow.

She gave Niall one last glance and smiled. He slept like a babe. His hair, black as ebony, fell across one eye. A very satisfied smile curled his full lips. Her grin widened. He'd made love to her this afternoon as though their lives depended on how totally they exploded. And when they were done the first time, he'd started again.

The urge to go back to him was immense. If she stayed much longer, she'd forget her promise to Mama and return to their bed. Shaking her head, she closed the door and headed down the hall. Ben caught her before she reached her mother's rooms.

"Lady Fiona," he said, huffing up to her, his old legs trembling from his exertions. "You've a visitor." He stopped talking to catch his breath.

Fiona waited patiently, sympathizing with his extremity. Ben had been with her godmother ever since she could remember. He wasn't young any more.

He took another deep breath. "The honorable Micheil Alpin is in the drawing room."

Fiona's face froze into a mask of polite acceptance. What did *he* want? No good. They'd been in Edinburgh almost two weeks, and this was the first time Micheil had called here.

Picking up her black skirts, Fiona reluctantly followed Ben through the hall and down the stairs. At the door to the drawing room, she stopped and took a deep breath.

"No need to announce me, Ben."

Without as much as a knock, Fiona opened the door and entered. Micheil was sitting in one of the pink-silk-covered chairs, his legs crossed at the knee and his arms folded across his chest. His face was pinched, his right eyelid twitched.

Bile rose in Fiona's throat.

"Hello, Micheil." She forced the words through stiff lips.

He jerked to his feet like a marionette whose strings had been pulled too hard. Whatever had brought him here, he was as nervous about it as she was loath to have him here.

He gave her a curt bow, little more than a nod of his head. "Is Niall here?"

She lifted her chin, wondering where this was going. "Yes. Did you want to see him instead? Ben is old and sometimes he doesn't hear well."

He shook his head, his wispy brown hair flying.

"No. You're the one. I was wondering if you know about Niall's latest duel?"

His tone was deceptively mild, belied by the air of tenseness that had settled over his body. Fiona's eyes narrowed.

"You mean Sculthorpe?"

His thin lips stretched into a sly smile. "So he has told you. Do you know it's set for tomorrow at dawn?"

Tomorrow. Dread ate at her, causing her fingers to tremble. During the last couple of days, she'd allowed herself to forget that Niall still intended to meet Sculthorpe. She hadn't wanted to remember, knowing she couldn't change his mind.

Tomorrow. He hadn't told her, but it would explain the desperation she'd sensed in him earlier.

Instead of answering Micheil's question, she asked, "Why are you telling me this? Are you hoping I can make him change his mind? And if so, why didn't you come sooner?" Her unease increased, and her temper began to simmer as she watched his eyes shift away from hers. "You've come to bait me. You don't care if Niall meets Sculthorpe. All you want is to come between Niall and me."

His feet shuffled on the thick, pink carpet. It told her louder than words that she was right.

His light tenor was unconcerned. "I came to warn you because I knew Niall wouldn't and I thought you should know. He may have married you, but he hasn't changed. He won't change. And when he's done with this duel, he'll challenge your brother and then this farce you call a marriage will be over."

Fiona's nails dug into her palms. She couldn't stop Niall from meeting Sculthorpe; she could only pray for his safety. But he had promised to leave Duncan alone.

"Niall has promised me that he won't challenge Duncan. Has he forgotten to tell you?" she asked, wanting to make it clear to this horrible man that he was not going to come between her and Niall.

"He's done what?" Fury twisted Micheil's face as he jumped up from the chair and stalked toward her. "You're lying. Niall would never agree to that. Macfie sent him to prison. Niall intends to kill the bastard."

Fiona stepped back at his approach. His complexion was livid; his hands were claws at his side. They reached for her. Her eyes shot wide open even as her vision blurred.

Vertigo took her and the nausea she'd felt earlier rushed back. She gagged, staggering away from him toward another chair where she could sit down. All the while, her gaze stayed riveted to his hands—red blood dripped from them, falling down to stain the pale, pink carpet beneath his elegantly shod feet.

It was her London vision all over again.

Perspiration beaded her forehead and sweat drenched her palms. The chair she was headed for bumped her knees and she sank gratefully into it, knowing that a second more and she would have collapsed to the floor.

"What's wrong with you?" His urgent voice penetrated the haze of horror surrounding her.

Before she realized what was happening, he was shaking her shoulder. Cold. Cold and hatred penetrated her flesh where he touched her. Bile rose to her mouth and choked her. She swallowed hard.

"Let go of me," she rasped, her throat burning. She shrank back into the chair. She tried to focus on his face. His eyes were slits.

"Are you with child?" His voice was soft. "Tell me," he demanded, his fingers tightening on her. "Did you get pregnant so that Niall can't leave you? That's something you'd do."

Fiona swallowed again, not answering. She sensed that if she told him she was pregnant, he'd kill her. Possibly right here—he was that mad.

It was all she could do not to throw up on him. She knew that if she looked to where he gripped her she'd see blood. It would be all over her shoulder and dripping down her bodice. She squeezed her eyes shut.

"Go away," she said in a hoarse whisper.

"Not until you tell me," he said, beginning to shake her.

The drawing room door slammed open. Niall's voice rose in a threat. "What the bloody hell's going on here?"

Relief washed over Fiona. Niall was here. He'd take care of everything.

"Release her," Niall said coldly.

When Micheil did so, Fiona sagged forward. Her stomach churned and her eyes burned so that she could barely keep them open.

"Niall," she whispered, one hand going out to him.

He was beside her instantly. Squatting, he wrapped his arms around her. Gratefully, she let her head sag to his shoulder. He was solid and warm.

"Are you sick?"

"She's pregnant," Micheil said from just behind Niall. "She won't admit it, but she is. There's no other reason for her to behave so strangely."

Over his shoulder, Niall gave Micheil a look that told him to shut up. "No, she's not. She's exhausted, or have you forgotten that in the last seven weeks she's been dragged all over Scotland and England and lost her brother?"

Affronted, Micheil stepped away, but did nothing to hide the hatred he felt for Fiona. It emanated from him in waves. Niall turned his attention back to his wife.

He smoothed the loose hair back from her forehead. He tilted her head away so that he could examine her. She was flushed and her eyes were glazed. He knew she'd had another vision, prompted by Micheil's presence. His heart began to pound painfully.

In a weary voice, he asked, "Why are you here, Micheil?" He heard his friend's feet scuffing across the carpet.

Defiantly, Micheil said, "I came to tell her about your upcoming duel with Sculthorpe."

Anger spurted through Niall's veins, tightening his muscles. It mixed with the growing dread over what Fiona would tell him when Micheil was finally gone. "Why, Micheil?"

Micheil sniffed, and favored Niall with a righteous glare. "Because I knew you wouldn't. I knew you'd decided to stay with her."

Weary beyond belief, sick to the core for the deterioration of his friend, Niall said softly, "You've done the damage you set out to do, Micheil. Now go away."

Not until he heard the door close behind Micheil did Niall speak to Fiona. "You saw something, didn't you?"

Fiona, still weak, nodded. "It was . . . it was the blood again. Only worse. So much more." Her mouth was dry, parched, and her head hurt. "He's killed, Niall. I know he has. And he's going to do it again."

Anxiety chewed at Niall. He didn't believe her. He didn't want to. Unable to remain squatting, needing to move, he picked her up and strode to the chaise. He sat down with her on his lap.

Tightening his arms around her, he said calmly, "Start from the beginning. There has to be another explanation."

Fiona took a deep breath and described all that she had seen. "It was the same as in London, only there was more blood." She wrapped her fingers in his shirt. "I tell you, he's a killer."

Unease made Niall's spine twitch. "It's not possible. Micheil has no reason to kill and no one to kill."

Fiona bit her lower lip. "He must. We just don't know what it is."

"He has none, I tell you," Niall said more vehemently. "He's the only son of a wealthy viscount. He's sought after by all the women, and the men admire him. He's educated, a good shot, and a good sport."

"A good sport?" She looked at him, disbelief in her eyes. "He's been abominable ever since I first laid eyes on him."

Niall frowned, his hands loosening their hold on

Fiona so he could run the fingers of one hand through his hair. "I can't explain that. It's not like him."

Fiona edged far enough away to see his face clearly. "Just as carrying tales isn't like him?"

She saw in Niall's eyes that her words had hit home. She felt his thighs bunch beneath her.

"I didn't want to worry you," he said stiffly. "And I don't understand why Micheil came to you with it, unless he hoped that by telling you he could prevent me from going through with it."

Fiona's mouth thinned. "He would do better to refuse to be your second. I think he came here hoping to cause trouble between us. That's what I've been telling you. Micheil isn't the wonderful, loyal friend you keep insisting he is. A friend wouldn't run to your wife with this story—no matter what his reasoning."

Niall stood abruptly, setting her down on the chaise. He paced to the window and flicked open the heavy, pink-velvet drapes. Outside snow was falling, and it was almost dark. He could barely make out the outline of the houses across the street.

"I can't explain Micheil's actions," he said finally. "He's been strange these last weeks; there's no denying it." His fingers gripped the windowsill.

Fiona watched his bowed back, her heart heavy with sadness. Niall was having to acknowledge that a man who'd been his friend all his life was that no more. Niall was having to see Micheil as he really was, and it wasn't a pretty sight.

When he turned to her, his face was dark. His brows were a black line across his forehead and his jaw was squared.

"All I can honestly say to your accusations is that you have no proof," he murmured. "Until there is evidence that Micheil is capable of the things you're accusing him of, I have to believe he's innocent." His eyes haunted, he added, "He's my friend."

Fiona had risen to go to him when the door opened again and her mother said, "Here you are, Fiona. . . . Oh, excuse me. I didn't mean to intrude."

Fiona gave Niall a regretful look and turned to Lady Mary. "Mama."

Niall, not wanting to continue the discussion, bowed. "My lady."

Mary, Countess of Colonsay, entered the room with her head held regally high. There were lines of strain around her mouth and a slight puffiness beneath her eyes, but they were the only signs of tragedy.

Fiona, seeing her mother's weariness and courage, put aside her worry about Niall and Micheil. There would be time later. Right now she had to do everything possible to ease her mama's pain.

"Mama, I'm sorry. I got caught up talking with Niall, but we can finish your packing now." She reached out her hand.

From the window, Niall asked, "Packing?"

With a smile that eased the lines around her eyes, Mary said, "Yes. I'm returning to Colonsay tomorrow. I've been away from Lachlan long enough. I miss him."

Her obvious love for her husband gave Niall a sense of warmth. With time and luck he hoped Fiona and he would have a bond like theirs. Meanwhile, Niall shook his head and looked out the window once again.

"You'll have a hard going. The roads already have several inches of snow."

The countess with a moue of unease, moved to the window and peered out. " 'Tis so typical. When I'm anxious to return to Lachlan, the weather acts up. Well, it's never held me back before. I brought several men from Colonsay for escort; we'll just travel by horse the entire way. We'd have to do so once we reached the Highlands anyway."

With an admiring shake of his head, Niall said, "You're a determined woman, my lady. Much like your daughter."

With a sigh, Mary said, "You might as well call me by my maiden name, Niall." She gave her daughter a wry smile that lightened some of the tightness in her own face. "It appears obvious that my determined daughter has decided to keep you, no matter how you first met."

Fiona, striving to follow her mama's lead, smiled roguishly at her husband. "He's magicked me with his skill at playing the harp, although it's been some time since I've heard it."

The last thing Fiona wanted to do was to add to her mama's unhappiness by telling her about her visions or Niall's upcoming duel with Sculthorpe. The countess believed in her daughter's gift; and Fiona knew that if she told her, she would worry. Her mother needed to return to Colonsay and her husband, not stay here and get caught up in whatever terror Micheil was creating.

The countess cocked her head in curiosity. "You play the harp?"

Niall's smile was self-deprecating. "It's a gift of my family."

"Ah, yes, the MacMhuirrich. Once the hereditary bards to the Lord of the Isles." The countess nodded in understanding. "Just as Fiona inherits her gift of sight from my mother, who—while not exactly able to see the future—often gets what she calls *hunches.*"

The door opened again, interrupting them.

"Here you all are," Lady Fennimore gushed, sailing into the room. Her plump figure was swathed in yards and yards of black silk, her acknowledgment of her goddaughter's loss. "I've been searching everywhere for you. Duncan's ship docked in Bristol . . . ah, let me see," she trailed off, reaching for the lorgnette hanging from her neck on a gold chain. She raised the glasses to her eyes at the same time she lifted a creamy sheet of paper to within six inches of her face. Shifting the sheet outward, she read, "This is dated two weeks ago." She turned the page over as though looking for more information. "And it only just reached here. Now, why would he send it to Edinburgh in the first place?"

Her puzzlement was exasperating, but Fiona took pity on her. "Did it come from London, ma'am?"

Lady Fennimore looked again, studying the piece of melted wax that had sealed the letter. "Why, I do believe this is Joshua Douglas' seal. He must have sent it."

Niall exchanged a glance with Fiona. They knew they were doing well to get that much information from Lady Fennimore. They'd have to read the missive themselves.

"May I see it, ma'am?" Fiona asked, stepping forward to take it from her ladyship's pudgy, white fingers. "Yes, it's from Uncle Joshua. He sent it here knowing we were coming to Edinburgh. And he hopes it reaches us in time."

"It damn well didn't," Duncan's familiar gravelly voice said from the door.

Chapter Nineteen

Fiona and her mother simultaneously rushed at Duncan, who threw wide his arms. Lady Fennimore hovered in the background, obviously wanting to be part of the welcome but not seeing an opening she could squeeze into. Duncan always had had a way with women.

Niall watched it all, his eyes hooded, his mouth curved sardonically. Duncan towered over his women, as tall as Niall . . . maybe taller. He hadn't changed much. His hair was coal-black and his eyes were gray. Broad shoulders and narrow hips were accentuated by his uniform. His captain's uniform.

It was an effort not to stride across the room and plant his fist in Duncan's face. But he'd made a promise to Fiona.

Duncan disengaged himself from the feminine arms. His head lifted, and he stared over Fiona's head directly at Niall. His gray eyes were murderous. "I'm going to run you through, Currie, for what you've done."

Niall took a step forward, blood rushing through his limbs in preparation. "You and who else?"

"Duncan!" Fiona cried, grabbing her brother's arm and digging her heels in. "Duncan, stop. You can't do that; he'll kill you."

Duncan, his eyes like ice chips, pried her fingers loose. "The hell I can't. He kidnapped you and did God-only-knows what else. He's going to pay."

Niall smiled, a baring of teeth. He might not be able to kill Duncan in a duel, but he damn well could knock him around. It was better than nothing at all. He went into a crouch, balancing on the balls of his feet, his hands hanging loosely at his sides.

Fiona, realizing she wasn't going to stop her brother, rushed to Niall. She launched herself at him, wrapping her arms around his neck. Knocked off balance, Niall grabbed her and struggled to keep from falling.

"Stop it," she said, clinging to him like a fashionable coat.

"Children," the countess ordered, her voice firm and in command. "Enough. I've already lost one son and a daughter; I don't want you killing each other."

Her words were a bucket of cold water. Niall, one arm around Fiona, stopped his forward momentum. Duncan froze in the process of removing his coat. Fiona cast an anxious look at her mother.

Niall sympathized with his mother-in-law; the lines of strain around her mouth and eyes were pronounced. "She's right, Macfie," he said. "And I promised Fiona not to fight you."

Duncan's silver eyes remained narrowed, but he

nodded reluctantly. "It appears that my sister would mourn your loss, but she always sympathized with the underdog."

Niall's face reddened. His shoulders bunched, and it was all he could do not to land his brother-in-law a facer. "Don't push me, Macfie. I'm sorry for your family's losses, but that doesn't mean I'll stand by and let your tongue get the better of your brain."

"Enough," Fiona said, stepping between the two men. "You're like two dogs facing off. I'll not have it."

"Oh, dear," Lady Fennimore wailed, wringing her plump, white hands. "Come along with me, Duncan. I'll show you to your room."

With one last scathing glance at Niall, Duncan turned away. "I hope it's not pink or purple," he said in an exasperated undertone.

Niall couldn't help but grin. It seemed Duncan had stayed with Lady Fennimore before. He hoped the man got a room that was all pink, and livid pink at that. It'd be some small revenge, and all he was liable to get.

When everyone was out of the room, Fiona wrapped her arms around his neck. "Thank you," she murmured, kissing him.

Luminous blue eyes full of love looked at him, and Niall realized that he'd do anything for her. He was truly crazy.

The room was still dark when Fiona felt Niall stir against her in the bed they shared. It was the morning of his duel with Sculthorpe. Her stomach clenched as she reached out for him. Touching his chest, her fingers curled into the black hairs.

"Don't go, Niall," she pleaded. "Let it go."

Beneath her palm, his heart beat strongly and slowly. He took her hand in his and raised it to his lips. "I can't, vixen. I promised myself that I'd avenge my conviction and imprisonment. If I stop now, I'll be failing myself and admitting to the world that I killed that woman—and I didn't."

She sighed, fighting back tears. Somehow she had to reason with him. "You aren't going to fight Duncan. Isn't that the same?"

"No, love," he whispered, pulling her head to his shoulder and stroking her hair. "I made the promise concerning Duncan because I love you and won't hurt you if I can keep from it. Sculthorpe is different. No one I love is worried about him, and he was my friend once. But Sculthorpe betrayed me by casting his vote to imprison me. I have to make him acknowledge that I was innocent. I have to hear him say the words."

Fiona bit her bottom lip to keep from moaning. "Please don't kill him, Niall. Don't do that to yourself."

His hand stopped the soothing motion. "I won't. Once I would have, but no more. I have you to return to. I don't want to have to flee to France and either leave you here or take you away from your family right now."

She knew he was thinking about the deaths that had so recently rocked her. Her love for him increased, if that could happen. She already loved him more than she'd ever thought possible.

Gently, he disengaged her fingers from his chest hair and set her away. "Go back to sleep, vixen," he said, kissing her on the forehead. "I'll be back."

Fiona put her knuckles to her mouth to keep from calling to him. She knew it would be futile. He was going to meet Sculthorpe, and that was all there was to it. All she could do was wait and pray. With luck, Sculthorpe wouldn't show.

He dressed in darkness. When Fiona heard the door open and close, she got out of bed and rushed to the window. Pulling back the curtain, she peered at the street below. It was getting light outside, and she could just make out the outline of the houses across the street.

It wasn't long before she saw Niall step into the road. A man on horseback appeared at the corner. The reins of a second horse were in the new man's hands, the animal itself trailing behind. Micheil was here with Prince Charlie, prepared to be Niall's second.

Fiona's toes curled against the cold wooden floor as she pressed her face to the even colder window, desperate for a glimpse of her husband as he disappeared down the street. Dawn was just starting to pink the eastern horizon. A spattering of snow fell fitfully from the cloudy sky.

Her hand strayed to her abdomen, and she prayed nothing would go wrong.

Niall and Micheil rode in silence, for which Niall was grateful. He was in no mood to deal with Micheil.

He wasn't sure he even liked him anymore, let alone trust him.

Neither did he want to tell Micheil about Duncan's arrival. It would only start an argument between them. Micheil had changed in the last weeks, and Niall didn't know him anymore.

In a barely audible voice, but accusing nonetheless, Micheil said, "She told me you aren't going to challenge Macfie. Is that true?"

He should have known Micheil wouldn't leave it alone. Niall gave him a jaundiced look. "Yes."

"What?" Micheil stopped his horse with a sharp yank on the reins. His cheeks were red in the pale light of dawn. "It's because of her. I knew she'd bring trouble. In just a couple of weeks, she's turned you from a plan you nursed for three years. She did what I couldn't."

Niall watched the hurt and anger that Micheil made no effort to hide. "I thought you'd be glad to hear I'm not doing it."

Micheil's face contorted. "You're still meeting Sculthorpe. But not Macfie. It doesn't make sense. If you want revenge on two of them, why not all of them?" He kicked his mount in the ribs, his lips pressed together. "It's because you love her."

There was a wealth of emotion in the last words, but Niall couldn't decipher any of it. "Yes," he said quietly, "I love her, and because of that I'm willing to let go of my hatred for Macfie . . . or at least not make Fiona suffer for it." He added the last because, in all honesty, he still loathed Macfie. Fiona was the only thing standing between her brother and Niall's vindictiveness.

Micheil's right eyelid twitched, but he didn't speak again.

Niall was thankful. There wasn't anything he could say. It was the way it was, and nothing would make him change his mind and cause Fiona further grief.

The remainder of the ride was cold, and the snow picked up. It would obscure their vision and make the duel more dangerous. You couldn't aim to hit a nonvital part of your opponent's anatomy if you couldn't see it.

It was uncommonly still when they reached the copse of trees where the duel was to take place. The snow made it hard for Niall to see if Sculthorpe was there yet. There were no tracks showing a horse or carriage had come that way, but then it would be only a matter of minutes before any tracks would be obliterated.

"Micheil, who arranged for the surgeon?" He didn't like the feel of this. Fiona would say he was having a premonition; he preferred to think of it as a hunch.

"Sculthorpe's second," Micheil answered, urging his mount into the copse as though the matter were settled and all they had to do was await the arrival of the others.

Niall followed more slowly on Prince Charlie. One look at Micheil's now-composed features, told Niall he was over-reacting. Sculthorpe was just late.

Jumping to the ground, Niall tethered his horse to one of the trees. He threw a blanket over Prince Charlie to ward off the cold before beginning to pace the small area. The wind knifed through his cape and coat and made his ears ache. He stomped his feet and clapped his hands to bring some warmth to them.

Micheil did the same, making rapid, jerky motions.

They didn't have longer than fifteen minutes to wait before Niall heard the muffled sounds of hooves. Lots of hooves. Sculthorpe was bringing more than his second and a surgeon.

Through eyes half-closed to keep out the wind-driven snow that was turning to sleet, Niall peered in the direction of the noise. He thought he could make out six riders. That was simply too many people.

He cast a warning look at Micheil and made for Prince Charlie and the dueling pistols. He was too late. Before he got within five feet of the stallion, they were surrounded. He considered drawing the knife he kept in his boot, but decided not to. They were outnumbered, and the dangerous looks on the faces of the six men around him told him that to provoke them would be sure death.

None of the six was Sculthorpe. The leader was Sculthorpe's second, Mackinsay.

The place between Niall's shoulder blades began to itch as he carefully kept his hands out and away from his body. From the corner of his eye, he saw Micheil taking the same stance. Careful he intended to be, but cower he wouldn't. "Where's Sculthorpe?" Niall asked in a level, commanding voice.

Mackinsay, his words a whip, said, "You know where he is—you bastard."

The itch became a tightness that drew Niall's shoulders back. Something was badly wrong. "No, I don't.

He's supposed to meet me here, not send a small army."

The urge to add a scathing comment was great, but Niall knew better. They were ready to kill. Already several of them were having trouble keeping their mounts still, which told him that the men's nerves were agitated and that was being communicated to the animals.

Mackinsay jumped down and strode to Niall. In one smooth effort, he swung at Niall's jaw with enough force to knock Niall to the ground had it connected cleanly. Niall hadn't been expecting the outright attack, not yet, but he instinctively turned with the punch so that much of the momentum behind the act was dissipated. Following through with the initial defensive move, Niall pivoted and went to the balls of his feet, his hands fisted and positioned for retaliation.

"Go ahead," Mackinsay dared him. "Hit so I can pound you into porridge. You're an animal and deserve everything I can give you."

He motioned to the men with him, and they jumped from their horses. Two grabbed Micheil and held him motionless so he couldn't help. The remaining three circled Niall. Niall's mouth curled in a grim smile. So, it was to be a fight. Well, he'd give them one they'd never forget.

In one smooth action, Niall whipped out the knife in his boot. He wasn't going to confront four men with nothing but his fists.

"Put it down," Mackinsay said in a deadly voice, pulling a pistol from the pocket of his great coat and aiming it at Niall. "Nothing would please me more than to shoot you where you stand."

Seeing death in the man's eyes, Niall dropped his knife. He'd try to reason his way out, but he didn't think there was much chance of that. Something had happened. To Sculthorpe, of course. But what? Niall closed his mind to the probabilities.

"What is going on?"

"You know exactly what's happening," Mackinsay said, closing the distance between him and Niall. "I'm not going to buy into this act of innocence. Grab his arms," he told the three men who'd been moving in on Niall. To Niall he said, "If you move or try to fight them, I'll kill you."

Niall wasn't surprised they weren't going to discuss it. And from the murderous look in Mackinsay's eyes, he knew better than to resist. Two of the men yanked his arms up behind his back. Pain shot from his shoulders, but he refused to acknowledge it. He wouldn't give them the satisfaction.

Defiantly, head held high in the continuing sleet, he stared at Mackinsay. Before Niall could do anything but duck his head, Mackinsay swung out with the hand holding the pistol. The handle of the weapon cracked against Niall's jaw, sending lights flashing in his head. The two men holding him kept him from falling. They showed no mercy. Mackinsay punched him in the gut. Niall would have doubled over, except he couldn't. His captors kept him standing.

"Before I take you to the magistrate," Mackinsay said softly, "I'm going to make you suffer, just like you made Sculthorpe suffer." He landed a fist in Niall's eye.

"Stop it," Micheil yelled. "He didn't do it."

No one paid him any attention. Mackinsay's fist connected again.

Niall sagged between his two captors. Mackinsay's possession of the pistol had ensured that Niall had no means to fight back. He had to submit to the two holding him cruelly, or be shot. Now all he could do was endure the attack.

Mackinsay hit Niall's other eye. With the part of his mind he kept free in times like this, Niall realized he'd have two black eyes by tomorrow and enough bruises to pepper a steak. This was worse than any beating he'd gotten in Newgate, and he didn't even know why they were doing it.

Nausea knotted his gut. Bile rose in his throat. His head felt as if it would explode at any time. The coppery taste of blood filled his mouth. Niall began to doubt he could hold onto consciousness much longer.

Vaguely, he heard Micheil continue to protest, but it didn't matter. Nothing mattered.

Shots rang out, spattering the snow-covered ground. The men holding Niall jerked, yanking Niall's arms up his back until he thought they would pull them out of the sockets.

"Let him go," Duncan's familiar gravelly voice ordered.

"Now!" a more familiar feminine voice screamed. Another shot exploded near Mackinsay's feet. "The next one will be between the eyes," Fiona promised.

The men holding Niall released him. He sagged to

the ground, bent double in an attempt not to vomit. His stomach ached and his head hurt. His jaw was beyond feeling.

"Niall. Oh my God, Niall," Fiona's urgent words filtered through to him.

Gathering all his determination and strength, he stood and gave her a lopsided grin. He winced as pain bolted from his jaw to his neck and down his spine. He vaguely registered the pistol she held. The end of the weapon still smoked in the frigid air. She must have fired one of the shots.

"Still a firebrand, vixen," he muttered in an attempt at levity.

She reached him and wrapped her arms around him. As much as he hated to admit it, it felt good to have her beside him. And she'd probably saved his life. Mackinsay might have mentioned a magistrate, but Niall doubted he'd have gotten there in one piece.

"Lean on me," she ordered, her shoulder propped under one of his arms.

Meanwhile, he was slightly aware of another figure following slowly behind her. This figure was tall and broad. It had to be Duncan.

"Step away from him," Duncan said, leveling one of the two pistols he held on Mackinsay. In an aside, he asked, "Can you stand, Currie?"

"Yeah," Niall said, spitting blood.

Micheil was beside him immediately. "Oh my God, what has that bastard done to you?" He pushed Fiona away and put his arm around Niall's waist.

Fiona, fuming so that she felt ready to scream like a fishwife, barely managed to contain herself. Hands on hips, she glared at Micheil. "He's my husband, not yours."

Niall felt the muscles in Micheil's arm spasm. "Let me go," he told the man who'd once been his only friend in the world. "Fiona's my wife and I want her beside me."

Niall didn't bother to look at Micheil, only Fiona as she rushed back to him.

Duncan, his guns still aimed at Niall's attackers, said, "If one of you moves, I'll shoot and worry about explaining it later. Now—" he turned his silver gaze on Mackinsay "—what's the meaning of this? This was supposed to be a duel, not a bloodbath. And where's Sculthorpe?"

Mackinsay's face contorted into a snarl. The pistol he'd dropped while he pummeled Niall still lay several feet away. "Sculthorpe is dead. His throat slit and his body sodomized. And this bastard you're protecting did it. Just as he did it to Winter and that woman." He turned to cast a look of hate and loathing at Niall. "He deserves whatever I do to him. He deserves to die a painful death."

At the words of Sculthorpe's fate, Niall felt Fiona stiffen against him and he knew that if he looked at her, her face would be as pale as a full moon. His probably wasn't any different. He felt sick.

"When?" he managed to get out of his rapidly swelling mouth.

Ignoring him, Mackinsay spoke to Duncan. "I found Sculthorpe this morning when I went to get him to come here. He was in his library. Thank God, he isn't married and his mother is in the country. No one—especially women—should have to see a sight like that."

Niall, his gorge rising, knew what Mackinsay spoke of. It was a grisly, obscene sight. But worse than that was knowing that the killer had followed him here. Winter hadn't been a coincidence.

Fiona blanched. Not even the warmth of Niall's body pressed against her could alleviate the chills spreading through her, chills that had nothing to do with the sleet still falling in sporatic spurts. Now Niall would have to listen to her.

She glanced at Micheil, who stood away from them near one of the trees, his face a sullen mask. Her teeth began to chatter.

"So," Duncan's voice intruded on her morbid thoughts, "you came here with a group to see that Niall suffered for the crime you think he committed. Not a pretty picture of you either, Mackinsay. You haven't even bothered to find out when the murder occurred and where Niall was at that time."

Mackinsay cast Niall a seething look. "I don't need to know. This type of killing has happened twice before. Once he was convicted; the second time he'd just challenged the man to a duel. Same situation as with Sculthorpe." He took a menacing step toward Niall before Duncan's pistol deterred him. "It's got to be him. No one else was there each time."

"You don't know that, and neither do we," Duncan said with a finality that succeeded in shutting Mackinsay up. Turning in Micheil's direction, he said, "Alpin, go back to Lady Fennimore's and have the carriage brought. Niall can't ride in this condition."

Niall, still leaning on Fiona, said, "The hell I can't. No little beating is going to take me out."

Before anyone could protest, he shook off Fiona's support and strode to Prince Charlie. His head spun and his jaw ached, but he could live with it. Taking the blanket off the stallion, he carefully folded it.

Duncan, a grin softening the harshness of his features, said, "Okay, Currie. You've proven your point." Bringing his attention back to Mackinsay, he said, "I'm taking Currie with me. If you want to follow—by yourself—we can discuss this further. Get the magistrate if you want."

Careful to keep the six men covered, Duncan beckoned to Fiona. She understood without his speaking. Picking up her own pistol from the ground where she'd dropped it when she rushed to Niall, she nodded. Next, she fetched Duncan's and her horses so that they could mount without taking their eyes from the men.

When everyone was seated, Duncan said, "Go ahead of me. I'll make sure they don't follow."

They made it to Lady Fennimore's without mishap. Ben opened the door for them, his mouth an *O* of surprise and shock.

"My lady," he said. "I'll fetch Lady Fennimore." His back bent, he shuffled up the stairs.

Fiona shook her head in exasperation. She could have better used him to fetch hot water and a clean cloth with which to wipe Niall's face. With a sigh, she said, "Niall, please go to the drawing room. I'll be right there."

Before he could protest, as she knew he would, she left. In the kitchen she got hot water from the pot on the stove. Next she went to the laundry and tore up one of her godmother's clean sheets.

When she got to the drawing room, Duncan and Micheil were there. Micheil stood by the window, but his attention was on Niall, who sat stiffly in one of the pink chairs. Duncan sprawled in another delicate chaise nearby.

Closing the door, Fiona joined them. She positioned a small table beside the chair where Niall sat. She dipped one end of her cloth into the water and started on Niall's blood-covered face. Tenderly, she wiped at the crusted material, careful to stay away from his darkening eyes and split lip.

"Ouch!" He pulled back, grimacing.

"You're going to have to be more stoic than that," she admonished him. "You're a mess."

"I love you, too," he murmured sarcastically.

Duncan laughed outright. "Best not to argue with her," he said around chuckles. "It accomplishes nothing and only makes her meaner."

Fiona gave her brother a minatory look. "I don't need you complicating the situation, Duncan." She dabbed at Niall's cut lip. "You'd do well to have a couple of leeches put around your eyes to draw off the blood and keep the swelling down. But we don't have any, and I don't imagine you want a doctor."

His face tensed as she continued to wipe. "No doctor. What I want to know is how you two got there in the nick of time." He gave Fiona a black-browed scowl. "I thought I'd left you safely in bed."

Refusing to let him intimidate her, Fiona took her time. She finished wiping the last of the dried blood from him and rinsed the cloth in the now-pink water. Next she wrung out the cloth and set it on a small dish.

"I couldn't let you just go off and kill someone," she said bluntly. "So I got Duncan."

Duncan's laughter was somewhat subdued, but there was still a hint of amusement in his voice. "What she means is that she woke me from a sound sleep whining about your going out to commit mayhem and worse. Luckily for her, and you, I had a pretty good idea where the duel was to take place." At Fiona's raised eyebrows, he amended it. "At least I knew of several places where it would probably be. You were at our fourth stop."

Leaning gingerly back in the chair, his face as white as a summer's cloud where it wasn't turning blue, Niall said, "I owe you a debt, Macfie. I think if you hadn't come along, I'd be horse meat by now."

Duncan, his silver eyes piercing, said, "You owe Fiona. She wouldn't give me any peace till I agreed to find you. She'd had a premonition that things weren't right; and when one of those comes over her, she's as persistent as a rabid dog until something's done." His face darkened. "I'd have left you, myself."

Micheil's sharp intake of breath was clearly audible in the ensuing hush. Niall nodded his head in acknowledgment of Macfie's refusal to take thanks.

Fiona, incensed at her brother's brutal honesty, hit Duncan in the arm. "You're supposed to stand behind Niall, you big oaf. Whether you like it or not, he's family now and we've precious little family left." She took a deep breath to calm herself. "But arguing isn't going to tell us who's doing this."

Upset as she was, she was still aware enough to catch the glance of warning Niall gave her from under worried brows. Belatedly, she remembered that Micheil was still here and all her suspicions about the man came flooding back. She had to get rid of him.

"Niall," she said firmly, "it's time you went to bed."

He stared at her. "I'm fine."

She glowered at him, aware of Duncan's silent mirth behind her. "No, you aren't. You're just stubborn. You need to be rested and have all your wits about you when Mackinsay finally arrives with the magistrate." She put her fists on her hips. "Or do you intend to enlist their sympathy the same way you did the Bow Street runner and magistrate in London?"

Her sarcasm wasn't lost on him. "Vixen," he muttered, placing his hands on the arms of his chair to push himself up.

"And that reminds me," she said as though having just thought of it. "Micheil, what did you learn from the runner Niall asked you to hire?"

His pale-blue eyes stared unblinking at her. Shudders chased one another across Fiona's back.

"Nothing."

"Then perhaps you'd better try to get a message to him, letting him know about this latest killing and that it's become imperative that he find out something." She spoke firmly, not liking the man and wanting to get him out of the house. "There's nothing here for you to do. Niall's going to bed, and I imagine Duncan will insist on doing the same—" she gave her brother a roguish glance "—since he lost so much of his beauty sleep last night."

Duncan rolled his eyes. "Perhaps you're the one who got the worst of this bargain, Currie," he said, rising from his chair.

Micheil whirled, his face livid. Duncan gave Niall a hand up, and Fiona tsked about Niall's stiff movements. Suddenly, the door opened.

Lady Fennimore stood on the threshold, fully dressed but with curling papers still in her silver hair. Wisps of gray stood out around her head like hat-needles. "Oh, dear. What is going one?"

Behind her came the countess in a dressing robe, her thick black hair hanging in a braid down her back. She looked regal in spite of her state of dishabille.

"Has Niall gotten himself into another scrape?" she asked, her gaze focusing on him. "Or is it you, Duncan?" She eyed her son with fond exasperation.

"Mama!" He gave her a look of mock hurt.

"It wouldn't surprise me. However," her gaze returned to Niall's beaten face, "it doesn't seem likely this time."

Fiona, wanting this over and done with so she could discuss her suspicions with Niall and Duncan in private, stepped around the men. "Mama, Lady Fennimore, please don't worry. Niall is all right, except for some cuts and bruises, but he needs to get some rest. It seems that . . ." She paused to take a deep breath. This was the hard part, the awful part. "Sculthorpe was found by his second. He'd been killed the same way Winter was."

Both women gasped. Lady Fennimore's face drained of color, and Duncan released Niall to grab the matron before she hit the ground in a faint. The countess was of sterner stuff. While she paled, she gritted her teeth and held her ground, head up, shoulders back.

"I see," Mary, Countess of Colonsay said softly. "But it couldn't have been Niall. He's been in this house all night."

"Exactly," Fiona said, giving her mother a grateful smile. It would go a long way toward keeping Niall out of prison to have the Earl of Colonsay's wife say he was innocent and that she'd vouch for his whereabouts.

Turning around, the countess put her arm around Lady Fennimore's shoulders and said, "Dorothy, we'd better go finish dressing. There's nothing we can do here." Before leaving she said to Niall, "I won't be leaving for Colonsay until after we've talked with the magistrate."

"Thank you," Niall said.

Fiona hugged her mother. "I love you, Mama."

The countess smiled at her daughter. "You'll need all the support you can get. It doesn't sound pretty."

While Fiona kissed her mother, Micheil hovered in the background. Fiona had sensed his presence as a faint crawling of her skin. She turned to him now. "I'll send a servant for you when Mackinsay and the magistrate arrive."

Instead of looking at her, he was watching Niall. His eyes held such pain and longing that Fiona's heart twisted in unwilling sympathy.

"I'll stand by you, Niall," he whispered.

Niall forced a smile to his lips, but it turned to a

grimace of pain when the cut opened again and started bleeding. "I know you will, Micheil."

As soon as everyone was gone, Fiona hustled Niall to their room. Once settled, she said, "I'm going to get Duncan. He can help us. We need to solve this before someone else is killed." Without giving Niall a chance to argue, she went in search of her brother.

Knocking on Duncan's door, she waited impatiently, shifting from foot to foot. "It took you long enough," she admonished him when he finally answered.

He raised his brows.

"Don't give me that look," she said. "It won't work. We need you."

Duncan lounged against the door jamb. "I need my beauty sleep, remember?"

Her mouth tightened at his jibing. "You need to keep your skin. Or haven't you figured out yet that both Winter and Sculthorpe were scheduled to meet Niall for a duel. Instead, they were murdered. Until several days ago, Niall had every intention of challenging you. That puts you in danger."

Duncan snorted. "Let whoever's behind this try. There aren't many men bigger than I am."

She shook her head at him. "Conceit will get you in serious trouble one of these days."

He grinned, but pushed away from the doorframe and followed her back to the room she shared with Niall. At their entry, Niall let go of the curtain he'd been holding aside in order to watch the front street.

"Thanks for coming," he said to Duncan. "I think I'm in serious trouble."

The three sat down in chairs they pulled together to

form a circle. Fiona told Duncan everything she knew. Niall did the same.

"There you have it," Fiona said, her hands clasped tightly in her lap in lieu of jumping up and pacing the room. "Every time there's been a murder, I've seen blood on Micheil's hands just before." She looked at Niall as she spoke softly. "And he was on that ship in America with the two of you."

Pain and disillusionment mixed in Niall's eyes. "I can't believe Micheil would do something like this."

Duncan rubbed his chin, a habit he had when thinking. "I wouldn't have thought it of him, either. But men can do strange things for strange reasons." His silver eyes met Niall's green ones squarely. "I don't think you can afford to rule him out. He's the only connection, other than yourself, that you've got."

Niall looked away, staring at nothing. "What reason does he have? None. And I can't believe he'd have done it and let me take his prison term. He's like a brother to me." His voice turned bitter. "He's been the brother my own brother's refused to be."

Fiona's heart went out to him. It was so hard for him to consider Micheil, and it hurt him so much to be forced into having to do so.

"Niall, I'm sorry," she murmured, reaching out to touch his hand where it clenched one of his knees.

His attention settled on her, and he gave her a slight smile. Then he squared his shoulders. "There's only one way to find out for sure. We have to duplicate the circumstances that were in effect with Winter and Sculthorpe." Standing, he said clearly, "Macfie, I challenge you to a duel of honor."

Chapter Twenty

Fiona sat as calmly as she could, listening to Niall tell the magistrate everything. But now that they'd decided upon a plan, she was impatient to set it in motion. Across the room, Micheil stood waiting his turn to speak.

They were gathered in Lady Fennimore's pink drawing room. The countess sat on the chaise beside Lady Fennimore. Mackinsay, unable to sit due to his anger, stood by the roaring fire, one booted foot propped on the grate. Duncan lounged in one of the pink-silk-covered chairs, looking too big for the piece of furniture's delicately carved legs. Niall sat opposite him and at a ninety-degree angle to the magistrate.

From her chair beside Niall, Fiona examined the magistrate, hoping to see something in his manner that would tell her he was on their side. A portly man with strands of gray hair combed meticulously over the bald dome of his head, he nodded after every sentence Niall uttered. His burgundy coat and cream-and-navy waistcoat strained around his middle. He was dressed like an overaged dandy, but his brown eyes were shrewd. Every once in a while, his gaze darted around the room to alight on the individuals present, as though to gauge their reactions to Niall's story.

When Niall was done and everyone had vouched for his presence in the house the night before, Lord Richardson, the magistrate spoke. "As I see it, Currie's the only suspect we have who seems to have had a motive in Sculthorpe and Winter's case." Fiona's gasp of outrage brought his noncommittal gaze to her. "However, in both instances, we also have a reputable witness who says Currie was with her."

Fiona's shoulders sagged as some of the tension left her. Her gaze darted to Micheil. His concentration was still centered on Niall. She shivered at the intensity he exuded.

Niall waited until Lord Richardson was finished before saying, "Sculthorpe was a big man. How did his murderer overpower him?"

"You should know," Mackinsay spat, his face crimsoning. He pushed away from the fireplace. "This is ridiculous. There's no one else who could have done it." He pinned the magistrate with his gaze. "You can't let him go."

The magistrate rose and spoke in a calm voice, but his gaze held Mackinsay's like iron. "I don't have anything solid to arrest him on. And he's brought up an interesting question. It appears Sculthorpe was hit from behind with a candlestick. My guess would be that he knew his murderer and was comfortable turning his back to him."

A pregnant silence fell over the room. It made perfect sense.

Fiona couldn't keep herself from looking at Micheil. His hands were jammed into his coat pockets. His eyes were a bright blue, almost feverish.

"Arrest the bastard," Mackinsay said, his lips drawn back against his teeth. "He's known Sculthorpe for years."

Quietly, the magistrate said, "So has every other man in this room." Blandly, he added, "Or am I mistaken, gentlemen?"

It was a leveler that no one could deny.

Picking up his cane from the table where it rested, the magistrate made a short bow. "I must ask that Currie not leave this house for a while. But other than that, I've nothing else to request."

Fiona watched the short, rotund man leave, relief washing over her. So far, they were succeeding.

But Mackinsay, his body shaking in fury, loomed over Niall. "Richardson's an old woman. I know you did it, Currie, and I intend to prove it."

Niall met Mackinsay's anger with coolness. "Go home and get some sleep."

Pride swelled Fiona's chest for her husband. Both Niall's eyes were swollen and black. His mouth looked like raw meat. Lines of exhaustion bracketed his lips, while more lines radiated out from the corners of his eyes. Instead of having a healthy color to his complexion, he looked gray. He was nearing the end of his endurance, and he still met Mackinsay's venom with calm authority.

Mackinsay, after a quick glance to see if there were

any support and not finding any, pivoted on his heel and stalked from the room.

Only Fiona, her mother, Lady Fennimore, Duncan, Micheil, and Niall remained. Fiona's breath came in shallow gulps. Perspiration slicked her palms. It was now or never.

Slowly, his eyes hooded and his mouth curled, Duncan rose from his chair across from Niall. "Personally," he drawled, "I think you did it. But since you're married to my sister now and she's made it clear that losing you would devastate her, I forbore to say anything."

Niall took several steps until he was inches from Duncan's scornful face. "Would you care to repeat your accusation?"

Duncan's smile didn't reach his eyes. "You heard me the first time." With careless grace, he sauntered past Niall toward the door.

"Brother-in-law be damned," Niall said, his swollen lips pulled back against his teeth. He strode after Duncan, his stomach spasming at the sudden movement that caused him to clench those muscles. "Look at me, you coward."

When Duncan turned insolently toward him, Niall slapped his hand across Duncan's right cheek. Duncan's eyes blazed, but Niall met that scathing look with unconcealed satisfaction.

"I challenge you," Niall said, distinctly and slowly, "to a duel to the death."

Gasps filled the room.

"Niall," Fiona said, rushing to her husband and grabbing his arm. "You promised me."

"Niall. Duncan, that's enough," the countess ordered, moving hastily to them.

"Oh, dear," Lady Fennimore said, wringing her plump, white hands. "I was afraid it would come to this."

Only Micheil said nothing. Fiona was acutely aware of that fact, her gaze sliding toward where he still stood near the door, ready to leave. Fierce light sparkled in his eyes and lent his face an aura of vitality. She realized that this was what he wanted. But why had he changed from the friend who wanted Niall to forget dueling and revenge? It didn't make sense.

"Accepted," Duncan said. "My second will call on Alpin immediately." Duncan, anger replacing the lazy insolence of minutes before, stalked from the room.

Niall watched with a wolfish grin of satisfaction that did nothing to dilute the black-and-blue texture of his mouth. "The sooner the better."

Fiona winced.

"Niall, I beg of you," the countess said, "don't do this. Duncan . . . is my only son."

Fiona watched the humility and agony mix on her mama's face and wished they'd been able to include her in their plan. But the fewer who knew, the better. If Micheil were to believe a duel was inevitable, everyone else had to believe it, too, and react honestly. But it was hard.

Niall's mouth twisted down. Fiona felt him tense beneath her fingers where she still gripped his arm. He didn't like this part either.

"I'm sorry," Niall said, "but his insult was unpardonable. I didn't kill that woman or those men. Duncan said I did. If I failed to challenge him, I'd be agreeing that what he said was true. It isn't"

Fiona left Niall and went to her mother. "Mama, come with me. There's nothing we can do here."

She put one arm around her mother's waist and extended the other to Lady Fennimore, who continued to wring her hands. The three of them left. Upstairs and away from Micheil, Fiona would tell her mother the truth. She couldn't bear to let her suffer any longer than was absolutely necessary.

Niall watched the three women leave. Fiona's straight, supple carriage and regally held head gave him a moment of great pride. She was holding up well. His only regret was the countess. The woman had suffered enough; he didn't want her to endure this as well. But there was no help for it.

Squaring his shoulders, Niall turned to Micheil, who still lingered. "Well, it seems I'm to fight Macfie after all." His mouth twisted into a sardonic curl. "That should make you happy. It does me."

Micheil stepped toward him, his eyes searching Niall's face. "What about *her?* Aren't you afraid she'll be hurt when you kill her brother? That she'll leave you?"

Niall forced himself to shrug indifferently. Every bruise in his torso and back burned, and it was all he could do not to grimace. "If she does, then she does. I couldn't let Macfie get away with what he said. You know that as well as I do."

Micheil nodded, but Niall knew his friend had never understood the honor that drove him to the duels in the first place. It had been the first time they'd ever disagreed over anything. Unfortunately, it hadn't been the last.

Hesitantly, Micheil asked, "Do you still want me to be your second?" He stopped just feet short of Niall.

Pain swamped Niall. He felt like a traitor, doing this, setting Micheil up. He prayed to God Fiona was wrong.

"Of course I want you as my second," Niall said. "You've stood by me since we were boys. There's no one else I'd trust with my life and my honor. You're the brother my own never were." Every word came from his heart.

The tight lines in Micheil's face eased. He inched closer until Niall could see the pores in his skin and the light shadow of blond beard on his jaw. Micheil hadn't gone home to clean up while they waited for the magistrate. Or he'd gone home, but ignored his person. That wasn't like Micheil, who was normally meticulous about his grooming.

"I love you like the brother I never had," Micheil said softly. "I'll find out immediately who Macfie's second will be and arrange everything." His eyes caught and held Niall's. "You can trust me with your life. I vow it."

Niall nodded. His throat was too tight to speak. He reached out and gripped Micheil's shoulder hard. It was as close as he could come to embracing his friend. "Thank you."

Much later, Niall lay sprawled across the large bed he shared with Fiona. One arm covered his eyes.

Twenty-four hours of ebony beard-growth covered his jaw.

"Love," Fiona said, sitting beside him, "don't torture yourself so."

"He's my friend, dammit. The only one I've had throughout this."

Fiona sighed and reached for his hand. "I know. And if he's innocent, we'll find out. If he's not . . ." She took a deep breath. "If he's not . . . we can't let this murderer stay free."

Niall groaned, his fingers squeezing hers. "This murderer only strikes when I'm getting ready to have a duel."

"That not always true," Fiona said softly. "There was the woman in America."

Niall shifted so that he sat propped against the bed's pillows and Fiona was nestled on his chest. "She was the first and for no reason. She had no money and nothing was taken. My lucky piece was planted on her along with the button from a British officer's uniform. God, I wish I could remember that night."

Fiona squirmed so that her eyes met his. "Could you have been drugged?"

An absolute stillness came over Niall. He gazed unseeing for long minutes. "Possibly. But I don't see how. I was with Micheil the whole night, or at least the part I remember."

The damning words were out. "Micheil again," Fiona murmured.

Niall's sharply indrawn breath was loud in her ear. "I won't condemn him, Fiona. There's got to be another answer, and I believe we'll find it out soon."

Unwilling to continue making him suffer over his friend, Fiona agreed softly. Her mouth settled gently on his, careful of his cut until passion overtook them. Her hand slid under his shirt and stroked across the hard muscles of his torso.

"There are other things to occupy us," she whispered against his lips.

The next day at breakfast, Duncan said, "Micheil wants to meet me this evening to find out who my second is."

Fiona's attention riveted on him. Her heart began to pound painfully with excitement. "Can't you send him that information by note?"

"Yes."

She looked at Niall. The pain moving across his face was enough to choke her. His bruises were turning brown and ugly mustard. She knew they hurt him. This was just more anguish.

Niall took a deep breath. "It appears that Micheil is doing everything Fiona expected him to do." He took a large bite of his kidney pie before downing his tankard of ale.

"It seems that way," Duncan said in his gravelly voice, neither agreeing nor disagreeing with Fiona.

"This is what we set out to discover," Fiona said gently. "We must find out if in fact it is Micheil."

Niall nodded and finished his breakfast.

"Where are you to meet him?" Fiona questioned, knowing Niall wasn't going to ask.

"At a tavern near the Port of Leith."

"The docks? Why there? That's far away. Micheil could come here or have you go to his house."

"You'd think so," Duncan said. "His note says he wants to share a bitters with me to show that there're no hard feelings on his part and that he thought I'd be more at home near the sea." He grinned. Then his gray eyes darkened in sadness. "Micheil doesn't know I've resigned my commission to go home to Colonsay and take up where Ian left off before his death."

"Duncan," Fiona said, "I didn't know. That will be good for Mama and Papa. They'll need your strength."

"They'll need my good, strong back," he said smiling. He wasn't the type of man to dwell on pain.

"That, too," Fiona conceded. She was finding this conversation depressing. Too many unpleasant things were happening too close together.

"What time are you to meet Micheil?" Niall asked, bringing them back to their original purpose.

"Ten." Duncan smiled roguishly. "The tavern should be full of business and twice as rowdy by then. A good time to meet someone without anyone else making anything of it."

"As much as I don't like the sound of it, you're right," Niall said, going to the sideboard where he helped himself to more kidney pie and a cup of black coffee. "I've developed a taste for this bitter stuff," he said, sitting back down and taking a drink. Demeanor serious, he added, "I'll be there."

After Duncan left to go about his daily business, Fiona put her fork down and said, "I'm going with you."

Niall laid his fork carefully down. "The hell you are!"

She lifted her chin. "I'm going with you. I'm as responsible for this as anyone. It's my idea. I'm going to see what happens. And besides," she sniffed disdainfully, "you might need me."

Niall reached across the short distance separating them and grabbed her wrist. "I won't allow you to come. Even if you're wrong about Micheil, a tavern on the docks is no place for a lady. And your coming will only increase the danger. I'll be worrying about protecting you instead of paying attention to what's going on between Duncan and Micheil."

A militant light entered Fiona's eyes. "I helped save you yesterday—or have you conveniently forgotten that?"

Niall sighed and brought her hand to his mouth for a lingering kiss. "No, vixen, I haven't forgotten. But you've failed to understand that the six men you helped save me from yesterday would never have harmed you. Whatever else they are, they're gentlemen first."

She snorted. "I know all about gentlemen. They're thus when it suits them. I'm going."

His mouth turned grim. "I want you to stay here where I'll know you're safe with your mother."

Triumph lit her face. "Mama is returning to Colonsay later this morning."

"Then stay with Lady Fennimore," Niall said, gritting his teeth.

"No. And if you continue to refuse to allow me to come, then I'll have to come on my own." She smiled at him. "You know how it is when I've been told no."

With a groan of defeat, Niall said, "Don't I just?"

Chapter Twenty-One

Niall kept a protective arm around Fiona and a watchful eye on the tavern patrons as they slipped into a booth across the room from where Duncan and Micheil sat. He was dressed like a sailor and Fiona had donned the clothing she'd gotten from the cottar's wife.

The room was poorly lit, with smoke from cheap tallow candles, pipes, and cheroots obscuring vision even more. And it stank. The smell of gin and ale mixed with the odors of unwashed bodies and the rancid fat in the stew being served to any customer with a stomach strong enough to handle it. The place was a cheap tavern and Niall had been in his share of bars just like it wherever His Majesty's Navy sailed.

When the serving wench came for their order, giving him a knowing wink in the process, he ordered ale for them both. When the girl returned with the drinks, he asked, "Are there rooms for rent above?"

"Reckon, iffn ye wants ter pay the price." Her eyes

skated to Fiona, whom she looked up and down with ill-concealed contempt.

Niall suppressed a smile as Fiona stiffened against him. "What about the alleys outside? Do they lead anywhere?"

Now the woman became wary. Taking a step back, she narrowed her eyes suspiciously. "And w'at ye be wantin' ter know fer?"

Niall realized he'd gone too fast. Reaching into his pocket he brought out a shilling and flipped it at her. "I've been 'round the world and I've made me share of enemies." He winked at her. "I intend to live to a ripe old age."

She caught the coin with a deft flick of her wrist and brought it to her mouth to test its authenticity by biting it. Convinced it was real, she smiled, showing a missing left canine tooth. She accepted his reason.

"T'at alley on the north leads to nothin' but a brick wall. Right dark back there, too. I wouldn't be goin' there iffn ye takes me meanin'. People 'ere what'd kill fer a meal."

Niall nodded slowly. "How 'bout the other?"

"Same," she said curtly, moving away as though she felt she'd said too much as it was.

"Nothing I didn't expect," Niall said for Fiona's ears only.

Her answer was to press closer to him. She was regretting the demand to be included. While she'd always considered herself a strong, resilient woman, she'd never been in surroundings as squalid and fraught with potential danger as this tavern.

She took a sip of her ale to calm her nerves. "Yuck,"

she sputtered, all but spitting the stuff out. "This is terrible."

Niall chuckled and took a big swig of his. "Ale is a man's drink."

She made a disgusted moue at him and pushed her tankard to his side. "Then you won't mind finishing mine."

Niall's chuckle deepened. "Are you wishing you hadn't come?"

Loath to let him know he was right, she pointedly looked away. "Hush, Niall. I need to pay attention to what Duncan and Micheil are doing."

"They're drinking their third tankard of ale since we arrived," Niall said dryly. "It seems they both intend to get drunk."

"They can't. Or Duncan can't," she amended.

As they watched, Duncan got up and left, going out a side door to relieve himself in the nearby alley. Micheil, with a casual glance around the room, extracted a small vial from his coat pocket. Under the cover of his hand, he uncorked it and dumped its contents into Duncan's ale.

"Oh, my God," Fiona gasped. "A drug."

Niall froze. He felt as if Mackinsay were slugging him in the stomach all over again. He wanted to deny the evidence of his own sight, but he couldn't. As they watched, Micheil secreted the empty vial back in his coat pocket.

"Stay here," he told Fiona, his face a hard, emotionless mask. "I've got to warn Duncan."

Using every table and every body as cover, Niall slipped out the door Duncan had gone through. It was the side alley the serving wench said ended in a brick wall, and it stank.

"About time you got here," Duncan drawled. "I was beginning to think one of the muggers would get to me before you did."

Niall was in no mood for any kind of levity. His world had crashed down around him. All he could do was keep his momentum forward. He had to find out why Micheil was doing this.

"He's drugged your ale," he whispered to Duncan.

Duncan's answer was a grunt. "I've had enough anyway. I'll manage to spill it and call it a night. I've already told him who my second is supposed to be."

"Go in ahead of me," Niall said. "Micheil's probably getting impatient. You've been gone quite awhile."

"It would have been shorter if you'd come sooner," Duncan said in a reasonable voice. With those words, he stepped back inside.

Niall watched Duncan's broad back disappear into the smoky light and squalid activity. He knew he should get back to Fiona. A woman alone in a place like this was inviting advances his wife wouldn't want to entertain. But he had to make sure Duncan was back with Micheil and that his friend's—pain shot through him at the word—attention was on Duncan.

He counted slowly to ten then slipped back in, keeping his face averted from Micheil's table and using every man, woman, and table he could for cover.

"Thank God for small favors," he muttered as he slid onto the seat next to Fiona. "I was afraid I'd come back and find I had to fight some sailor for your virtue."

Fiona was too engrossed in what was happening across the room to pay him any mind. Duncan, swaying slightly, bumped into the table where his and Micheil's drinks sat. Losing his balance, Duncan fell onto the table. His right arm shot out and swiped across the oak top, trying to find someplace to rest and support his weight. In the process, he knocked both his and Micheil's tankards to the floor.

Micheil jumped to his feet and said something neither Niall nor Fiona could hear over the noise and distance, but his face was livid. Duncan, in a performance good enough for Drury Lane, stumbled again. The fall looked real, and Fiona was gladder than she could say that they'd seen Micheil pour the drug into Duncan's drink, otherwise her brother's lack of coordination would be all-too-real.

With ill-disguised contempt, Micheil led Duncan from the tavern. Duncan, putting on the display of his life, reeled into one of the serving wenches, sending her armload of drink and food crashing to the floor.

"Come on," Niall whispered, grabbing Fiona's hand and yanking her from their seat. "He's doing it to give us a chance to beat them onto the street. We're going through the alley."

Fiona's nose wrinkled at the stench as they stepped into the night-shrouded alley. "Couldn't we have gone a different way?" she muttered through clenched teeth in an effort not to breathe anymore of the noxious stench than she absolutely had to.

"Bad," Niall agreed. "Come on, and draw your pistol. You may need to protect yourself, and I can't be worried about you. If the drug means what we think, Micheil's got to be planning something pretty quick."

Sticking close to the tavern's outside wall, they made their way to where the back passage entered the street. Just then, the tavern door swung open and Duncan tumbled out, barely managing to stay on his feet. Micheil followed.

Once the tavern door was shut, the only light came from the moon. It was so cold out that the moon was haloed in silver when it shone from between the snow clouds. Ice and puddles of water dotted the dirt and wooden walkways.

Micheil steered Duncan down the street away from the direction they needed to go to return to the city. He maneuvered him right past the alley on the other side of the tavern from Fiona and Niall's hiding place.

The two men entered the shadow cast by the building and there was a flash of silver as Micheil stuck his cane between Duncan's legs.

"Wha—" Duncan's shout rent the frost-riddled air. He fell to his knees in an icy puddle.

Two figures sprinted from the alley and fell on Duncan as Micheil backed a safe distance away. Niall, sick at heart, but responding to the danger, dashed into the street and sped to Duncan's rescue. He shot one of the two pistols he carried into the dirt near the attackers. He didn't want to kill them; he wanted to scare them into running.

"Let him go!" he shouted, skidding to a halt not five feet away.

His pistols had two shots each, the one with only one shot remaining he pointed at Micheil. The other he aimed at the two men who had released Duncan as if he were a burning coal. He motioned with his weapon in the direction of the docks.

"Get out of here now," he said, "and I'll forget your faces and what you've done. Stay, and I'll kill you."

The two ruffians stared at Niall, their faces dark from beard and dirt. Their clothes hung in rags about their lean frames, and their hair hung to their shoulders in greasy strings. Niall almost felt sorry for them.

"Let them go, Niall," Micheil said in a voice wrought with weariness and despair. "Here." He tossed a bag in the air at them. It landed with the jingle of coins. "The money's in there. Take it and get out of here."

Duncan rose to his feet lithely, all pretense of being drunk gone. Moving to Micheil's right side, he drew a small pistol from his coat pocket and aimed it at Micheil. Fiona came forward until she formed part of the circle surrounding Niall's friend.

It was all she could do to look at Niall and the naked pain on his face. Realization had come to him in the tavern, but in this moment he was faced with the fact of what previously had only been a possibility.

"Why, Micheil?" Niall whispered, his voice hoarse with the need to cry that he denied himself. "Why did you do it?"

Micheil, so calm until now, crumbled in on himself. His narrow, beak nose seemed to fall into his face. His mouth appeared to shrivel. And his eyes welled with tears that fell like tiny shards of ice down his cheeks.

"I had to," he whispered, one hand rubbing his temples as though they ached horribly. He didn't pretend to misunderstand. "I had to kill her. She saw me. She saw me with the man . . . and she threatened to tell if I didn't pay her. After that, I had to get rid of her. I knew that if I didn't, she'd tell eventually, no matter what I paid her. She was that kind. I would have lost everything. My title. My commission. My father's love."

"But so brutally?" Niall's shoulders hunched inside his wool coat and heavy cape. He wanted this to be a nightmare, but he knew it wasn't.

Micheil shrugged. "She was only a whore."

His friend's lack of remorse was awful. It was worse than hearing Micheil's lack of understanding when he'd tried to explain honor to him.

"What about Sculthorpe and Winter? They weren't whores. They were your friends." Niall's voice was devoid of emotion. The only way he could get through this was to stop feeling.

Micheil's eyes beseeched Niall's in the wan light from the moon that had just peeked out from between two mountainous snow clouds. He took a step toward Niall. "I had to, don't you understand?" His voice was plaintive, his face screwed up in tears. "They might have killed you if you'd fought them. I couldn't take that risk." His voice fell to a whisper. "I love you."

Duncan's harsh voice broke the silence. "You're a homosexual, and the woman knew it. So you killed her. But why'd you frame Niall? You just said you love him."

Micheil's pale-blue eyes looked wild and bewildered. "I . . . I don't know. He'd been with her earlier and come back down with a smirk of satisfaction on his face. And he told me to go bed her, that she was good." He gulped in big heaving sobs of air. "He always did that after bedding a whore—offered her to me. It made me angry. He was mine."

"Oh God," Niall moaned, hearing Micheil's confession. The horror of it threatened to overwhelm him. "We were brothers, Micheil."

Micheil sneered. "That's what you thought. But I've loved you since we were boys, and you never even considered me that way. You always chased after the girls, and then the women. You didn't want me." He shrugged, a change coming over his face. Now, instead of suffering, he was angry. "You goaded me that night, telling me I never seemed interested in women. You even went so far as to suggest I seek out one of the men. I hated you in that second. That's why I punished you."

The anger left him, and suddenly he looked like a rag that's had all the water squeezed from it. "When I realized what I'd done, it was too late. You were convicted and put in Newgate." His voice became pathetic. "I did everything I could to make your imprisonment as easy as possible."

There it was, Micheil's motivation for all of it. And it explained everything. Niall was sick.

Another transformation came over Micheil. He began to whine. "What are you going to do with me? If you turn me over to the magistrate, my secret will come out and the law will keep me from inheriting my title and estates. You know they don't let homosexuals inherit. And my father will kill me. He'll hate me." He fell to his knees in front of Niall. "You know how it feels to have your father hate you. You can't do that to me. Please don't."

Niall stared down at Micheil's bowed head. The revulsion and sympathy that twisted his gut was worse than anything he'd ever felt. He'd rather be back in Newgate than see Micheil like this. He fell to his knees and wrapped his arms around the man who'd been his best friend, his brother, and held him tightly.

Fiona felt the cold wind hit her tears, stinging her cheeks. This was all so sad, so horrible. She moved to Duncan for warmth and comfort. He put an arm around her and pulled her into the protection of his side. Together they watched Niall lift Micheil to his feet.

Niall turned a stricken face toward her. "I can't condemn him to that disgrace, that dishonor. Even after all he's done, I can't find it in myself to do that to him." Releasing Micheil, he said to him, "If you promise to go to the Continent and stay there, to never come back to Britain, I'll let you go. But you must stay there the rest of your life. If I hear that you've come back, I'll expose you. I swear it."

Micheil stood shaking. "I swear . . . on my name as an Alpin."

Niall was glad he hadn't sworn on his honor. He wouldn't have been able to believe Micheil if he had.

"Get out of here," Duncan said flatly. "Niall's soft enough to let you go, but I'm tempted to shoot you where you stand. The things you did were unforgivable. Thank whatever god you worship that Niall's a better friend to you than you ever were to him."

Micheil cast Niall one last anguished look, then he

started running into the night. The moon went behind a cloud and darkness fell on them. When its silvery light broke free, Micheil was gone.

Fiona rushed to Niall and wrapped her arms around him hard. He clung to her, burying his face in her hair.

"He wasn't evil," he murmured, "just confused."

"Ha!" Duncan said. "He was twisted inside."

Niall repositioned Fiona so that she was tucked into the crook of his arms. His swollen lips formed a sad smile. "He was still my friend. In my heart, he'll always be the boy I grew up with who ran the hills with me and learned to ride and shoot with me." He took a deep breath and looked down at Fiona. "He'll always be my friend, but thank God I have you."

She smiled at him, wanted to hug him so tight nothing could separate them. She loved him. She loved him for his unwillingness to condemn his friend, for his determination to find something good in the man who'd wreaked so much death.

Still smiling, she said, "And soon you'll have a son to care for."

Niall's face lit up. Some of the pain so recently felt dissipated. "You're with child? How long? When?"

She laughed at Niall. In the background she heard Duncan snort, but ignored him. "You should be a father in about seven months, give or take a month. Just in time for spring."

Healing laughter broke out from Niall. Exultant, he grabbed her about the waist and lifted her high in the air. "The best thing I ever did was kidnap you." Setting her back on her feet, he whispered, "I love you, vixen."

Rising on tiptoe, she kissed him wildly, passionately.

Epilogue

Early Spring, 1816

Helping Fiona ashore, Niall asked, "Why'd you want to come here? The midwife says you're due in three weeks. We should be back at Colonsay where you'll get the best care."

Fiona, her feet finding precarious purchase on the wet rocks of Skye's shoreline, smiled tenderly at her husband. "Relax, love. I have plenty of time."

She picked up her heavy skirts and allowed him to assist her to more stable ground. Her stomach was large enough to make her sense of balance something not to be trusted.

Watery sun shone down on them. Spring was coming to the Highlands and islands, but it wasn't completely here yet. She was glad they'd packed plenty of blankets and warm clothing.

After Niall finished beaching the boat and unloading their supplies, he came back to her. "It's a long climb to the castle," he warned.

Her smile widened. "Don't I know that? If I could make it that first time, something like a little pregnancy won't stop me now."

His black brows drew together in worry. "I don't want you over-exerting yourself. The midwife said you were to take it easy." His face cleared. "You stay here while I take these on up. I'll come back for you and carry you."

Fiona laughed at him. "Don't be ridiculous, Niall. I'm perfectly capable."

To prove it to him, she set off on her own with the largest strides she was capable of, burdened by the babe as she was. She hadn't gone three yards before he was upon her and scooping her into his arms.

"I'll not let you do it, vixen. And that's that."

His arms tightened around her as he took off up the rocky hillside to the ruined castle. Strapped to his back, his harp banged against him with every step. Fiona felt for it and brought it around and into her lap.

"I'm glad you brought this," she said, holding it reverently. "It was the first thing I liked about you—your skill with this instrument."

He smiled rakishly down at her, his breath coming a little faster than before. "What was the second?"

She clucked at him. "Flattery?"

"Why not?"

"I think it was your help in dealing with Blackie. You didn't have to hold him for me, but you did."

He shook his head. "You're daft. If I hadn't helped with that crow, I'd never have heard the end of it. Even that soon after meeting you, I knew that much about you." His eyes turned thoughtful. "Is that why we're here? To find the crow?"

"You know as well as I that you can't find a wild animal," she said. "I wanted to return to the place where I first began to fall in love with you. It seemed right, what with our first child almost here, the babe we created that one morning down on the beach."

"Ah," he said, his chest lifting and falling with more definition as the climb with her weight burdening him began to tell on his stamina. "We're here for *auld lang syne.*"

"Precisely," she said, noting the strain that was beginning to slow him down. "I'm not as light as I used to be."

"You're no more than a thistledown," he countered. "But I'm glad we're here."

She looked away from him to see the ruined castle keep appear over a shallow rise, almost as though it'd risen from the ground itself. "I knew this place was magic," she murmured. "It brought me you."

He set her on the ground, her swollen belly a barrier that neither one let keep them apart. "Fate and my vengeance brought me you. I was blessed that you're the woman you are. Another would have left me to my hell."

Gently Fiona rested her finger on his mouth. "We're both lucky."

"Yes," he said, bending down to kiss her and carry her to the ground.

From overhead, the raucous cry of a crow interrupted them. Glancing up, Niall muttered, "That must be your crow. No other would be so importunate."

Fiona giggled as the bird came to rest on the ground beside their prone bodies. The crow's bright eyes shifted from one to the other, then he walked pigeon-toed toward them.

"Blackie," Fiona crooned. The bird came to her.

Niall snorted in disgust. "Come back later, old man," he said, gently pushing the bird away.

Blackie did as instructed.

MAKE THE
ROMANCE CONNECTION

Come talk to your favorite authors and get the inside scoop on everything that's going on in the world of romance publishing, from the only online service that's designed exclusively for the publishing industry.

With Z-Talk Online Information Service, the most innovative and exciting computer bulletin board around, you can:

- ♥ CHAT "LIVE" WITH AUTHORS, FELLOW ROMANCE READERS, AND OTHER MEMBERS OF THE ROMANCE PUBLISHING COMMUNITY.

- ♥ FIND OUT ABOUT UPCOMING TITLES BEFORE THEY'RE RELEASED.

- ♥ COPY THOUSANDS OF FILES AND GAMES TO YOUR OWN COMPUTER.

- ♥ READ REVIEWS OF ROMANCE TITLES.

- ♥ HAVE UNLIMITED USE OF ELECTRONIC MAIL.
- ♥ POST MESSAGES ON OUR DOZENS OF TOPIC BOARDS.

All it takes is a computer and a modem to get online with Z-Talk. Set your modem to 8/N/1, and dial 212-935-0270. If you need help, call the System Operator, at 212-407-1533. There's a two week free trial period. After that, annual membership is only $ 60.00.

See you online!

brought to you by Zebra Books

KENSINGTON PUBLISHING CORP.